THE CONSPIRACY

Phoneme Media
P.O. Box 411272
Los Angeles, CA 90041

ISBN: 978-1-939419-99-6

This book is distributed by Publishers Group West

Cover design and typesetting by Jaya Nicely

Printed in the United States of America

Phoneme Media is a nonprofit media company dedicated to
promoting cross-cultural understanding, connecting people and
ideas through translated books and films.

http://phoneme.media
http://cityofasylumpittsburgh.org

Book #2 in Phoneme Media's City of Asylum Imprint

ISRAEL CENTENO

THE CONSPIRACY

TRANSLATED FROM THE
SPANISH BY GUILLERMO PARRA

CONTENTS

To the memory of my father,
José Félix Centeno

"...I'm convinced that he not only knows every detail of
'our' position, but that he knows something else besides,
something neither you nor I know yet, and perhaps never
shall, or shall only know when it's too late, when there's
no turning back!..."

— Fyodor Dostoevsky, *The Possessed*

"We will not act with the same ingenuousness as before,
I can assure you of that. I know from the most reliable sources
that the possibility of an assassination is being considered."

— José Vicente Rangel, *El Nacional, Caracas*, 4 May 2002

PARIS IS BURNING

In Buenos Aires they called it mist. In Mexico City, smog. When the wind from the Sahara blew and covered Santa Cruz de Tenerife, the islanders knew it as haze. In Caracas there was soot, and I was moving through smoke and ashes on the day I went out to kill the president.

A persistent fire was ravaging Mount Ávila. The flames had never reached such heights. The forest ranger stations were overtaken and the neighboring zones began to burn. In the outskirts, toward Sartanejas, in Fort Tiuna, where they trained the battalions of recruits, the pines were burning. The pines were burning in Caracas. These weren't the Christmas pines you find in bazaars nor pinewoods from an exotic garden. Those who liked to quibble might have questioned whether pines actually existed in Caracas. They did. And they burned like they might anywhere else. And the resin—an oil that burns itself up—filled the air.

I had been fleeing from my comrades for two days now. Silvestre was escaping with me. They set a trap for us during a meeting. Lourdes had always lent herself to helping set up traps; she was a government agent, I kept telling them and they'd laugh, accusing me of being paranoid or horny or jealous. "The comrade has a nice ass, and that makes you talk shit," they said. But there's no doubt Lourdes was a government agent. I insisted and they kept laughing and insinuating things; there was no need to speculate too much anymore to reach the conclusion that the entire party had been infiltrated. Dominguín says we'll become the government and that we're winning at this moment in the process.

They called us so we'd put down our weapons. They invited us to a definitive meeting. Silvestre and I decided to wait.

The days passed. We continued to focus on the tasks inherent to conspiracies. We knew that the people from the organization were looking for us, urgently calling for us to meet with them. We hoped we would do what had to be done. But we remained weary; decisions don't change from one day to the next. Silvestre and I hid in one of those safe houses that you never reveal, even to your lover. We shared a few places just in case, never all of them. They insisted on seeing us, they wanted to meet in Pinto Salinas; that smelled rotten from the start. We tended to meet in Pinto Salinas at the house of a friend of Lourdes, during the clandestine years. It had been a while since we had gone to the house of Lourdes's friend and in formal terms, we were no longer clandestine. Silvestre took two additional charges, for his Raging Bull .44. I wore a .38 and tossed six extra bullets in my coat pocket. Before leaving I took a grenade from a shoebox. I remembered what Abelardo had once told me, it's never a bad idea to bring something that makes a lot of noise. I will always ask myself why we went and in order to not reach drastic conclusions that might compromise my comrade, I maintain it was due to discipline.

Lourdes's friend lived in an apartment on the twelfth floor of one of the superblocks. We didn't go up through the stairs, as was our habit. At first we thought we'd go up in the dilapidated elevator. We smelled something bad. They'd never expect us to use the elevators. We changed plans when we got to the door. We wouldn't go up. We moved between buildings stealthily. We decided to first go to an acquaintance's house and send a messenger to the people, changing the meeting place. Our friend lived in one of the houses located alongside the basketball courts, and he would let us use it without a fuss since back when we were still not in power.

We crossed the apartment blocks, got lost in their dark corridors. It was eight at night, the courts were empty, generally at that hour the usual gangsters drink their bottles of anise with rum and burn chunks of crack. We crossed the field. If we had gone through the stairs or the elevator to the house of Lourdes's friend, they would have killed us as soon as we started to climb the first steps. But they had a second plan, this was it, if we didn't go to the blocks, they also knew about our acquaintance. Since when do these dogs care at all about the gangsters? Why had they scared them off? We finished crossing the block, from entrance to entrance, letter to letter. Now, we were some experienced men, we knew a thing or two about fate; we couldn't go back because they had surely closed off our rearguard. At some point I said it was a matter of discipline. It was a dark night, the bulbs on the streetlights were burnt out and the mountain at our back was burning, the glow of the flames barely drew shadows in the slum. We had no choice but to jump onto the zinc rooftops of some houses that emerged beneath a slope at the start of a trail. The noise was thunderous. The mountain was burning and the fire was illuminating a couple of men who were sprinting as they plunged into the rooftops of shantytown homes. The shots began to sound at intervals, one, two; we didn't respond, I sank into the shadows up to my chest, the zinc sheet from one of the roofs gave way, a spray of bullets rained down on us.

"Let yourself fall, motherfucker," Silvestre shouted at me, I didn't understand him, my suit was torn but I had been able to pull my revolver from the holster.

"Let yourself fall into the fucking house."

Silvestre returned fire, six shots in a single blow. I got out of the trap as soon as I could and crawled, shot back two times, reached an edge of the roof and let myself fall into one of the alleys, I could barely glimpse a tall man with his head shaved who was aiming at me, he brought his whole body against me, why wasn't he shooting at me, his head exploded. Silvestre had plugged him at the base of the nape with a bullet from his .44. As soon as I stood up I had to get rid of another guy who was lunging toward me, this time I got him right between the eyes. We ran downhill, until reaching the avenue. Silvestre jumped head first onto the windshield of a Fiat Uno that was descending, while I grabbed the girl at the wheel by her hair, I barely glimpsed her eyes, brown, black, shining, her white teeth, perfect, her chest agitated and her breath metallic, I threw her to the pavement, I realized I felt a warmth between my legs, as though I'd pissed myself, I checked with my hand, looking for blood, it was likely they'd wounded me, but it was an erection, a damned and simple erection. Silvestre opened the passenger side door however he could and we took off, I was laughing, I was fucked up but I was laughing. Silvestre found a box of cigarettes in the glove compartment of the Fiat, he lit one for me and put another one between his lips.

"We barely escaped," I let loose with a puff of smoke. "And now who's looking for us? The organization or the government." Silvestre took a deep drag and kept the smoke in his lungs, he released it with the same strength as when he inhaled it.

"It's the same shit. Aren't you injured?"

I smiled with the cigarette in my teeth.

"No, I'm fine. Even got a hard-on." He shrugged, didn't understand anything. I asked him the question in the voice of the mouse in the comic books: "And what'll we do now, Silvestre?" He didn't think, he had nothing to think about, he had already thought about it since birth, he was an illuminated one, destiny was in front of his eyes. "We'll kill the president."

What better day than the Day of the Homeland? The Day of the Homeland had turned into Homeland Week. We all knew how much the President liked to celebrate the day and week of the Homeland. We didn't have much time. The shell we were hiding in was safe. Nobody in the organization knew about it. We had what we needed, a rifle with a telescopic sight that gave a margin of error of about half an inch.

Some people preferred bombs for assassinations. Unless they were inside jobs, they didn't work. The possibilities for failing were abundant. A rifle could also fail, it's true, it was a matter of logistics. And what about us, did we have logistics? It was precarious. In this case the precarious could provide results. We didn't have anyone on the inside, there was no way for us to choose a place where we could set up what could be an invisible point. We were always exposed to monitoring by intelligence agents. We would kill him on Los Próceres Avenue. I told Silvestre I didn't like the place, that's where the assassination attempt against Betancourt in the sixties had failed.

"That devil was targeted by the right, we won't fail with this one."

This conviction of Silvestre's was total and unfounded, no one could guarantee the success of an assassination attempt merely by its political alignment. It was best not to think like a defeatist, the old school knew that and I was from the old school. I remembered that after I insisted to Abelardo, he, in one of those moving letters, full of phrases, named me a pioneer of the revolution. I wasn't just any pioneer, I was a pioneer of a struggle that conceived itself as armed. I felt happiness and couldn't wait to see myself incorporated to its ranks. Later on, the organization would use me for important tasks, which only a boy of my age could have accomplished. For the time being, I was happy to memorize the steps for taking apart, cleaning and putting back together a nine millimeter pistol, following the instructions of a manual written on a tiny piece of onion skin paper, Abelardo's handwriting illegible for everyone except me.

I would take apart the rifle, pull down the canon and chamber, set them on one side of the bed, I was sitting on one of the two beds in the room where we were hiding, adjusting the springs, using a towel and the little brush, I used a little

3-in-One Oil and applied myself to the military procedure. The
canon, the chambers, the tiniest pieces, all free of any particles
that might block them; then I would put it back together and
take it apart again. We wouldn't place the rifle ahead of time
at the spot where we intended to shoot. It was a public place,
though not too public. Silvestre knew that it was the room for
an old chimney alcove where the smoke from the burnt trash
escaped. It wasn't public because the superintendent had set
it aside for himself as a workshop. That's where he repaired
washing machine and refrigerator motors. It was a small room
with openings instead of doors and windows, it looked like a
cabin. It only had a work table, a rickety tool panel and a few
motors, it wasn't very big, but two people could move easily
within the space. It was three hundred meters from the objective. The organizers of the parade had scheduled a stop at the
beginning of the avenue from where the reserves of the revolution would march; they were militias, civilians. The place was
chosen by the people who handle the protocol, at that point the
avenue is no longer run by the military, it's still part of Los Ilus-
tres, and this way they would avoid offending the high command with the informality of a parade that didn't keep to the
orthodox standards of a military ceremony. This is where our
man would be surrounded by the crowds as always and, as he
tended to do, he would make the feint of breaking with protocol. No one believed me about the feint, but I knew about it, I
spent two days on the president's security team, it was the first
job I was given after they came into power, his baths of pop-
ularity weren't such, or they were such only to a degree. He
would break the security ring in order to hand himself over to
the actual security ring that was mixed in with the crowd, each
person was identified, each one was monitored by the agents, it
was a Cuban technique, we called it three in one, one sovereign
and three agents, the multitude was sighted in a short, tense
and precise aim. There was no room for a successful attempt. I
never guarded the president's back but I did for one of his gov-
ernors, it was the second day, I hadn't been given training, the

Cubans hadn't arrived and everything was more relaxed, they trusted in my experience as a guerrilla and that I would memorize a few procedures. I ruined everything when I hit an old woman at the base of her ear with the butt of my pistol when she tried to hand a little piece of paper to the governor. Everyone stood still and they carried the lady out to a good private hospital, along with the paper and its petitions. She had been carrying a cheap hairbrush in her hand but, regardless, I hadn't struggled all my life to end up as a bodyguard for a bureaucrat.

The buildings would be under surveillance, in general one man per rooftop is the norm. What made our building special, escaping immediate vigilance from the military house and intelligence? Nothing, it would be under surveillance just the same, but they wouldn't place a man on the rooftop, we knew that ledge would be monitored by another ledge and that it was enough for them to check the place thoroughly and with the helicopter's aerial view.

We had two more points in our favor. The superintendent was a collaborator of Silvestre's, who had told him we were going to be on a counterintelligence job, because we suspected a movement might take place at the reserves' militia stop. As always, we would be on the margins, we told him, and as always, our labor was to shadow. The second point was definitive: we didn't plan on escaping alive from the action, we would have one opportunity, one shot and then we'd be dead.

I was crossing the mist, the haze, the smog, the ashes and dust of a blurry Caracas that was on fire. Silvestre had left me on the corner, I was carrying the rifle buried under vegetables and groceries, wrapped in a green towel, taken apart, at the bottom of a bag. I passed through the security rings without a problem, I was modestly dressed, a cotton shirt, blue jeans, with some Catalonian sandals. I carried the newspaper under my arm and blended in with other pedestrians who were taking advantage of an open-air market's good prices, early in the morning. I knocked on the superintendent's door, he lived alone, he always wore khaki shirts and pants, he was covered in grease, in tube grime, his face was immense, with a crooked mustache and a squinty-eyed look, it almost seemed monstrous to me. I told him I had to go up to the room and he shrugged, that was my problem, he gave me the key, his arms were covered in dirt, he didn't smell bad, nothing could smell bad with all that smoke. I got on the elevator and pressed the floor, as it was reaching the last one, I once again felt a warmth between my legs, my tearful eyes glimpsed Lourdes, I felt her mouth tighten around my glans, grip it firmly. I had the certainty I was going to die that morning and all I wanted to take with me was Lourdes's eyes, the intensity of her observation when she stuck my glans in her mouth, the glow of her eyes when it seemed like she would swallow my cock, all that cruelty she reflected at the moment of licking, taking. They say the hanged man dies with an erection, I think I'm going to die with my loins warm, and the mouth and tongue and eyes of Lourdes, right there, fixed like a butterfly on cork waiting for me to come. No one suspected me, I entered the ledge with no problem, opened the little chimney room, it was full of smoke, they didn't burn trash anymore, the crematory had been eliminated a while ago, it was smoke from the city, from the hills, the barracks. I remembered the chorus: "Paris is burning, Paris is burning..." and nothing else came out of my head, it would mix together with the anguish and porno sequences that would inhabit me until the moment of my death.

Morning was rising quickly, you could hear the noise from the avenue, martial bands, deafening protest songs blared from megaphones on trucks, the motors of the buses that transported people to the march, the ice cream man's bells, the shouts of the street vendors selling red berets and other revolutionary souvenirs. "Paris is burning... Paris is burning..." the smoke covered everything and the sequences ran, Lourdes's mouth moved closer, that ate and took, that sucked and I was crouching and he was bathing in the masses behind the smoke, Paris was burning... the militias arrived, you could see them in formations, you could hear the voices of command, the turns, the helicopter started to circle, the president was on his way. I took out the vegetables and groceries and started to unwrap the disassembled rifle, I was still crouching, I spread the opened towel on the floor, one by one I picked up the rifle pieces, someone had come on stage and was talking to the crowd, he harangued them and cheered them on and recited the virtues of the process, the people didn't listen to him, they made noise, lots of noise, I assessed each part of the rifle, carefully, serene, I sang and looked, Paris was burning and Lourdes was sucking me off, she had beautiful tits—Lourdes, they're not big but they're beautiful, well formed—the martial band imposed itself, and the drums and brass made noise, the parade had begun, the shouts made noise in the morning, someone was describing the volunteer battalions, their sections, regiments, virtues, a unit passed by at a trot shouting, it's not a slogan, it's not a chant, it's the name of the president spoken with martial strength. I remembered that Martial was the first political overseer I had, his pseudonym was due to his origins, not the Latin poet. He was an officer who deserted from the army. He honored his name, he was a bastard about discipline and punctuality. The unit shouting the president's name passed by, the crowd was waving little flags and was also cheering the president's name, for a while it was all smoke and the president's name, then I thought maybe the president wasn't within range, that it was unreal. I felt like I was situated wrongly, I leaned a little to stand up slightly, I barely peeked out to see if he was within shooting range. Yes, the place from where the president was going to speak was within view. I returned to my original position, I put the rifle between my legs, I put the bullet in the chamber and pulled the bolt, it would be one shot, a clean and straight shot that would launch us into the arms of revolutionary uncertainty. The man who served as a dam for the revolution would be erased by history and in this case history was me. Actually, Silvestre and me. Us.

The parade reached the end, the masses were stirred, they roared and threw the leader's name into the air. I remembered that at first they yelled out other names, even Bolívar, but then, in the wasteland, in the desert of voices from the masses, all that could be heard was the indisputable leader's name.

I heard his voice, he was clearing his throat, it was the smoke. Paris is burning...the wet lips, the erect breasts, the intense eyes. The president began to wave, his martial and absolute voice made the crowd quiet down, his firm voice was giving me a foothold for my entry into history, I got up again, I could barely see him, his profile... Paris was burning, was moving toward me with her wet mouth, I adjusted the viewer, came toward me and looked at me from below, stuck her tongue out, I lifted the rifle and stepped back, my back bumped against the superintendent's worktable, it was clean, it didn't have any motors on top of it, I needed space to point comfortably without losing sight of the target, if I lodged myself against the table it was impossible for me to miss, Paris was burning and I felt a sea of sperm swelling from within that would be spilled onto Lourdes's mouth, her face, her chest, I adjusted the finger on the trigger, I had got him fixed, I saw the skin behind his earlobe which was my objective, Paris was burning, they kicked the door open, Silvestre pointed at me with his Raging Bull .44, I didn't understand anything, he should have been covering the rear guard, Lourdes remained fixed at the center of my body, she sucked vigorously, I needed to launch my sperm into history, I shot, ejaculated inside, deep in Lourdes's mouth, she was drowning, she vomited, Caracas was burning, the smoke made me cry, I barely felt Silvestre's punch against my shoulder, the president didn't realize history had just incrusted itself into an acacia, just behind the nape of his neck. I gave it back to Silvestre, without knowing exactly what I was doing, a blow with the butt of my rifle, I could feel them shooting at us, three projectiles entered the room, Silvestre crowded into the corner and let himself fall, lifted up his knee and pointed at me. Lourdes had already left, I looked for my revolver, I didn't understand this historical play, my comrade put the gun to his mouth and blew his head off. That motherfucker ruined everything and left me alone, I stopped thinking, Paris was burning... Paris was burning, I left the room and they shot at me from the helicopter, I don't think, Paris was burning and I jumped from the building's ledge where I stood right when some men in black burst onto the deck, I fell onto an awning almost on my knees, I bended them, turned around and threw myself again into a window that led to a hallway, a spray of bullets rained on the naked rooftop, I made my way down the stairs, I knocked over a man who was walking up with his dog, I got tangled in the animal's leash and fell head-first, I let go of a shot and caught a neighbor who came out to see what was happening, she was bleeding from her chest, this wasn't contemplated in the historical move, I smiled, dragged myself and saw there was a big window, I didn't think about where it led, I jumped again and fell on a mountain of trash, I made my way with my hands, moved them blindly, flashing the revolver, through an alley, death waiting for me at the end, I ran toward it and remembered that a girlfriend once told me we had to be like butterflies that move toward the light and burn up, the light was truth my grandfather would say, the truth will burn me and keep me safe. You could hear the screams of the multitude, someone said they'd placed a bomb, there was a great disorder beyond the alley, where the flames awaited me, I ran toward it, closed my eyes and smashed into two women who were running, they weren't officials dressed in black, they were two ladies, one of them grabbed her thigh, between sobs she screamed that it was dislocated, they hadn't realized I had a revolver in my hand, I let it roll on the ground and stood up asking for help, a woman had dislocated her leg, she pulled her thigh, women at that age who dislocate their legs could die, a mob started coming in this direction and with them the officials dressed in black, they cordoned off the zone, entered the alley and began shooting, the multitude forced me to return to the building where I was hidden, I managed to see the stage, they'd already moved the president, I fixed my shirt however I could, I cleaned my arm, I felt like my face was burning, I thought I'd scratched it against something in one of my many falls that day, I cleaned it with the palm of my hand, there was no blood, a dirty sweat, smelling of smoke, Caracas was smoke and people, the people wanted to break the cordon, some agitators started to scream slogans against repression, I passed through the multitude in front of the building's entrance, they pulled out two bodies, one was Silvestre, the other the superintendent. Who could have taken out the superintendent, there was confusion and they let up on the siege, they asked people for their papers randomly and special squadrons wandered through the crowds with dogs, the area was flown over by two helicopters then, you could hear patrol sirens and ambulances, where they were previously shouting in support of the president. A group of reservists, militia men who were in the parade, ran in a squadron and made their way through the crowds, they carried clubs, assault daggers and sticks in their hands, I imagined their order was to lynch the assassin. I felt so tired, my right cheek hurt, I was aching everywhere, I felt the need to hobble, but if I limped I was dead, I had to follow the mob, think that Paris hadn't burned and that Lourdes wouldn't extract my virile liquid.

It was midmorning already, I wasn't safe. History had been intervened in swiftly, so much so that not a single leaf on a tree had moved. The trees of Caracas were diverse, I couldn't name a single one. I knew there were acacias and mahoganies; the avenues had small trees, withered trees, insignificant bushes, some were green, others dry. The smoke fell on the city like a disgrace and took air away from us. My eyes were burning and I was already resenting the blows I received when I fell. Why had the course of history continued to be the same? I didn't have any answers, the city was stirred up, all the police were on the street, they were looking for me, I was walking as if nothing had happened, amid the people, in the mist, with my eyes red and wet. I'd already walked away from the avenue,

I'd left the site of the attempt behind, but I needed to find a safe spot. Where? I couldn't go back to the hideout I shared with Silvestre. I still didn't know what made him abort the mission. I wouldn't have been safe there. I should have at least gotten myself to the other side of the city. I looked in my pockets and saw that I had enough money. I should have taken a taxi. I would have rather walked for a while, I'd already exposed myself too much. The taxis were always driven by government people, ever since the distant years of clandestine living it had always been inconvenient to escape in a taxi, they were managed by cops. Abelardo told me on one occasion, either you robbed one or you found a friend who could take you. Actually, public transportation was preferable, you were just another passenger, if you were unarmed and your papers were in order, you weren't in danger. I wanted to take the subway but the entrance was flanked by police with dogs. They weren't stopping anyone but I didn't want to take a chance. I could have crossed the university, but it was surely one of the most guarded places. Its autonomy turned it into a de facto refuge for people who were escaping. I paused at a bus stop and grabbed a bus. I got on. I would go East. I had no destination, to begin. The East sounded good.

I was aching everywhere. My whole body was throbbing, my head was killing me. I stood the whole way, the radio never stopped sounding, the music was noise, the landscape didn't come through the windows and the door, ashes did, people were coughing, the driver was glancing back in the rearview mirror at the ass of a black girl standing next to me, at times it seemed like he was looking for something. They interrupted a vile changa song on the radio and gave updates about the events that morning. *The security organisms had dismantled an international conspiracy to assassinate the president and leader of the revolution, right where the parade was taking place, on Roosevelt Avenue, a suspect had been shot. The superintendent of the building from where the reprehensible act was going to be perpetrated was found dead from a shot to the head.* —If it wasn't the police, who the hell had killed the Colombian?— Silvestre. They'd already raided several houses and a syndicate leader and an ex-director of a small company had been arrested. They didn't say anything about a third suspect, they weren't naming me, that meant I was dead. Where did they invent the part about an international conspiracy? What the hell made them think we worked for the right?

Based on the people they had detained, it was assumed as obvious that the assassination was planned by people in Miami. Anyways, my cheek hurt, I felt like my eye was about to fall out, I realized that my shirt was ripped down one side. A stretch of traffic had stopped, it was too loud in the van, too much smoke and too much coughing, the driver wouldn't stop staring at me, or he wouldn't stop staring at the tits and ass of the black girl who was right beside me. The police and army must be asking people for their papers, they must have set up checkpoints all over the place. On the radio you could hear the president's voice, it was roaring, going crazy, it was deafening. I regretted not turning the course of history forever. You could see military cars on the street, on the corners they had tanks. "The parties that destroyed the country have tried to stop the process of change, they have plotted this time with arms against the process and I repeat to the political parties that destroyed the country, this process will take my life, my commitment is to the people and with the voice of the people I will say..." The van braked and I took advantage of the moment to leap onto the street, avoided a few cars and reached the sidewalk, limping, I was slow but safe. And sure enough, they had set up checkpoints and were asking for papers, looking through people's bags. I had nothing to fear, I wasn't carrying anything, my papers were in order, with a name that wasn't my own, but in order. I could pass through any barrier. And what if they knew about me? If Lourdes or Dominguín himself had warned the police that two of the men from the organization were out of control? I had probably been uncovered, they had probably found the hideout where Silvestre and I would lay low. They would have the order to kill us, Manuel Roca would have given that order, Roca was now the party, the organization, the government's black hand.

I decided against taking any risks and walked toward a mall, I saw my mirrored image in the display windows. I was a disaster, I looked like I had been in a fight. I passed my fingers through my hair, straightened my shirt, there was nothing else I could do. The mall was also full of police. I felt surrounded, I didn't have many options, I considered the idea of turning myself in, of lying, of involving Roca in the assassination attempt.

A police officer was coming towards me, it was inevitable that he'd stop me, I was broken, my morale was in shreds, but all of a sudden I pushed a door and entered a record shop. There weren't many people, only a few stragglers who were searching through the compact discs and a badly groomed woman listening to the earphones she had on. I stood in front of her, it looked like we were a couple. The woman was very young, her face was thin, her lips thick, she was beautiful and strange, disheveled. We were both disheveled. The police officer came in and glanced around, saw me in front of the lady, I was smiling at her and she was making signs at me, she made her hands rotate as though she were moving a crank, her fingers barely peeked out from the sleeves of an ugly denim jacket. I responded to her with improvised gestures and took the risk of grabbing the CD case she was holding. The officer assumed we were a couple, a strange couple, and decided to leave us alone.

The store was pleasant, clean, well-lit. The cash registers and shelves were organized in a geometrical order that resembled ancient observation towers. What am I saying—observation towers? Do I actually have any fucking clue what observatories look like? I imagined Stonehenge, not at all, that room had nothing to do with it, but I insist it gave the impression of being inside a place from where astronomical points of reference are registered. The place could seem, with its plastic angles illuminated by neon, to have figures to fit the scale of the Peruvian desert. But I wasn't in the mood for these things. I had a beautiful woman in front of me, quite disheveled, with a thin face, dishcloth hair and full lips. She kept moving a crank with her hands, then I realized she had her eyes closed. She opened them, let her glance fall on my face, made no gesture, not even a sigh, grabbed the cuff of her jacket, turned her eyes and balanced her head, I followed her rhythm, then she bit her lower lip. She was strange, I wasn't up to figuring her out, I was making time and almost dancing with her. It was silly because I wasn't wearing the earphones, I moved my head closer to hers, listened to a little bit, it was a trumpet, she continued to balance herself and I thought that I'd like to free myself from everything, escape. The woman took off the earphones and without ceasing to clamp the sleeves of her jacket with her hands, she made a gesture to me, I returned it. I looked stupid, but I couldn't think of anything better to do. She finally let me look into her eyes, she hadn't allowed me before, they were green, dark, so dark they seemed black, like Lourdes's. God, I felt chills. She was my type, most definitely. What use was it anyways that she be a distortion of Lourdes, and that my entire face become covered in drops of sweat? If they caught me as soon as I left the record shop, they'd liquidate me in an alley. I suddenly understood that neither my companions nor Roca were going to let them catch me alive. I don't know why I supposed I was the victim of a conspiracy I hadn't yet managed to figure out.

"And where did you come from, cute kitty?" the dancer finally asked me, my distorted mirror image of Lourdes.

"From a cat hunt." I don't know why I responded with something so stupid. I looked like a dumb hippie, a fool who tries to pick up another New Age fool.

"And the kitty's a player. Besides, your glance is like a dog's," she answered.

"I look however I can," I told her, "and dogs like the music of Gato Barbieri." I remembered that I had a girlfriend who listened to Barbieri, just the soundtrack to *Last Tango in Paris*. She half-closed her eyes, they were as green as they were deep.

"Is that the only thing you know about Barbieri?" she challenged me.

"Probably, I don't remember anything beside the soundtrack, I like to remember the soundtrack to **Last Tango in Paris**." She left a crack open, a green firefly glance.

"Really, how come?" she asked.

"Because it reminds me of a woman."

"It makes me think of many men. " She came closer, held my glance, I felt her breath, it was sweet, syrupy, she offered me her whole mouth.

"Do you like to sodomize your lovers?"

Had I heard right?

"I don't have time for lovers," I answered, I was faltering for the first time, I was intimidated by the conversation, I had forgotten that a few hours ago I had tried to kill the president and they were looking for me, to kill me.

"What are you doing?" she took charge again, grabbed me by the arm as if we knew each other, set the earphones down.

"I'm looking for a record," I answered. I had become conscious of my true situation.

"Do you believe in ghosts?" She asked me another question that broke the logic of any decent discourse.

"In the beyond and those types of things? I don't believe. I don't know." I almost laughed. She smiled at me. We both smiled and she held on to my arm tighter.

"Are you alone?" I asked her.

"Almost always. Whenever I'm not in a pack," she responded.

"Can I accompany you?" I returned a question to her.

"Only if you'll go to Puerto Píritu." I thought of the sea. Yes, I wanted to go to the sea. I wanted to be swallowed by an old town. I remembered Puerto Píritu, we had buried an informer near there. I remembered its beach with murky, furious waves, its nights, the nearly eternal breeze, the white cathedral, yes, I wanted to go far away, to the sea, to a port, to a town with a port, a solitary town, I wanted to get lost from history and its plays, a place far from the laws of the dialectic, the dialectic was a big lie.

But this woman who was stuck to my arm, this couple for one dance, was she crazy? I looked at her closely, even though she was wearing rags, the rags were on purpose, she wore them with style, and underneath them was the outline of a delicate body—fine—I wanted to grab her by the waist, but the situation was absurd. She was probably playing. The similarity with Lourdes excited me. I was hoping she'd take me by the arm to the parking lot, put me in her car and take me out of this damn situation I had gotten myself into.

"Let's go," I said.

"All the way to Puerto Píritu?" she asked.

"Wherever you want to take me," I answered. She wanted to play and I was playing along.

"Are you sure? Would you sign on it?" she asked.

"Definitely, let's go to your car," I inquired.

"I don't have a car." I moved her hand from my arm, I felt like shoving her against the display case, she looked down, grabbed my arm again, I wanted to kill her. With this crazy bitch I was fucked. It wasn't possible for circumstances to play against me, now that I thought I was safe. I couldn't believe it. These disheveled girls have giant cars, it's the law, at least that's how things should be. Christ, it's the law.

"You told me you were sure about coming. C'mon, dude, let's go. I'll get you out of here." I had no choice, I gave myself over to her designs.

"What's your name?" she asked me.

"Sergio." Sonia went up to the cash register and paid for her purchase, grabbed the package and held it in her free hand, she was still hanging onto my arm and even then with that insignificant acrobatic act, she was trapping her jacket sleeve with her fingers. We were an impressionist and murky fresco, leaving the store, it was already getting dark out. God. A whole day. Quickly, in darkness, a whole fucking day lost in the haze, the mist, in the ashes and smoke of a New York that wasn't, of an impossible Caracas, of a Mexico that was a stranger to itself, of Santa Cruz and its Sahara airs, thick, asphyxiating.

I have had friends in life, though none like Abelardo. Abelardo wasn't my friend, he was one of those father figures, one of many. Our friends are father figures, all of them, even female friends, that's what I ended up thinking. But Abelardo was my friend, my first friend, a father figure, of course, but my friend. He said revealing things, at one time, when I didn't have a clearly defined idea of socialism, that necessary theory that must go beyond equality and the struggle for the poor, the theory that tells you that to each his own according to his productivity and such, and not just a slogan. I had slogans, I think I still have them, I fight for slogans and set phrases, my theory is the party and the party explains itself to me, that's what I think, but back then I needed a clarification, a transcendent vision. "What is socialism?" was the question that day. Abelardo, practical as ever, told me: "It's fascism, but of the left," another slogan. Another phrase that demanded another answer, "What is fascism?" The answer came, but Abelardo wasn't always so practical.

He pretended to live his life with a philosophical sense, I remember he called himself a Zen Marxist. He'd tell me life was a river and that this didn't contradict the dialectic, that I shouldn't get too worked up about it being a river, to remember that no one bathes twice in the same river, for me to reconcile this idea without intellectual pretensions with the premise that you have to let the river flow. And since I let situations flow, of course, a point of contradiction would immediately follow: if I let it flow I wouldn't do anything to change it, and that was a metaphysical idea. What the fuck was metaphysics?

Well, to be an idealist. What the fuck, according to Plekhanov's manual, did it mean to be an idealist? It didn't mean being a man with ideas, he was clear about that, it's so hard to handle theory without it becoming a mess, but we need to reconcile things. Abelardo would say, he could say, let it flow as a tactical expression—to let life flow didn't mean refusing to change it, it meant allowing for the laws of the dialectic to impose themselves, that they occasionally escaped from the individual need for change, that the river was a collective will, called history, and we had to let the river flow. That was Zen Marxism.

So letting myself be guided by Sonia was a collective will, to walk out into the sunset with Sonia wasn't my will, this was obvious, it was the will of a hidden force, of the dialectic.

We left the mall. We passed by police officers with their dogs, with my appearance, with my blows, with my fears set aside. We passed a military checkpoint and I realized the army was in the streets, I had already seen tanks and men in green; now I didn't notice anything, I knew they were in the street, the street belonged to the army and yet nothing was happening, traffic was infernal, people were moving on the sidewalks, between cars, on the avenues, disrupting their walks, they sat on benches in the plazas or crowded the subway station. The mist was pink, a pink fire like the sunset, it was neither mist nor haze, it was a fire, ashes, smoke, it smelled horrible, it covered us. Sonia wasn't taking me to a parking lot, we weren't getting into her car and taking off, we joined the collective that was mixed together with the dogs, the police, the soldiers, that was glowing red until it grew dark, that ended up being the afternoon that had gone by and was becoming night and then we were brown beside all the city cats. They probably would have caught me in Sonia's car, in the parking lot. They were stopping cars, the parking lots were being monitored, soldiers and police were asking people for their papers, I was thinking about it and I knew I would escape. When would I escape from Sonia? It wasn't convenient to leave; it wasn't convenient for her to leave me. I had nowhere to go, I had lost my shell, the collaborators within the party were probably waiting for me so they could hand me over—my people were looking for me and I'm sure they had orders, because I was on the periphery. "Not having an organization is not having a family," I thought. I had no choice, I had to let myself flow with the river, with history, with life, with Sonia.

We took a bus that opened a path between other buses, we were standing in the crowd, all squeezed together. The situation was repeating itself. The driver was blasting the radio, the president was speaking, with the same voice as always, willing, metallic, he dragged his *r*s like a good troop commander, he was high-pitched. He said nothing to the crowd, they were tired of listening to him, the faces they made were the same as ever—yawns, a smirk of annoyance or anger, someone managed to pull out a joke, someone else hugged a friend, we were packed in and we were in the habit of being crowded together on the ride home, it was the habit of the collective in which I was moving. The president's speech didn't exist even though it was being broadcast on the radio at full volume. It didn't matter that he was announcing special measures, or that he was suspending some guarantees in the best constitution in the world while the conspiracy was revealed, the right had wanted to restore the opprobrious regime of previous years, his own life didn't matter, he owed his life to the people, he was the process, he had respected and would respect all democratic and peaceful forms—but what State doesn't have the legitimate right to defend itself when faced with the treachery of dark and reactionary factors? The detentions and the dismantling of a few labor unions that obey conspiratorial designs would continue. I remembered the early morning when we were supposed to go out into the street to support the coup attempt. That was a while ago, we would finally create the revolution, so many guerrillas, so many persecutions, so many projects were justified with the rebellion of the revolutionary soldiers. Our handler recalled that the Bolshevik revolution would not have been possible without the participation of soldiers. "It was a revolution of workers and soldiers, if that term had existed," our handler kept repeating, "the October insurrection would have proclaimed itself as a civilian-military manifestation..." That's how our handler kept talking while we waited for the order to go out into the streets and we ended up waiting all morning and half the day. They never called us, Roca never appeared with the order for insurrection, they left us stranded like a small town bride and they, the glorious revolutionary soldiers, lost their riot, and the man who is now president during his minute in front of the TV cameras asked them to wait for a better time, to lay down their arms and wait for more suitable times. "The rebellion was lost because they didn't trust civilians, " our handler said. "They underestimated us," he screamed, "they gave us four guns and pushed us aside. They underestimated us." "And what will we do with the weapons?" asked one of Ruperto Lugo's companions. "Bury them!" exclaimed Roca. "We won't get rid of them. These weapons belong to the people, we have to find a place for them."

We left downtown in that despicable bus, packed together, with Sonia clinging to my arm. We crossed the Eastern part of the city, making our way through ashes, soldiers, dogs, the president's speech and the smoke until we reached the outskirts, arriving without delay at the Eastern bus terminal.

I was immune. I realized I was immune, that I had to keep vaccinating myself against reality.

We got off the bus and went in to the terminal, my arm in the hands of that woman I had just met in a record shop, and she clinging to me, almost dragging me, she stumbled as she walked, she never stopped clamping the sleeve of her jacket with her other hand. And we talked. We talked a lot, we were like a couple, we said things that had nothing to do with anything, absurd things. I realized that amid all the situations I had gone through, I had always kept reading, it was an inheritance from Abelardo. He read all the time, even the writers who had been killed by Stalin, he devoured books. And I did the same, which is why many people said I sounded like someone who had graduated from the School of Arts at the Central University. I was vague and pretentious, I was a romantic guy with his girlfriend on his arm. That's how they must have seen us: absent, gone from the world, because nothing touched us. That night was tense, the president had settled into his speech and he promised to extend it until dawn, the troops were on the streets, people weren't whispering like they had in other similar situations, they seemed to give no importance to the event, they didn't speak about a coup or countercoup, much less about the unveiled conspiracy. They were recommending horses for a race or making plans for a round of beers.

It was time to abandon Sonia, it made no sense to go with her. She was a vague entity, she had no conclusion, she had no grasp on an idea, she would vanish, I vanished alongside her, I shared her virtue, her phantasmagoria. Her similarity to Lourdes kept me in suspense. But I needed to leave.

I was outside the city, in a bus terminal, a place for meetings and departures, a platform for big cars with wheels. I could go anywhere. But I had no fucking clue where I should go. We sat down at a cafeteria. I ordered a coffee, started to drink it, while I watched myself reflected in Sonia's dark green glance, which had emptied itself to reflect me. I realized I hadn't eaten all day, my stomach was aching, an unpleasant pressure in my esophagus. I was hungry. I had gone nearly twenty-four hours without eating, without drinking. I was like one of those movie heroes who pass through circumstances well beyond their needs. So it was true, the action of my life could be continuous, offer no explanations, it could proceed without anyone saying you need to stop acting so you can shit, piss or eat. No, the movie runs, and you run. I felt all the necessities at once. So then all life's miseries crashed down on me and I felt like crying. Between pouts I told Sonia to order me a beef arepa or an empanada, a Coke or some tea, that she ask for both of them, more coffee, I searched my pockets and pulled out a bill, left it on the table and went to the bathrooms.

The men's room was empty. It was one of those nights with very little transit in the terminal. I let myself fall onto the tiles above the urinal, I let my weight pull me, I felt like I was carrying the world on my shoulders, it was something mythological. I had to push in order to start pissing, at first a short, dry stream came out, a shot. Then the river flowed, with its history, the collective, it was moving, I felt the hair on my arms stand on end, my eyes began to water. A feeling, a bitterness, a hoarseness, everything was mixing together inside, I hit the wall three times with the palm of my hand, it wasn't the first time I did it, I would always do it after drinking a few beers when standing in front of a urinal and the emptiness, the uselessness would come to me, all those petit bourgeois emotions that, according to Abelardo, make men want to shoot themselves in the mouth.

Facing the urinal, in the bus terminal, I had to hit the wall and its dirty tiles, give those three slaps to conjure fear, rancor, uncertainty. I didn't want to ask myself anything, I was pissing and I felt a sensation of painful, special relief, a small orgasm, I felt like I was emptying all my sperm, it was like getting lost in a painful and contradictory orgasm, I felt like the light would go out, that I would die. Soon I was empty, without any piss in my bladder. Soon I was quiet, listening to voices in the hallway, I was empty of everything, inert. I zipped up my pants and went to the sink, opened the tap and once again the water came along with the idea of the flowing river, life was there, I could see it in the mirror, with a swollen, red cheek, my face dirty and deformed, my eyes much too expressive, revealing a desperation I didn't want to confront—shit—how could it be they didn't catch me, I asked myself? I'm so obvious, such a case. I threw water on myself, wet my hair, cleaned dirt and blood off my face—I was dirt and blood—I looked like a mechanic after a bad day's work.

A box, a motor, an accident. My life had exploded into piec-es and I was facing the mirror, with a blow to my right cheek, eye closed, I then realized I was looking through one eye only, or one and a half, there I was and the smoke was entering the bathroom, that cursed smoke, cursed fire that never ended. My life. I asked about my life. My stomach was hurting and I left, first I had to kill my hunger, then decide about myself and life, about the flowing river, the smoke, history, the collective.

I returned to the table. There were two empanadas on a plate.

"They don't have any beef arepas," Sonia told me.

"And what are these?" I pointed at the plate with a gesture that started at my mouth.

"Empanadas," she answered, and took a cigarette out and offered me one. I declined, I would smoke later, I had also for-gotten how to smoke.

"I asked for ham and cheese, you eat," I shrugged and sat down. I ate with desperation, quickly, without thinking. I or-dered another empanada and drank the iced tea, opened the can of Coke, looked at Sonia who was now squeezing the sleeves of her jacket with her fingers.

"The bus leaves in half an hour," she told me. "You'd better hurry."

"Yeah, I imagine it would be good if you hurried, too," I answered. Sonia squinted at me. "I don't think I want to go with you." I took the empanada and nearly ate the whole thing in one bite.

"You promised," she screamed, standing up and pulling at her jacket sleeves with her hands. "You signed!" She puffed up her chest, it was big, round, voluptuous, her shape was marked in a precise manner, she was wearing a cheap woven shirt, with mediocre stitching, with stupid flowers. She stretched and screamed, under her shirt she wore a t-shirt and nothing beneath that, she showed me her belly button: it was pierced, a little silverfish covering it. I saw her skin, not on her face, burned by the sun or by the city smoke, I saw the skin of her belly, flat and taut, young, I saw her tanned skin, she had been born of bronze, her whiteness shone in the bronze, this is what I thought while she screamed.

"You can scream all you like. What the hell do you think I'm going to do in Puerto Píritu?" I said to her and lifted the coffee I had ordered to my mouth.

"Nothing," she spat out with anger. "But you promised me and you should honor your promise, no one can be saved if they don't stand by their word, and you need to be saved."

I stood up from the chair, took another bill out of my pocket and threw it on the table, it was an ugly gesture (that's how you pay a whore), but I was paying for my food. To honor a promise, I thought, I should honor a promise, I didn't give a fuck, her rhetoric of salvation seemed like shit to me, but why would I save myself by honoring the promise, the matter seemed gothic to me, I wanted to ask her about it, but I turned my back to her and started to leave her behind, she was losing perspective, I was moving to the front, a close-up toward nowhere, she was going out of focus, two soldiers appeared in front of me, dogs—fuck—fate appeared in front of me once again. That's what it's about. Where could I go now? My cheek was throbbing, I felt all the blows I had received that morning pulsing, my stomach hadn't stopped being resentful, now it was accusing an abrupt plenitude, my reality was those terminal spaces, the shots were blurring together, I went to the restroom and entered one of the stalls, threw up everything. The coffee, empanadas, Coke, tea; history, the river, life, vomit, they all flowed.

I left the stall and leaned on the sink, I turned on the tap, I threw water on my face, I was red, swollen, bloated, I looked like an infected glans. God, what an image. I had to step out of there with a firm step, but I couldn't, my knees were buckling, I was trembling and the bathroom ceiling was spinning, I thought, *I'm about to lose the famous good foot that will take me out of here, I'm about to faint, I feel disgust.* I kept myself from falling and dragged my shoulder across the wall, all the way to the bathroom door. Once again I was in a close-up, alone, the soldiers and their dogs outside, with their assault rifles, their daggers at their belts, their helmets and metallic voices dragging the *r*s, their voices would tell me to stop any moment now. I couldn't fight this battle, I needed to avoid a confrontation, my guerrilla tactic. I turned my back on them and felt the voice that was about to tell me, "Hey, you!" It was about to shoot at me, "Stop!"

I picked up the pace, I staggered, I left them behind, out of focus, I was sweating, my face pearly, drenched, soaked—shit! All the water had left my body, the platform came into focus.

"Which buses are heading East?" I asked, no one able to tell me exactly which one was going and to what town, I insisted and got onto a bus, dimly lit, almost empty, in the third row to the right I saw Sonia, clamping the sleeves of her jacket with her hands, I felt tenderness, peace, I think I felt a strong desire to hug her, I smiled at her, she looked at me, I couldn't see her face, she didn't smile but she looked at me, I thought of her eyes as dark green embers full of hate. I walked towards her, asked her if I could sit down next to her, I sighed.

"You're right, a man has to honor his promises, that's the only way he can save himself."

She looked straight ahead, breathing very tranquilly, her chest rose and fell, I wanted to lean my head on it, I wanted to sleep or die, as that crazy prince said. The driver got in and closed the door, we began to move, backwards at first, night had finally arrived and it was quite late, dawn would arrive soon, we picked up speed, connected to the highway and moved along the road, I pulled the curtain aside, everything was dark out there, even the darkness of the orange flames, the brushwood that burns darkly in the hills, that burns and burns and produces all the smoke of a world we were leaving behind. Sonia barely smiled.

THERE ARE BLOWS IN LIFE

Manuel Roca was a correct, disciplined, tidy man. Manuel Roca was behind the president the moment they shot at him. He was his Minister of Social Affairs. Until the Military Staff cleared the stage, he didn't flinch. He was a cold man. One of the guards grabbed him by the arm and he resisted. "What's the matter?" he managed to ask, as he was freeing himself from the security pincers, looking at his coat, it had been ruined by the soldier's assault, he ended up feeling annoyed.

"They've shot at the president." Until that moment he had been Manuel Roca, the grey minister, with a low profile in the cabinet, a political favorite. Before they put him in the car heading to the presidential office his fate was already decided, "there are blows in life..."

When he reached the antechamber he was called to an emergency meeting and was told that from now on he would handle the office of Internal Affairs. He received the news without moving a muscle in his face. In his hands he held the regime's domestic policy, he held the domestic policy of power. He remained standing in the meeting room, he knew it would be a private meeting, that it wouldn't be a tedious cabinet meeting. The guards stood at attention when the president walked in, he took off the military cap and unbuttoned the front of his military uniform, revealing the bullet-proof vest. There were no preambles.

"Manuel, you've made a commitment to me, to the process and to the people. You must lead this stage," the leader spit out. He took a handkerchief from the hands of his aide, first wiping his entire face with it, leaving him dry, with no shine, matte; then he insisted on wiping his forehead. He took the cup of coffee another soldier held out to him, and he drank it in one gulp.

"I'll proceed immediately," was all Roca said.

"Do whatever you have to do and don't inform me about the details, you assume that responsibility, I trust you, but there are things for which only you will be able to answer." He asked for another jacket and the aide told him they were ready for the national TV and radio broadcast. The president, who was on his second coffee, extended his hand to Roca, his hand was small, delicate, it didn't correspond with the rest of the body, at times imposing, despite revealing the initial corruption of obesity. Both men looked at each other, Roca remained sober, the president squinted his glance slightly. He turned his back to him and left.

From the presidential office, Manuel Roca was led to the offices of his new ministry. He didn't see his surroundings, he didn't stop to notice the details the departing minister had left, he picked up the phone that was free of monitoring and called Lourdes and Dominguín, his two party companions, demanding their immediate presence at his office. Then he called the State Police Commissioner and asked him for a meeting with the Chief of Military Intelligence, while he ordered him to not let the ex-president of the state oil companies escape, that they take measures in the airports and detain Durán; it was the moment to dismantle the syndicates he led. He requested that they raid the headquarters of a few opposition organizations and detain all those who were on file as enemies of the revolutionary government. He immediately demanded a call with the Attorney General of the Republic and with the People's Defender, he informed them that some constitutional rights had been suspended, but that regardless he wanted them to guarantee the physical integrity of all those detained, a few legal procedures would be ignored and whoever had to go to prison would go, but both the Attorney General's office and the Office of the People's Defense must tell the world that human rights were being respected. He received a call from the Minister of Defense in which the latter informed him that the troops were on the street, the headquarters of the National Assembly was being guarded and there were no reports of disturbances, the situation was under control, they had found the weapons they needed to find in Durán's house. Roca smiled, now is when things are about to become difficult for Durán, he told himself.

Lourdes and Dominguín arrived in an official car, they were immediately invited to step into another official car where the minister was waiting for them. They drove out into the street, took one of the main avenues and then a highway, feinting as though they were leaving the city. The minister trusted no one and still didn't have a safe place for meetings. Which is why they would drive around while they discussed a few details.

"We're in power now," said Roca. "We finally have actual power. What about Silvestre?" He took out a handkerchief and covered his nose, even through the air conditioning, the smell of smoke was everywhere.

"Silvestre did a half-assed job, he's dead," said Dominguín. Lourdes was looking towards the right, along the highway they passed billboards, buildings, light posts; the city was passing by outside, foreseen, through the smoke that was falling over it. She was looking at tanks. The military was mobilized.

"I understand that Sergio escaped."

Yes, he had escaped, the man had been swallowed by the earth or the smoke. It shouldn't have happened. He should be accompanying Silvestre in the morgue, he should have been exposed to the press.

"It's a matter of time, " said Lourdes, "before they photograph his corpse." She tried to smile. Roca was tense, but he didn't stop looking at her with fondness, he was staring at her chest, she had medium-sized but ample breasts, nicely shaped and firm.

"We have to correct whatever mistakes were made, all of you in the organization now become a shadow army." He gave Dominguín a folder. "Here's a list of people who need to be quiet. I don't want to know anything about them, ever. And for tomorrow I want Sergio where he needs to be." He told them that the process had entered the stage where they had to organize anarchy, that the ground had become a matter for the army, that whomever took over even a yard of ground would do so only to be buried under it. The revolution was now about order. This was how things had changed and it was a real shift that everyone must have been made to feel, not as a message, but rather as the government's order and will. He ordered the driver to take the car toward a town in the city outskirts and he told Dominguín that he should only contact him via the agreed upon cell phone number. Dominguín opened the door, paused and waited for Lourdes.

"She's staying, we've got work to do. We'll talk soon." Dominguín found himself alone on the sidewalk of a town in the outskirts of Caracas, he watched the black car disappear amid the smoke. While he scratched his head he thought how unnecessary it had been for them to leave him out there. He lit a cigarette. The comrade was already making us feel the power he wielded. He thought with annoyance that he would have to figure out how to get back to the city, he didn't realize a man was lifting his arm behind him, aiming and destroying his occipital bone with a gunshot. The body fell without drama, the papers with the to-do list disappeared from his side.

Manuel Roca was recalling "The Night of the Generals." He had watched it at one point in his life. Maybe in Paris, after meeting with the old Khmer Rouge man. His life was the life of a long time ago, he saw himself in the rearview mirror and looked at his face, watching the many years that had passed through him, he remained the same: cold, beautiful, attractive. His face was lined by various wrinkles, its texture was already like parchment, his black hair now sparse. He was anguished by the loss of his hair in recent years, he would have to come to terms with it. He had lived through enough to face the ravages of baldness without being ridiculous. His eyes were glowing with the same intensity as ever, which made him feel strong, vital. It wasn't the glow of passion, he never had that particular glow, his eyes had the cold light of intelligence. He felt proud of that. All his colleagues who had carried the glow of passion were dead. Or alone. Or crazy. Most definitely, disgrace had touched them. He didn't consider himself a survivor. An unfortunate man. Abelardo would often tell him, "Only survivors gain access to power, one can only remain in power by surviving." For him, Manuel Roca—now Minister of Internal Affairs, the man who was leading a maneuver of the revolutionary government—it had all come down to being alive, not merely surviving, but being alive in permanent exercise, life was a demanding routine, one must know its equations, erase the empire of feelings, that vain tyranny. To live means to calculate. To calculate was to establish distances. A contradictory game for a Marxist—collective power did not reconcile with the power of the cadres of the revolutionary vanguard. The minister left those contradictions to the theorists. He was considered a theorist by his party colleagues and by the president himself. They were wrong, he privately defined himself as an executive of the revolution.

Manuel Roca had been born in a town at the foothills of the Andean mountains. The illegitimate and incestuous son of a municipal schoolteacher and a landowner who grew coffee and raised cattle. Roca's mother was the sister of the farmer's wife. His conception and birth had been a scandal. He and his mother had been banished from the family and the town.

He was raised in a village neighboring that of his parents. They weren't protected from the scandal, but his mother was accepted as a teacher in a rural school, despite the doubts and thanks to his father's influence throughout the region. His first years were spent in a rural school. He remembers as his home those damp classrooms, the smell of the wooden desks, the smell of the children in that school. It is a particular odor, he recalls, the smell of the whole school along with that of the children, the sum of childhood smells. The chalk dust, the gum erasers, the smell of glue and the wood of the pencils and desks, the sweat, to those smells were added the ones from the day, the morning one had to do with the greasy paper in which breakfast was wrapped, the afternoon one included the lunch smell, almost always beef vegetable soup, noodle soup, always soup and wheat arepas. The afternoon smells would be roused by running in the patio, it was a rancid, acidic smell and this is how he remembers the light, like the afternoon smells, the light that began at noon, the light that would impose itself when the sky cleared in the mountain, the light that came with the air around the cow dung, with the earth and its potatoes and onions, with the passing of carts, the transit of rough men, the men who spoke of his mother when they gulped an anisette in the cantina, the ones who would look at her as though she were a whore. They, who would grab the yoke of the oxen and plow the black earth of the mountain foothills, they also smelled of afternoons in the school.

He remembered his early childhood in a small room with a portable coal oven and a latrine at the end of a patio. He remembered the smell of his mother, the smell of sweet skin, warm skin; his mother had long hair that she would patiently brush each night in front of a piece of a mirror she had nailed to an unpainted wall. His mother was warmth, the only warmth that had ever satisfied him. They slept in the same bed and before sleeping, he remembered his mother would read to him; she was ill, he would never forget that. With a pale grimace she would read a sad story to him—his mother's life had been sad—she couldn't help reading Dickens, it made sense that she read *Oliver Twist,* it was just and necessary. As the priest said in church while the altar boy swung the censer: it was for someone who had never felt happiness, who never had emotions, someone sad, that's how he remembered his mother, a sadness that would enfold him each night with her skin, a sadness that was extinguished with a great deal of pain.

They buried his mother in the town cemetery. Manuel Roca went to the burial accompanied by a thick, tall man, with a single gesture on his face, a grimace that seemed cruel to him. Not many people went to his mother's funeral. Of her warmth, of her sadness, he is left with everything or actually, nothing. The school principal, the priest, his father, and himself.

He was beginning his life. His early childhood had not seen the light of life but rather that of his mother's sure and sad nonlife. His early childhood was a damp school and many smells, the portable oven and the ripped bedspreads, a cavern.

He was starting over, now with brothers who barely spoke to him and who referred to him as the other cousin, the bastard, the bitch aunt's son. He was starting his life on his father's hacienda, a large house on a plateau, a cold place, permanently covered by fog. He never ate at the table with the family, he never saw his father's wife, he was always with the servants and his cousin, the other cousin, he never understood why they called her the other cousin. Or he did, she was the other sister. Life seemed sad and miserable to him like that of the boy from Dickens, but without the consolation of adventures and happy endings. His life was miserable and confusing while he was on that hacienda of black earth and permanent fog, his other cousin would besiege him, she would climb into bed with him at night and pull his pants down. He resisted at first but she would cover his mouth with her manly hands, his cousin would stir him up, touching him between his legs. He didn't have to learn anything about sex, that incubus revealed everything to him brusquely. His other cousin would masturbate him until he was irritated, she would put his little penis in her mouth and suck it compulsively, she would no longer silence him with her hands, he had learned how to remain quiet. Each time he tried to protest, the other cousin would threaten to tell about what they had been doing. His nights grew long, he barely slept, when he recalled those nights his back would become drenched in sweat, it is a recurring memory. His cousin enjoyed herself and he began to enjoy an early nightmare in the house on the hacienda of perpetual fog. One time, under threat, he was forced to pass his tongue along his cousin's genitals, they were very red, bare flesh, nearly hairless, he remembered the smell of his other cousin, it was a thick smell, sweat and salt; sweat and acidic honey, stale honey, frightful honey, honey and radishes, honey and dirt. He would eat her each night. Long night, without any conclusion in time, life night, of tenuous light in candles, night amid his existence that was just beginning, his oblique nothingness on the hacienda, on the ledge of a plateau, a night that ended when they were caught by the father. The light goes out, a dry blow to the mouth, the taste of blood, its thickness, the viscosity, his own honey. This was how another life began.

He was sent to a seminary in the city that was the capital of the state. One could say that until then he had been unfortunate, he was no different than the miserable characters in the novels by Dickens that had been read to him by his mother's sadness or by his mother.

He didn't change much, he could say like Vallejo that he had been born on a day God was ill and when he saw the heavy rains fall, he could say he would die in Mérida on a rainy day.

In the seminary he had no deviant experiences, though it was assumed to be the norm. Everyone talks about deviant experiences in seminaries, they tell of mistreatment and abuse, but he found some peace, he could devote himself to studying, he learned the liturgy, he submitted to discipline in order to save himself from nostalgia, he thought it would be good to study and be a priest, to live apart from the world. Which he otherwise considered despicable. He didn't have many friends,

his first friend tried to touch him like his cousin and he immediately managed to distance himself from him, he was cautious, rarely spoke, then he made another friend, Joaquín. Joaquín was the son of a poor peasant. He studied in the seminary
because it was a way of not having to share the misery of his
siblings. Besides, one son for the militia and another for God,
the rest for hunger, his father would say.

His relationship with Joaquín was cautious at first. But they
shared tastes in reading. They would spend hours in the library, reading the church priests' books, the history of the martyrs, then they read the permitted classics, which is how they
came upon the Greeks and would even recite rhapsodies from
The Iliad by heart. They were glorious times, life had meaning,
they thought as they read the Greeks, as they were washed
over by the tragedies. That's as far as they got. Father Serafín
lent them a book that contained some epigrams by Martial and
a few poems by Catullus. That turned them into learned boys,
beyond the class discussions about the apology of Socrates or
Plato's *Republic,* literature that led them to St. Augustine, they
were already reading the profane authors, they began to mark
a distance from philosophical digressions and to drink from
the poems of Teresa of Ávila, St. John of the Cross and Sor Juana Inés.

Thanks to the clandestine exchange they kept up with Father Serafín, their intellectual restlessness transcended that of
the other seminary students. They saw the world as the only
place where a glorious life could be lived. It was a blasphe-
mous concept, but they eventually discussed Christ's mission,
his mission in the world, beyond the church of his own time,
a glorious mission to the degree that he established it among
fishermen and publicans, among whores and gluttons. Their
reading of books of chivalry convinced them. Tirant lo Blanch,
Amadis de Gaula and the Quixote defined their future. The
mission of life was to be found in life itself. But what had life

itself been for Manuel Roca? Until that moment: impressions, the memory of sadness, banishment, abuse, damp smells, the cold and sordid relationship with his father. Life was a place without echoes, a weak light.

The seminary reminded him of his first years, the filtered light of the classrooms in the school where his mother taught. The damp room of his nights. The grotto, the cavern, beyond the world, noisy with its rivers and breezes, within his mother's warm skin. But the seminary ended with his readings, he had to make a decision, he could have kept studying to be a priest, but his heart was overflowing with texts that had awakened an excessive appetite to reaffirm himself in life, in the world. Once he finished high school, he would go out into the world, this is what he had decided with Joaquín, his first brother in arms.

And where would they go?

To the capital.

It was the beginning and end, when they would conquer the world. They would go study at the university. Father Serafín served as their bridge, he secured them places to study law at the Central University, the University City had recently been opened, they could already use the student dormitories and find jobs at night, teaching a few hours of classes. The difficulty would be to go to the capital and begin to exist outside, among people.

The night had been long. He had been forced to make decisions, this is what he told Lourdes. He had spent his life making decisions, some of them good ones and others not quite so. Now he was sure he was on the right path. And staying on the path meant making decisions.

Manuel Roca lived in a hotel. He had transferred his convoy to the hotel. He had time to rest for a few hours. The army was on the streets, civil rights were suspended. Power rested in the hands of the executive, nearly everything had gone well.

Sergio, that was the only loose thread and he could turn into the fuse for a stick of dynamite. He had already sent instructions for his capture, for them to plant him. It had to be done. Everything else was on schedule, he had started to dismantle the party's apparatus. Without Dominguín and with Lourdes by his side, the other commanders were under his orders, they would start to change from being commanders for the party to commanders for the government, or they would disappear, if the rigor of the State's necessities continued to impose itself. All processes need elite groups for executing indecorous tasks. Every process has its indecorous tasks; it is romanticism to believe otherwise.

Lourdes helped him loosen his tie. She was standing behind him, pressing her body against his back. She was tall and beautiful. Manuel Roca had never been with a physically lacking woman. There were times when he was criticized for his habit of exhibiting himself with beautiful women. But just as he was recognized for his impeccable taste in clothes, his discipline, his political instinct and his good taste when it came to food and drinks, people also recognized his style when choosing a girlfriend. It was his signature.

It was late in the evening, but Manuel Roca hardly slept at all. He let Lourdes undress him, then undress herself, place her hands on his pectorals, press her nipples against his back, while her genitalia, her damp and warm cunt, heated his ass. He was breathing deeply, he almost recognized the aroma of happiness. An exclusive suite in a five star hotel, with plenty of room, lit with adequate lighting, cream curtains, a comfortable bed, clean sheets, a new place each night, room service nightly, with no other heat besides his own and that of his companion, with no connotation beyond that of an exclusive suite in a five star hotel, without permanent service. Nothing that might tie him down, nothing that might make him feel like the owner of a space. To own a space quantifiable in square feet would circumscribe a man, that's what he thought. To own a home would detract from a revolutionary. The revolutionary must inhabit the elements and there was no better way to do so than being in a hotel. He hadn't always been in a five star hotel. When he began his major at the university he shared a room with other students, just like in the seminary, living in the dormitories. At first he adapted his space, made it his own, placed a few books and put a poster on the wall. He hung up his change of clothes and kept a strict order among his things.

He began to attend meetings for the Patriotic Council. He was won over by the idea of overthrowing the dictator. He applied himself to the tasks they assigned him. These had to do with propaganda and agitation. He would go to high schools and organize cells for the council, he would set up demonstrations, he served as a messenger between the high school cells and those at the university; then he began to maintain direct contact with activists from the Communist Party. Joaquín also participated in the conspiratorial dynamics. He didn't have time to be in the dorm, later on he began moving to other ones, so as to avoid being identified by National Security.

The demonstrations exploded. Manuel Roca moved between high schools and universities. Many activists were arrested, among them Joaquín. He would spend the last days of the dictatorship in the prisons of National Security. He was tortured and left incommunicado. But the dictator ended up fleeing the country and the sun came out on January 23, 1958, with people in the streets, making caravans with their cars, waving flags, singing hymns. Roca didn't join the festivities, he had always been a man of responsibilities and from that moment on he knew he would become someone marked by power. He went with a group of activists from the party to the Government Palace, they wanted to radicalize the revolution, go further, take over the offices and hand them over to the party. He had fallen out of line, he wasn't interested in the dictator's fall as a conclusive event, they must have gone further. They were detained by a military unit that obeyed the new Government Coalition and were placed under the control of an activist from the coalition. They listened to his speech, steps had to be followed, they couldn't just burn through the stages quickly. What bull-shit, they thought, and they demanded the freedom to act, they were told that was pure anarchy; however, they were released. They ended up in front of the National Security headquarters, where they began to lynch the henchmen of the dictatorship alongside the overflowing crowds. They hung the regime's tor-turers from light posts and the prisoners were freed.

Manuel Roca went back to the university.

The Communist Party made him a member of its youth.

And the years of armed struggle came. The years with Abe-lardo came. As did his trips to Eastern Europe, his stay in Paris, his years of theoretical formation, Havana, his predilection for hotels, his office at the Tricontinental in the Habana Libre, the guerrilla.

That's why he was considered a notable figure.

Now, under the shower, Manuel Roca let Lourdes pass the sponge over his body. He gave himself over to her kisses. He al-ways expected kisses from his women, it had always been like that, ever since the days with his other cousin. His women did things for him; his women invaded him. He didn't like bathing in Jacuzzis, he considered them vulgar, in poor taste. But that night he let himself be submerged in one, he had to loosen his body, relax himself so he might exercise power comfortably.

To kiss Lourdes's nipples, as though it were an imposition, left him in a blank room, abandoned him to the vaporous hu-midity of her body, she would force him to caress her, to sink his head into the water between her legs, to stick out his tongue, conquer the water, arrive at the plateau of the submerged cunt and lick, bite, come up for air and return. It was a form of tor-ture. He remembered how, at the start of the armed struggle, he was captured and taken to the army's theater of operations. They laid him down on a strip of zinc that served as an oscil-lating board over lumber, when he went down he was doing it to a cowgirl, a place where the cows drank water, half his body was submerged while they applied electric shocks to his fingers and his balls and in his anus. He swallowed water and could barely move, he was tied down, he would half-close his eyes and dream; he would remember the other cousin, her pink and living cunt, like a snail's skin, her honey, he remembered her pushing his head, twisting in bed, her, twisting in bed, he, without air, with the other cousin's honey and spittle, with the shit and water of the cows, tortured in the theater of operations. They didn't kill him, he passed the test, the peasant who fell alongside him, after various fakes, was shot dead. With him they went no further than the cow trough and he ended up in prison for two years.

Lourdes was drying him with a long, fluffy towel, a modest cloth. Lourdes took him to the wide bed, threw him down on the sheets and jumped on top of him, rubbing herself against his body. She loved him. She was his right hand as well as his woman. He had always had women as his right hand. In his office at the Tricontinental in Havana he had Gloria, a big, blonde Uruguayan, with clear eyes like the bottom of the sea in Varadero. A daughter of communists. They worked on logistics, tracking the help provided to the groups that maintained themselves, creating the three, four, five Vietnams of Commander Guevara. Gloria was dominant, rude, strict. She executed a colleague in the Congo because he had let off a shot by mistake. That detail captivated Roca—the forced humanity, that's what he called her.

Forced humanity, Manuel maintained, was the ethics of the new man. Forced humanity had no compassionate feelings toward the individual within his values. Compassion was a bourgeois sentiment. The bourgeoisie were capable of compassion, revolutionaries were only capable of justice.

Gloria gave him a daughter. And she gave him unforgettable moments when they worked together in the school for cadres. She was capable of reaching extremes, she would transform herself in the execution of her tasks. And yet she was passionate in bed, one time she even subdued him with weapons, took him prisoner, handcuffed and blindfolded him to simulate a firing squad. Manuel counted that particular lay as the most didactical lay of his revolutionary life. It was more than a lay, it was the rupture of conventional values, it was a rehearsal of power. Sex is the practice of power, and the practice of power is not romantic—power submits and humiliates, power gratifies by means of those mechanisms. One cannot maintain a revolutionary order without repressing the spontaneous responses of reaction, that manifest themselves because they have been internalized within the collective consciousness for centuries. I learned, he would say, that those spontaneous forces had to be humiliated and repressed, and then gratified, never the other way around.

Gloria left on an internationalist mission. She never returned. They told him she was executed in a struggle between Maoists and pro-Soviets in Africa. Her daughter was adopted by the grandparents and educated in Moscow.

At this point he wouldn't sleep, dawn was shifting into morning, he would soon have to free himself from Lourdes's body and get dressed. On his agenda he had a meeting with the Minister of Defense and the army's intelligence services to fine-tune a few details. He looked at Lourdes. Lourdes looked back at him. She passed her fingers over the minister's lips.

"It's almost a paradox, I'm about to direct the revolution's repressive apparatus," he said.

"You shouldn't look at it that way," Lourdes hugged him, tossing the sheet over them.

"I'm not making problems for myself, really. One time in Havana we talked about whether we should use the same methods as the enemy in order to guarantee the power of the revolution and there were some who felt scruples when they mentioned torture," he touched Lourdes's belly with one of his hands. "I never had any doubts about it, the enemy is the one who has set the rules of the game, if we don't follow them, if we skip them, they win the upper hand."

"What's going to happen with Sergio?"

"Sergio doesn't exist, kid," he stood up from the bed.

"The problem," Lourdes sat down, took out her round, medium-sized and firm breasts, threw her hands around Roca's waist, grazed her lover's glans, opened her mouth, barely sucked and lifted her gaze, "is that he exists and we don't know exactly where he's staying."

The sun was coming up. Lourdes drew the curtain. There was smoke outside, the smell of ash was still there, the mountain couldn't be seen in the distance, only shadows. You could barely make out the red lights of the cars. Dawn had passed. She was exhausted, she wanted to sleep a little. She thought the time would come for a vacation, she imagined going to a secluded beach, an island. She thought about her childhood in front of the sea, about her years at the university, she had never stopped going to the sea, of immersing herself in its waters, she felt a passion for the sea. Now the city full of smoke, the revolution and the hardening of the process all imposed a sensation, she had somehow lost the sea, there were no solitary beaches, nor islands, only this process and the need to consolidate it. She thought about Dominguín, part of the process was also seeing how friends got lost in it, the process leaves no alternatives, Dominguín had played a dangerous card, individualism, he had a very particular way of looking at the process and there is only one process, either you're with it or you're outside it. The risk of losing was too high. That forced humanity imposed itself like an ethics, the extreme demands of revolutionary humanism. Dominguín came up against that humanism. There was no need to lament. She would have done the exact same thing.

Lourdes had studied anthropology. It was almost the exact result of an equation. To study anthropology predisposes one. That's what the Argentine military thought when they took power. The humanities departments of the universities were raided. To be a student in one of those departments generated a file. The Chilean military agreed. They were centers of communist formation. But in Cuba, the party had also raided the various departments, had imposed a vision, a line; the dialectic, scientific materialism and historical materialism were what was studied there. In reality they had turned them into departments where they formed cadres. Lourdes could have taken the wandering path through the school, she could have completed her major with a less fundamentalist view of history. It wasn't necessarily an equation. But she was limited by her reading, a relationship with an extreme left-wing activist and one or another slogan. She was locked in there.

Her father was a history professor. A professor who sympathized with the Communist Party. She had gone to Barcelona with her father when she was a child. He had taken a sabbatical year, writing a text about the Conquest. She read it years later and it added nothing to what Galeano said in his *Open Veins of Latin America*. It followed the same course. When she asked herself about her father, she saw him at the table in the apartment overlooking the Maragall Gardens with two or three big books lying open, she saw him so handsome when he would throw on a raincoat before heading out to the library. She accompanied him to Sevilla, she shared in the moment of religiosity when together they entered the General Archive of the Indies. Everything was there, her father had told her, one didn't need to invent anything, everything charged them with genocide. He maintained the Spaniards had committed genocide, she thought he had learned this while reading Galeano's book aloud, but her father wanted to go further, he intended to prove the thesis of slave work, of unpaid hours of work, of the added value that the indigenous work force had created, of the added value that had been created by slave labor, that was the main point, his difference with Galeano, to detail the pillaging in order to move towards an international litigation and demand that the peoples of the Americas be compensated.

Lourdes had a boyfriend in Spain, Toni, who was from Madrid and would occasionally eat dinner at her house. He was involved with the socialists and was a defender of conscientious objectors. But he was too liberal for her father. They once had an argument that almost led to a break up. Her boyfriend couldn't accept the Russian invasion of Afghanistan, he said it was comparable to the North American intervention in Southeast Asia. That position generated the first fracture, an eternal silence at dinner.

Lourdes's mother took the plates off the table, brought in dessert and some Venezuelan coffee. She turned on the TV and turned to a talk show, making a jocular remark about Rocío Jurado and nothing changed. Lourdes's father had turned red, ill, he had somehow choked on his dinner, he hadn't asked the young man to leave so as to not break the ties he had with his family, who were history professors at the autonomous university of Barcelona. He would have to swallow the impertinence of the liberal social democrat. On another occasion, Toni created a definitive, unbearable atmosphere. He pointed out to Lourdes's father that he didn't disagree with him, the conquest was brutal and the Indians were coerced into forced labor, but that was only part of history, it wasn't history, history couldn't be reduced to an inventory of bloody actions. The Spaniards left a series of institutions. The conquest was irreversible, just like the independence of the American republics, but there was room to ask oneself why those of mixed race, the Indians and the blacks were in many cases fighting on the side of the Spanish against republican soldiers. Why did the war of independence become, at least in Venezuela, a civil war? One had to ask what those free republics had done for the Indians, up to what point had they taken the extermination to extremes. If compensation had to be sought, how much would have to be paid by the republics that were born after independence? The matter had to be reevaluated. The Spaniards didn't conquer Latin America by themselves, they were aided by Indians who had been persecuted and oppressed by the dominant races, which was the case with the Aztecs... At that moment Lourdes's father stood up and nearly screamed, gesticulating and puffing up his chest, what Toni was saying was inadmissible, if he had to continue his thesis outside Spain he would do so, but that social democrat son of a bitch would never again enter his house and Lourdes would leave, far from Toni's life, from his reformist poison, she would go to Paris, immediately. He was sweating, red. It was summertime, and there was no air. The boy laughed, made a gesture with his hand and excused himself. Before he left he seemed to have said, *at least that's how Lourdes remembers it,* that the discussion wasn't worth it, that a discussion couldn't exist without room for debate, he would eventually have to face a committee, one had to be quite naïve to think that thesis would be accepted without discussion. He went away leaving that dart. Her father fell into the sofa chair and stared at a Spanish TV show, saying nothing.

The next day Lourdes left for Paris, her father finished his thesis, but he never submitted it to a committee for discussion. He never published it, he didn't even show it to his friends.

When Lourdes studied anthropology she wanted to vindicate her father. She studied the pre-Hispanic cultures in depth, confronted her professors' positions, gradually radicalized herself until she reached a certain level of stupidity. Just like her father she wielded an argument that accepted no discussion. Her father had died of a heart attack. He died before the process began. He died without seeing Marcos's entrance into Mexico. He died without having a premonition that an indigenous revolution was looming in the Americas. She was now vindicating him. She kept seeing Toni in Paris. She lost her virginity to him in Paris. She never answered a single letter from her father. She felt embarrassed for him. She saw him as being conceited, dogmatic, wearing his raincoat, with four ideas he never varied. *Why the hell did they come to Europe?* she'd write her mother. And she was gradually left alone, without the man who took her virginity, without her father, alongside a group that called itself millenarianist, cultivated skepticism, thought it had discovered in Cioran the bearer of a supreme truth, that would incite Cioran to break the balls of any fool who might try to convince them of man's virtues, the virtues of the future, of life's reason. She hated the commonplace, hated her father, hated Toni, hated anyone who sustained a possibility for salvation, whether in dictatorship, in democracy, in fascism or in communism. She hated all exits, and the people who reaffirmed themselves in the species. One day, it must have been during the winter, everything was grey, there was the weight of lead in the atmosphere, the lover with whom she'd spent the night told her she was an imbecile. That didn't affect her. He told her that Cioran had put together the commonplace of desperation. That hardly registered for her. That to feel desperation was as pathetic as living with hope. "So what?" she told herself. He told her that being indifferent was the sum of both ridiculous stances. That Cioran was uncultivated. That Cioran's readers were a bunch of middle class fools who wanted to feel unfortunate. That regardless they remained uncultured. That they didn't even take the time to read the Romantics. That they would never look at themselves in the Greeks nor in their tragedies. That they never went beyond the cigarette hanging from their mouth, the vinegar they drank in the bars, and the bags under their eyes. Cioran gave order to a pose, he gave body to a cliché. It was a means of living on the cusp of hopelessness. Shit, it was fucking shit, there was no room for illustrated skepticism, nor for her in the world. Her lover screamed at her, got up from the bed and smacked her, spit at her, pulled her hair and made love to her violently, with contempt. He left her, told her to not look for him again, that he wouldn't go back to bed with scum. Lourdes was left naked, in a fetal position on her bed. The days passed in this manner, thus the winter ended, she lost weight. She decided to return. She decided to go back to her people. She had no arguments and she needed to find ones she could make her own.

Her father died thinking she was a nihilist. Her father died thinking she was a lumpen.

Manuel Roca was shaving in front of the sink. He was looking at his face, he hadn't aged. His torso was naked, he kept his figure. He wanted to grimace in front of the mirror. Day and night had passed and a new one was starting. He believed it literally.

Lourdes received a suit at the door and laid it out for him on the bed. A grey suit, white shirt and a silk tie, very red, like blood. She picked up the cell phone and made a call, setting up a meeting with the people from the party. She received a call from the Ministry of Defense, told them the meeting would take place outside the offices. That was Minister Roca's wish. They would have it on the hotel terraces, in the open air. It wasn't advisable to use the rooms until they had been swept. Decisions had to be made without microphones. She set the phone aside and went to get dressed, she put on a salmon-colored silk dress, let her hair down, loose, barely combing it. It was reddish and abundant. She felt beautiful. She put on some high heels that the minister's valet brought her.

Both of them, Manuel Roca and her, were ready to go out. They hadn't slept. There was no time to sleep.

Their first meeting was with three comrades from the party. They still insisted on calling themselves a party. Lourdes explained the line they should follow at the juncture that presented itself to them after yesterday's events. Comrade Roca was Minister of Internal Affairs for the revolutionary government. The party must become the executive arm of the revolutionary government's internal affairs, they said. Dominguín had left on an internationalist mission. They had to suppress any type of deviation within the heart of the organization. They had to be ruthless with elements that might move forward with spontaneous acts. They condemned Silvestre and Sergio. Silvestre had killed himself after the failed assassination attempt against the president. Sergio had not been so sensible. He had to be executed the moment he was found. He had acted on his own and in favor of the interests of the right. They had to investigate up to what point Sergio and Silvestre had infiltrated the organization. They were the government now and they had to act coherently in order to maintain revolutionary power and governability.

The meeting lasted barely an hour, it didn't take a day's worth of discussions. There were no debates, as there had been in the past. This was not a plenary and no consensus was sought. Left and right positions did not exist. There was a single position and one programmatic line. They had to assimilate themselves to the work of state security.

Before meeting with the army intelligence officials, Manuel Roca and Lourdes asked to eat breakfast. It was a frugal breakfast: toast, jam and tea. Ash was falling on the hotel terrace, the day was gloomy, the sun had risen behind the smoke.

"We have to dismantle the organization, Lourdes," said Roca. He lifted the perfumed handkerchief to his nose.

"But some of them can be assimilated. We told them and they accepted it."

"No. They have too many theoretical vices. I think they've misread the Marxist classics. They have to go." He took her hand and kissed it. All his mornings had been premonitory. His mornings at school beside his mother. The mornings on his father's hacienda, the mornings at the seminary. The mornings during the fight against the dictatorship. His morning in Prague. Mornings in the mountains of Falcón. But that morning in the hotel sitting in front of Lourdes, the morning of power, was simply morning. The instant for which he had been born.

"We can't get rid of them."

"Remember, we have to force our humanism." Roca didn't say this ironically, nor cynically. He was convinced there are moments when a revolutionary must demand of himself an absolute detachment from any affection that might alienate his practice.

"How far will you go to force your humanism, Roca?" Lourdes asked. She felt sadness, an inner trembling, she suddenly felt she had been ejected into Sergio's reality. Something told her there was an element of monstrosity in that idea of

forced humanism. That was related to the thesis of the Cambo-
dian communists, which had to do with extermination camps.
It meant superimposing the reason of the new man, the values
of the new man, above the values of the species. You can't force
an ethics. It all started to sound like the rhetoric of extermination to her.

"As far as I need to," answered Roca. He shifted in his
seat and picked up a piece of toast, without ceasing to stare
at Lourdes. Mistrust had been born. She mistrusted his forced
humanism and he mistrusted her suspicion.

"As far as you need to has no end, Roca," Lourdes spit out.
She felt that somehow her future in the revolution was at stake.
She once again felt the spit of her lover in Paris, the crumbling
of her hopes, the mirror in front of her and the faces of Silvestre
and Domínguin staring back at her.

"Look kid, I'm going to tell you something that isn't new,
that can be found in the classics. Something I stand by. The
class struggle must be taken to its maximal expression, the
class struggle doesn't end once you take power, this is a law.
If we ignore it, they'll sweep us aside. History will pass right
over us." The minister loosed one maxim after another.

Lourdes finished her toast and asked for a coffee with milk. She
was overwhelmed by events. She needed to go rest, take some
time. But how could she ask for a leave without raising suspicion. If she asked for a leave she would be eliminated by Minister Roca's forced humanism. She needed to get away from
the city, needed to see the clear sky, see that it was blue, see
the ocean. She had been part of a machinery of extermination.
She had provoked Domínguin, Sergio and Silvestre to take
positions. She had whispered to them that the president was
becoming a prisoner of interests outside the revolution. That
they had to create conditions for assaulting power. She voted
for destabilization, for the invasion of land, for breaking up
the official syndicates, for the revolutionary boycott. Isn't that

what the Bolsheviks had done? But she knew that was all part of a plan that Roca managed and would carry out for his own ends. Now the balance was one. The organization dismantled, its leaders eliminated, the future of the rest of the comrades was uncertain—they fell under Roca's concept of forced humanism (she herself fell under Roca's forced humanism). She knew he had voted for Gloria and her group to be executed by Maoists; Gloria, his girlfriend, the mother of his daughter, the one who passed on to him the lesson of his life.

Lourdes wasn't planning on deserting. She wanted time. She wanted to step aside for a bit, a few days, to be outside the game. To gain a perspective. In her heart she didn't want to assume new responsibilities. She didn't see herself as a functionary for a police regime. She felt like she'd gotten her hands dirty. They wouldn't make an Amerindian revolution, they wouldn't even make a classic, Marxist-Leninist revolution. So then, what type of revolution would they make? She had closed her eyes when they abandoned Dominguín in the outskirts of the city, she didn't hear the shot. She hated her deafness. She knew that Dominguín was no longer living. She felt tenderness toward Dominguín. A brusque man. Crude. A bad lover. Simple, with fixed ideas, but within the measure of what the puddle of shit of a process permitted, he was a good man. Sensible? What was good sense? Dominguín would have ended up killing Roca. Everyone would end up killing someone and death would make pasture of the new men.

"It's not a good idea for you to be at the meeting with the intelligence people," Manuel said to her as he lifted the napkin to his mouth.

"But you said you'd keep me by your side. That I'd be your ally in these meetings."

"It's not a good idea, I know why I'm telling you this." He took her by the chin, pulled her closer and grazed her with his lips. Lourdes thought he was giving her the kiss of death. Maybe she was tired. Maybe she wasn't thinking clearly. Who did Roca's forced humanism respect? Was it limitless? He no longer needed anyone. He had known how to free himself from all ties throughout his revolutionary history. She remembered that he had ordered Joaquín to be killed. His best friend. The friend who had taken him out of the seminary. His logic functioned in an implacable manner. Joaquín was a functionary for a bourgeois government, someone in charge of social affairs, a man who caused a great deal of damage with his reformist policies, with his populist social democracy, a nuisance for the revolution. Besides, he was one of the president's men at that time, which is why his friend from the seminary, with whom he discovered Sor Juana Inés and Martial, had appeared in a dumpster, with his hands tied and his body riddled with bullets. Another example of Roca's forced humanism.

"I don't want to step aside from this," Lourdes replied in an attempt to save her life.

"You're already outside dear, for a little while. I'll call you." He kissed her again, this time on the cheek.

"But who will coordinate the assimilation of the comrades?" she insisted.

"There won't be any assimilation, Lourdes. I told you, you have to be strong. Go on, I'll call you." He said goodbye to her with a slap on the ass.

She stood up haltingly. She knew he had sentenced her to death. Why hadn't he ordered for her to be executed alongside Dominguín? At what moment had she disappointed him to the point of activating the perverse logic of his humanism? She crossed the terrace, put her hands on her dress to prevent the wind and smoke from lifting her skirt; it was useless, her long, perfect legs were revealed, the dress was fluttering about and showing her legs, it was a beautiful and desperate image. She ran to seek shelter, she thought about going up to the room, but she was scared of being kidnapped, they would be waiting for her in the room. She walked through the hotel lobby, went into a bookstore, she wasn't showing her anxiety. A well-dressed man, tall and with sunglasses, entered behind her. Typical. She hurried out after buying a magazine at random, accelerated her steps and headed toward one of the restaurants, burst into the kitchen, the man was following her. She had to lose him, but she was wearing that damn silk dress, she took off her heels and started to run without worrying about how she looked. She left the kitchen and went into the service room, grabbed some dirty clothes that were hanging on a rack and put them on over her dress, she hid her hair under a cap and opened a window that looked onto the dumpsters, and she saw no one outside—the truck that took the trash away was leaving with its load. The pursuer abandoned the service room and pulled out a weapon from his holster, ran toward the parking lot and stopped the truck. He looked inside, there was the driver and his assistant. He climbed onto the truck's flatbed and looked: there was trash, kitchen waste. He pointed randomly and shot at the load of trash, nothing moved. He got down and left the parking lot.

A man walked through the trash. He carried a frayed sack. He gripped it with one of his hands, as though he were gripping a neck. He rummaged through the junk, he had followed the same routine for years. The landfill looked like the landscape of an asteroid. He was accompanied by a dog whose ribs were exaggeratedly visible. Behind him walked another companion, a man with a sack over his shoulders. He rummaged.

Smoke was the perennial reality of the dump. From its entrails rose exhalations, columns: a persistent, unequivocal breathing. The dump breathed and the vultures flew above it, they drew circles over the white, pustulous asteroid.

The landscape included children with pants ripped to shreds, nearly naked. They were dispersed over a plateau of trash, eternal waste of recent cities. The sound of the trucks could be heard, the scream of a carrion bird disputing its precariousness with someone.

"There's nothing."

"Just bottles."

"The other day Matías found a gold tooth."

"How's that?"

"A gold tooth, my man."

They passed the bottle back and forth and drank, wiped themselves with their arms and remained with their mouths open. They looked like reptiles.

"The corpse must be around here somewhere."

"That's what I said."

"Though a tooth without a corpse could arrive."

"What do you mean?"

"It could be that the corpse was left somewhere else. Maybe it's never left the place where it's already a corpse."

They shrugged and dedicated themselves to checking a little hill that had recently been dumped from a truck.

"What if we find two gold teeth?"

"Then it would be a day of good luck."

"Well, look."

"No, it's not a day of good luck, José."

"There's the corpse."

"Which one?"

"The one with the gold tooth."

"Don't be an idiot, José. This dead person just died recently."

They both ran over to the body and started to circle it, looking at it up close, they turned it over with what was left of their shoes.

"It's a woman, José. Hurry up, the thieves are coming."

Some children were approaching. "Look closely, she probably has a necklace, a watch. Open her mouth, she probably has at least a gold tooth." The children started to crowd around the naked torso.

"Get out of here, you fucking pickpockets, this is our dead body."

They jumped towards her and so did their dog. The woman turned around, she was holding a revolver with both hands. She was pointing at them firmly. Her glance was cloudy. Green and cloudy. She was wearing a silk dress, at her side were the workingman's pants she had taken from the hotel kitchen. She was wearing her evening dress, that could have been salmon colored, in which she would have begun her life as a functionary of the process, now partly frayed.

"If you assholes don't want an eye in your forehead, you'll hit the road. Understand?" She got on her knees atop pieces of cardboard, rags, papers, shapeless and bundled matter. "And you, little rats. Would you like to become big rats?" She addressed the children. "So, what are you waiting for? Run!"

The two trash collectors and a band of naked children started to run, the woman gesticulated with the weapon and they spread out in various directions. They were graceless figures that made levers with their legs on a landscape at the end of the world, the smoke moved, from east to west, it came from the holes, from the entrails of the filth. Lourdes stood up and walked amid the scraps, with her right arm hanging, beside her leg, with the weapon. She had pulled her .38's firing pin. She walked like an automaton, thinking about her years in Paris, she thought how she had eventually considered life to be trash, the meaning of life as excrement, hopelessness. Her lover pissed all over her face. And life changed. Life was her country, her house, a career at the university. Life knocked her over and from upset to upset she made herself a ruthless forger of revolutionary humanity. Then she was in the trash once again. Without revolution. Without a project. Outside the process. In a landscape where the world's hopeful wandered looking for a bit of cardboard, a piece of aluminum, dirty papers, a gold tooth. They were searchers, they hadn't given up, they rummaged through shit and lived off the items of value they rescued from the shit. On an asteroid, outside the world, the Earth's last hopeful people. She with her .38 in her hand, undecided, with no course, amid scavengers, she had to shake them off by means of threats—*the hopeful are dangerous, they are carrion eaters,* she was thinking.

Lourdes walked in a circle. She was just another image amid the smoke. A svelte and dirty shadow, walking reluctantly, with a dark glance, lost, toneless. She repeated herself in the spaces of the asteroid. She was being followed by the cross-breeds, the beggars, the ragged of the earth; no one had ever thought about them. Not even the professional revolutionaries. They didn't fit in the world. They were strange.

Lourdes was thinking that she was already transiting through the infernos of hope. That she had seen the sea, that the sea was detritus and bums. She would go no further. There was no safe haven outside. They were looking for her to liqui-date her. Where would she go? She raised the weapon to her mouth, swallowed the barrel, let herself feel it on her palate, she recalled how she had once told Roca that his penis was a warm barrel that spilled a little death on her palate. She felt embarrassed by the memory, it made her feel ashamed. She was ashamed to have had the minister's glans in her mouth. Presumptuous. Cold. Too cold to have been a good lover. And yet he was. He paid attention to details, he wouldn't push her head to hurry an ejaculation, he didn't call her a bitch, nor my little whore, he never told her he loved her, not even that he cared for her, quiet, attentive to details, to the partial caress, to good wine, to artichokes. He was a man of details.

She would die at the foot of the plateau. She would roll down a cliff of trash and hope, she would lie there, lost to the world.

"Hey, miss, what are you doing?" screamed a uniformed man, through the pestilent fumaroles.

Lourdes took the gun out of her mouth and shot at him. Once, twice. She jumped from the plateau toward the cliff, rolled, turned around, lost her weapon in the fall. When she reached the bottom, she found herself on tamped dirt, amid tin shacks, a labyrinth of tin shacks. Hope had metastasized. She ran through it, making way through the shadows, from the frames that served as doors, the uncombed heads of the shadows peeked out—the shadows were on every corner—she recalled Ulysses in Hades, the shadows didn't reflect him, she was not reflected by the tin city and its inhabitants. She leaned over while holding on to a rusted wall, and vomited. She thought she was dead, that she had managed to shoot herself. What would the social theorists say about the perverse hope of extreme misery? Why they prosper, why the rusted ivy, the vine shoots and zinc panels, the toothless smiles. She had descended to the infernos. She kept running, she didn't want to stop, she forced herself, set a rhythm to her fleeing; she wouldn't stop fleeing until she was struck down, unconscious. She hoped for a more significant death in unconsciousness. But the labyrinth had an exit, a conclusion, she crawled up an irregular dirt ramp and reached a paved road. She was outside. Beyond hope, she was at the edge of the road. She stretched out her arm, asking to be taken somewhere. Once again.

She didn't remember how, but she arrived at a town.

She had to make a call.

She entered a dispensary. A doctor saw her. She said she'd had an accident. The doctor said he would call the police. She asked him to please not do it, that she would trust him, that she had no one to trust, that she would put herself in his hands, she was crying, and she realized she was using a detestable resource. But she wasn't using any resource, she was truly crying, crying like she did when her lover pissed on her face in Paris, she was wounded, she saw herself like a wolf, like a wounded dog.

"Are you involved in the conspiracy?" the doctor asked her.

"No," Lourdes answered.

"Then why are they looking for you?" He took her face, stretched the skin on her cheek, looked into her eyes—they were dark, green, very dark and green. The eyes that had venerated Roca, that had felt sympathy for Dominguín.

"They're looking for everyone. Everyone who's been opposed to this government," she responded, leaning back on the cot. She fixed her dress, covered her legs a bit. She became aware of her modesty and lowered her gaze.

"Are you part of the opposition to the government?" the doctor asked.

"I was a member of a syndicate, and went to a few assemblies. They've jailed my boss." She passed her tongue over her lips, which were chapped. She had a bad taste in her mouth. "Is there any way I could clean myself up?" she asked and stood up. She was facing the doctor. "Are you a Cuban doctor?" She felt fear.

"No, does it sound like I'm speaking with a cigar between my teeth?" He smiled. "I just graduated and I'm doing my residency here in this village.

"Where am I?" Lourdes was beginning to realize she was lost, that it was the first time in her short and stupid life that she felt a sensation of complete uprooting. She remembered Dante's verse: "I found myself within a forest dark / For the straightforward pathway had been lost." She began to cry again.

The doctor wiped the tears away.

"You're in a town on the road to Oriente province."

Oriente was the Levant. Rising. Life was giving her strange signs. The road to Oriente.

"Are you going to turn me in?" her voice quivered. She felt like vomiting once again.

"Wait, this sounds like the dialog from a spy thriller."

"But, are you going to turn me in?"

"No, I won't. Have you eaten?"

"I don't think so. I don't know how long I've been fleeing. Don't turn me in."

"No. Let's go, I'll take you to a place where you can shower and then eat and make a phone call." He took the cheek with his hand. "But you have to get out of here, it'll be night soon, I'll find a way for you to leave town. If you stay, someone's bound to say something to the National Guard."

The doctor took her by the arm and led her to the room where he stayed for his residency: it had a small outer courtyard, with a bathroom in the back. Lourdes walked through the place, there was an orange tree that dropped its leaves on her, she remembered the autumn in Europe, her walks through

Luxembourg Park—there aren't any orange trees over there, but the forests light up and the leaves fall and the season is beautiful, blood red. Like the rising sun, like the sun in the evening. When she reached the bathroom door she turned around, sought the doctor's glance. She felt like she was crumbling, that she was being conquered by fear, her utter solitude.

"I can't do it."

"What?"

"I can't bathe alone, I can't keep going without someone hugging me."

Lourdes didn't see the night from the window in the small bus. There was nothing out there. There was no moon. If it was there, it was barely a smile. Outside was darkness, a landscape that hid in the night. Lourdes thought, and she concluded that she had lived these past few hours in a free fall. She couldn't explain events to herself coherently. She couldn't conceive the random circumstances and framework that led her to a little bus with no clear destination, a small and ancient port, in the Oriente region of the country.

Many theorists say that beyond chaos, and the collapse of institutions, revolution is a science. What is established collapses and is substituted by a revolutionary order. In her exact calculation of things she saw herself alongside and within the new order. That's what she thought. But did order fit within revolution? All it took was twenty-four hours, the sharpening of the process, the concretion of Manuel Roca's plan, for her to be left out.

When she joined the organization, in the Department of Anthropology, revolution was the objective, the chimera. That's where she met Silvestre, Dominguín and Sergio. They introduced her to Roca. Although they were no longer an armed group, they believed that revolutions had to be armed. Along with the customary ideological discussions in their study groups. they received military training, they went to the Sahara.

Not everyone in the organization did this. Only the elite. When the coup attempt occurred, someone informed them they were involved, that a military-civilian coup would take place, that they would be the civilian vanguard of the disturbance and they were secluded in a house in El Valle. The insurrectionaries would deliver arms to them and they would form small and effective columns that would serve as support from the slums for the rebel soldiers.

When the military coup attempt happened, Lourdes was trained. She had already gone to the Sahara with Sergio. It hadn't been Sergio's first time. Sergio, Dominguín and Silvestre had gone to many other places, they kept up to date with the use of arms and with the techniques and tactics of war. They were cadres, at their full capacity.

Everyone was impatient that night. They recalled Roca's face when he burst into the shell.

"The order hasn't arrived. Something must have gone wrong. Regardless, our military comrades" —when he said military comrades, Lourdes recalls how the old fighter stuttered— "have taken Maracaibo, Valencia and there are battles going on in Caracas."

Hours later they watched undaunted as a Lieutenant Colonel, in a trance, with cloudy eyes, tired, precise in his words, surrendered and called on his companions to lay down their weapons. Roca wheezed. He said they had lost the revolution, that the soldiers had excluded the civilians. If they had taken the people out into the streets accompanied by columns of well-trained combatants, they'd now be celebrating the triumph. He immediately demobilized them.

The night had closed around the little bus. It had closed around Lourdes. She was headed toward an uncertain destination and would be taken in by a friend of that helpful doctor who had taken care of her and bathed her, who had kept quiet. Silence reigned inside the bus, everyone was sleeping, you could barely hear a few spasmodic moans. Up ahead, beyond the windshield, you could see a thin road, the lights were crossing and sweeping the pavement. A landscape was opening like the cupola of a forest or the nave of a church, as they continued their transit. The dark night above them, this is the last bus, history was not traveling on it, the passengers were asleep, Lourdes knew she was on the outside, persecuted. Sentenced to death.

Elmer was a tidy man. Thin and small, with a firm and nervous bearing. Elmer didn't smile, but he had a permanent grimace, the grimace of comedy; he looked like he was smiling. A wide forehead with his hair brushed back, fixed in place with gel. Elmer was a man with a long trajectory, with an orthodox formation. He was a pilot in the Sahara, where he trained the people Roca would send him. In recent years, before "the process" took off, he lived in desert camps. He knew how to avoid the "empire's" satellites, he handled technology as though it were an assault rifle. They never discovered any of his training camps, he knew how to make use of props and was knowledgeable about insurgencies and counterinsurgencies. He was a man who was valued by the leaders of the desert and many subversive organizations would fight for him to train their men.

Unlike Manuel Roca, who had reinserted himself in the armed struggle in Venezuela, once the Tricontinental was dismantled, Elmer had remained abroad, at the service of global revolution. He decided to transmit his knowledge and to wait for the future.

He had trained Sergio, Dominguín, Silvestre and Lourdes. They lived in the Sahara for a year, in caves, beneath the sand; in improvised, portable camps. They learned the rudiments of the war of resistance, they learned how to move platforms around unnamable places to create airports, and above all to survive in extreme conditions.

Now Manuel Roca was calling him so he could rise to greatness with the process. Why would a man who had found serenity and recognition in the training camps of the Maghreb now abandon his refuge to serve a bureaucrat and a revolution of uncertain destiny? Elmer had a historical debt, a debt to the past. It was the moment to apply his knowledge in his own country; besides, the minister promised him substantial incentives. The world was becoming smaller for the great artisans of subversion, some of his old allies were growing uncomfortable with the presence in their territories of a man like him, at the moment when they were negotiating their insertion back into the world. Their points of view had shifted a great deal since the distant sixties.

Before the assassination attempt against the president, he had been in charge of the reservists, he had been assigned the responsibility of arming the revolution's militias. And he had done it well. Once the revolution's militias had been armed, what purpose did Roca's party serve, a miniscule group that had survived a forty-year struggle whose cycle was now closing? None. Which is why he chose to suppress it.

Elmer arrived late at night to the hotel where the minister was staying. He didn't stop in the foyer, he immediately walked into Manuel Roca's bedroom, where he was asking to be served a whisky.

"What'll you have, Elmer?" asked the emergency government's hard man.

"Evian mineral water, please."

"You're too predictable to be a counterintelligence man," said the minister, and he let himself fall onto the easy chair, taking out a Cuban cigar, "sit down, my friend."

The room was taken over by silence. You could hear the ice tinkling in the crystal glass Roca was holding, the lighting of a match, the inhalation, exhalation and a sigh, but you couldn't hear the water poured into the cup, silence and smoke, smoke inside and out. "City of Smoke," they had started to call Caracas in the newspaper headlines.

"You know I wouldn't have asked you for this if it wasn't important," the minister broke the silence.

"How's the president?" Elmer asked.

"In good health and in full spirits."

"Ah."

"You can speak, Elmer." He made a gesture of annoyance. "I've ordered them to sweep this room with three early detection systems, there are no microphones, no hidden cameras."

"They say Vladimir Montesinos ordered all his interviews to be recorded," the instructor smiled.

"That Montesinos, he has a morbid mania for archives," the minister smiled, "you know I don't like to leave any evidence."

"Everyone leaves traces, Manuel," he answered and lifted the glass of water to his lips. Elmer drank very little, he barely wet his lips, it was his habit. In the desert you don't drink more than that, you drink in sips.

"Let's not pontificate about traces and the dialectic of class struggle," Manuel Roca smiled again, then he squeezed the cigar in his teeth.

"You're just going to tell me about the president's health, you know he lives with few complications," Elmer insisted.

"He has his concerns, as you know. We have to fortify his health," answered Roca.

"And have the doctors taken measures?" Elmer insisted with his mocking grimace, a fixed mockery, an immoveable mask.

"Cut the crap, Elmer." The minister sat up, puffed on the cigar furiously and blew the smoke into the air. "I've got two people who are out of control, two fighters I wasn't able to suppress. They're out there, they could be causing damage. If they reach conclusions and talk, they could do a great deal of harm to the revolution."

"And you believe in the revolution?" Elmer was insisting while he drank his water sip by sip.

"Well, in the process, you know we have to take care of this thing. We're in power and any pretext can take us out."

"Do you believe in the process?" Elmer asked once again.

"What do you fucking think, that I'm leading this because I don't believe?" Elmer shrugged his shoulders. "Regardless, this is what we're left with."

"The end of the road, old man."

Manuel Roca walked across the living room, retraced his steps, unbuttoned two of his shirt buttons, served himself ice and more whisky, moved one of his hands across his forehead and puffed on the cigar again, exhaled noisily, slapped himself on one of his own thighs and let himself fall back on the easy chair again.

"Look Elmer, I have a bunch of things weighing on me. With this movement I'm putting all my cards on the table, I don't have any other ones, I only have one option. I'm the one who harmonizes the elements of the process, nothing can be out of tune, our relationship with the Colombian guerrillas, the delivery of arms, the jailing of government enemies, the confiscation of their goods, the pressure from people who've given us their money, the fiscal measures to keep the media quiet, the pressure groups, the organization of the militias and the surveillance committees, I have to do all of it and it all has to happen, one thing and another, no matter how contradictory things might be. A few undesirables have to disappear, we have to direct the class struggle from the ministry, everything has to be in order, the muscle of the process can be seen in this ministry. So now you come and ask me whether I believe in this shit or not. Of course I believe, I have to believe, there's no alternative. The president is as healthy as the ministry says he is, that's the answer, he's healthy now and we're going to make him healthier and you'll walk out that door with that goal in mind."

Manuel Roca remained silent. He was a man of short speeches. He had never spoken much. He was known for being laconic. He was famous for the absence of eloquence in his speech. Now he felt like talking, saying whatever came to his mind, suddenly giving an endless harangue, crying. He realized he wanted to cry. He recalled the portable oven, the room where he spent his early childhood, the humidity and his mother's smell. A salty smell, of weeping, of inner turmoil. He had always carried his pain within himself, from that cursed room, with hardly any light, cold, unbearable. His mother bequeathed it to him and he had apprehended it. She bequeathed a salty warmth that was always with him, that assisted him in his already long and solitary life. "Why didn't you stick to the original plan?" Elmer burst out. The minister felt rats crawling in his stomach. He half-closed his eyes. He took a long drink. He seemed to be looking for something with his glance, this time sweeping the walls, furniture, curtains, armoire, the windows. There couldn't possibly be anyone recording them, unless Elmer was wearing a wire. He felt he needed to be cautious. The feeling was mutual.

"There was no original plan, there was always a plan and it's the one that was put into place."

Both men remained silent. They wanted to relax. It was best to let oneself be won over by silence.

The nights in the desert were cold. The sky was a wide cupola, dotted with stars. Elmer tried to recall faces. He had had hundreds of people under his charge, the car bombs, the bullet that crossed through space and entered silently through a window and reached its target, the buildings that were brought down with a load of C4, the planes that never reached their destination, these all had a certain style, Elmer's style. Now he found himself in a hotel room at the disposition of an old and mediocre companion. Why? Because he wasn't wanted in the desert anymore, the desert had decided to clean up its image, the desert countries now held seats in human rights organizations. The desert countries would hand him over to a Western intelligence agency. For that simple reason he was there under the obtuse, cloudy and cold glance of a man who did the dirty work for a lie. That's why he was letting things slide, waiting for the rain to stop, for the rainstorm to pass by, for this infinite refuge—the desert—to open up for him once again.

He tried to recall faces, to classify them, to find Lourdes's face, eyes and body. She was there, in the past, there were three Venezuelans, they knew very little about arms, they would hesitate when they dismantled an assault rifle, they forced themselves not to piss in their cargo pants whenever they launched a surface-to-air missile, they grew pearly with cold sweat when manipulating plastic explosives, he remembered them, they were losers.

"I don't know how, but Sergio escaped," said Roca, placing the rest of his cigar in the ashtray.

"A beginner's mistake."

"What do you expect, I wasn't in charge of all this at the time," he puffed.

"And what happened with little Lourdes?" asked Elmer, who had already stood up from the armchair where he had drank his bottle of Evian water.

"I underestimated her. I think I expected to have her at my side in this matter. I miscalculated," responded the minister.

"And where do you think each of them might be?"

" If I knew I wouldn't even have answered your previous questions," Roca smiled bitterly. "We've raided all the places they could have gone, their friends are no longer with us." His mouth jumped with a tic. "We've carefully dismantled the apparatus to which they belonged. They have nowhere to run."

"You should have left the possibility of a hideout intact." He raised his voice without changing the perennial mocking grimace on his face. "Now they could be anywhere. Two people who could be anywhere, that's difficult."

"Not quite," responded the minister. "They'll eventually leave traces, the country is taken over, they don't know how to live outside an organized structure, they will eventually reveal their movements. My biggest fear is that the information's been filtered and someone else is looking for them."

"Who?"

"We've blamed the assassination attempt on the ex-president of a small company, on the right, and on a union."

"I'm aware of that."

"Well, I think we've hit them pretty hard, but we haven't finished off the opposition," Roca said. "On the other hand, outside intelligence agencies are seeking to corroborate our version. We've planted the matter of false clues; if they fully believe us they'll stay put, they have no other choice, the state of emergency is legitimate, unless an undesirable person reclaims the assassination attempt."

They were quiet. Elmer picked up his coat, stared out the window for a while. It was an ample window, the view was ruined by the smoke and ash. In the distance the city was boiling, the noise of motors, and the horns, despite everything the night continued to be pure noise. He felt a great unease. He thought he wouldn't have much patience. The rain would not stop, time passed, he was in a country that would end up becoming muddy ashes, far from home, from the Sahara's icy nights. Training reservists had become arduous for him, they were men without morals, they had no ideological convictions, they marched only for a plate of food and a salary. Roca didn't have a militia, he had an army of mercenaries.

"Don't worry," he said like a jail sentence, "I'll pluck them out of the smoke. I'll make magic with my hat and two rabbits will emerge and I'll roast them on the grill." Without extending his hand to Manuel Roca, he leaned his head down slightly, turned his back to him and began to exit, while he thought that he must already have an executioner assigned to him (he was a very old man in the business of violent revolutions), he knew they were playing for time, everyone was playing for time, Roca knew this and did the same.

"Consider them dead."

THE LAUGHTER OF WOMEN

A woman was laughing. I thought this, looking at Sonia and the laughter of all women. It wasn't a grimace. La Gioconda laughed. She didn't smile. She laughed like all women do, with seriousness. She maintained satisfaction and desire, grace and misfortune, she was the mouth that denoted an inexact movement, the cheeks that accused a demand, the glance and the eyes, both in perfect harmony; there was the laughter and all the laughs of all women.

I was tired. I could only digress. I didn't think of the future. It didn't exist, I was dead. Roca had killed me, the party had sentenced me, the process had decreed my death. A summary trial of the story that had escaped my finger and the trigger for just a second. I remembered Abelardo's dialectic, the same as Heraclitus, the one about the river, about the river that flows and lets the river flow. I told myself, I'm Sergio, I've almost never used my last name, I have used last names, there have been many, a few others for my first names, now my name is Sergio. They were looking for Sergio and Sergio flows in the river or by the river of Heraclitus, he was accompanied by a woman who laughed in profile, in the penumbra, in the deepest night of an escape to nowhere. Puerto Píritu was nowhere. When I awoke from my latest dream I never considered going anywhere or to Puerto Píritu. Life had left me no alternative, or history or that cursed day of mist, smog, ashes.

Nothing fit. There was no puzzle. I couldn't look to the immediate past. I looked at a lump of flour: shapeless mass, transparent tumor.

The process had to be radicalized. Silvestre would mention this to me again and again. He insisted on stellar actions. He believed in the solitary acts that foster great movements in societies. The anarchist who killed the archduke in Sarajevo never imagined he would be the unrecognized father of the Bolshevik revolution. We had no alternative. Revolution or nothingness. Now that the bus was moving over the pavement, silently through the Eastern night, under the first dawn stars, now with Sonia and her laughter, I would have almost affirmed that revolution and nothingness were synonyms. I was empty. This is not an idiom. Not at all. It's the stone that rolls through a chandelier. That crashes into the accidents of an internal cave. That produces a sound and projects itself; it's unpleasant, a frightening echo, life returning without having found any resonances.

When I went up into the mountains for the first time, I knew I was taking the path of violence. I made an end of death. It is not a slogan, it's an end. I never supposed I would assault power, I was convinced I would die during the assault. I thought of myself as a martyr and I enjoyed it; however, I knew how to cover my ass well. I wasn't in the mountains for too long. When I went up, the guerrilla fronts were starting to be dismantled. The return to the city was inevitable, to the work in cells, in the organization and the small assaults, attacks, blows. But having been in the mountains, having formed a small column that traversed quite a few ravines, two or three springs, three or four scrub valleys and avoided a confrontation with the army, that took over strategic villages and trained comrades for a long march we never made, this was all fundamental. It was the crusade for the crusader. To go to the Holy Land, look after arms and renew vows. The world and its multiple meanings didn't matter. It was the end or the beginning. We returned to the city much more aggressive. We performed several commando missions, expropriated the banks we had to expropriate and kept a minimal apparatus formed to take up once again a struggle that we considered armed. There was no other. There was no such thing as a bloodless revolution. I met Dominguín. He came from another party, from other people who had taken up arms. Dominguín used to talk a lot. He was one of those comrades who knew how to speak just the right word, he wielded the phraseology dictionary of orthodox communists, unintelligible and convincing. To a certain degree, he was like Abelardo. Roca was the factor that created a cohesion between us and, along with Lourdes and Silvestre, we finished our military preparation abroad. We strengthened the muscle. We spent nights under the desert stars reviewing insurgency manuals. Nights in the desert were like nights on the open sea. Where are you now, you fucking bitch? Lourdes, she was the one who set the trap, I had a feeling about it. She, the perverse one. While we were training with Elmer, she knew how to turn the teacher's nights into passages from *One Thousand and One Nights.* I was objective when I thought about what a whore she was. Elmer was the sultan. Elmer set up his encampment under the sands, in the depths of the caves, and there he would delight himself. He knew when to spread out the Bedouin tents in the immensities of the Sahara. He knew about radars and concealment, and once he was in them he would lift up true fortresses of black silk; inside, old blue cloths, edged with silver, crimson pennants, carpets with heraldries of Moorish nobility; the teacher would lose himself warmly in his comfortable robes and along with him, Lourdes, the green eyes of Lourdes, the tall and prominent bearing of Lourdes, the great whore, the great bitch's daughter who mocked security in order to get fucked by Elmer; she would always roast in pairs, when she returned she would ask Dominguín to fuck her firm and sharp in the ass, the whore, the one who had betrayed me. Man doesn't live from putting up tents in the desert, he sets up traps and bombs and launches surface-to-air missiles and runs platforms and makes himself resistant. And we learned about intrigue and counterintelligence matters. We who loved each other so much and out of love made... we were combatants and we were learning, at every moment, how to die just before the assault against power.

That was the mistake. Others had assaulted power. And we hadn't died. That was the logic that functioned despite the logic that should have; I was watching Sonia lean her head on the bus window and listening to Lourdes's exhausting breathing. I shouldn't have survived the coup attempts, I should have died on the day the soldiers refused to give us weapons; we should have gone out, the handful of us from the party, to fight to the death instead of the soldiers who laid down their arms and surrendered and who later would assault power, denying us a death in the assault, postponing death, making my death and Silvestre's, such heavy death, my martyrdom, the necessary immolation, an act of ridiculous and demoralizing betrayal.

I closed my eyes. I needed to sleep. My head was spinning. I was dizzy. Tired. My thoughts and memories were riding a carriage on a carousel, I was listening to its bell, that circus bell in the desert that wouldn't let me sleep.

It was dawn already. I had barely exchanged a few words with that girl who clamped down on the sleeves of her jacket with her hands. Who laughed like all the women in the world laugh. She, who had me, who was taking me to an appalling, solitary, decayed port.

The bus balanced itself tenuously on the pebble-strewn road. We were in front of the church Our Lady of the Conception. The door opened and we stepped off. We received a strong, persistent blow from the warm breeze. I recalled the desert. This is where we would stay. Completely alone. They wouldn't take us into town. We were wrapped in the night in front of a church with tall, robust walls like a military fort, old and generous, white in the darkness, Our Lady of the Conception.

"What now?" I broke the silence, cutting the fresh breeze. "We arrived, I kept my promise." Sonia showed me the lines of her teeth, somewhat irregular. I thought she had the teeth of

a witch. Witches must have teeth like that, including the Gioconda and all women, even when they're perfect they have the
irregularity of the laugh. She shrugged.

"We have to walk or wait to see if someone will take us near
the shrimper."

"What the hell are we going to do at the shrimper's?"

"Go home," she opened her arms so that her body looked
like a cross, a divine image. The church wall rose up behind
her. She was a saint; useless, I thought, stupid. I thought. I was
a moron and a fool. I thought. What house. I asked myself. She
stretched her arms so far into a cross that she turned her jacket
into a cape. She revealed a silhouette I assumed was naked, a
thin silhouette, a smooth belly, a piece of metal shone in the
center, in her belly button, she left her teeth and eyes and hair
in the warm, dry air of dawn; everything against or beyond, it
was the first time I felt I was dealing with the ineffable.

She was incorporeal, a mockery. I feared she would vanish
and leave me in the middle of my great nothingness. Alone.

"Home, what home, your home? I don't have a fucking
home," I said. She turned around and began to run toward one
of the church walls, she passed by the ditch. I followed her. I
stopped when I got to the ditch and I thought that more than
one heretic had been thrown in there. I was reminded of Poe's
"The Pit and the Pendulum." Would they throw me into the
pit? I felt cold. My bones were freezing. Sonia kept running,
she would crash in the darkness against the high, military
white wall of the church. I looked up, noticed the stars, they
were twinkling. How long had it been since I looked at the
twinkling stars? Shit, I started walking again and yelled at her:

"Tu casa es mi casa!"

Sonia was whirling and repeating the phrase like a little
song, "Tu casa es mi casa..."

I hurried and reached her. I grabbed her by the waist. She
threw her body backwards, she was stretching as though she
had been sleeping at the bottom of the ditch of the Inquisition.
I squeezed her waist, lifted her up and we whirled around,

she clamped down on the sleeves of her jacket with force and opened her arms in a cross. I had her in front of me, thin, a beautiful form. That scene was frighteningly absurd, quite tacky. I felt like I was in front of a reverse Lourdes. It made no sense to find myself whirling around with the image of betrayal while the sky began to turn a rose shade in the east, barely twenty-four hours after having tried to change the course of history by blasting a hole in the president's head. Now I realized that my entire life made absolutely no sense and there was no reason for it to begin making sense. I had to follow the river's flow, Heraclitus's river, Abelardo's river, the river of my contradictions. I stopped and pulled her towards me, I felt her eyes fix on my lips, her lips exhaled a sweet breath that overwhelmed my nose, gave me life, took it from me. I turned the dance into an embrace and pulled her closer to me, I squeezed her firmly, stuck to her, I wanted to blend into her, die in her, hide and escape in her. I kissed her. It was a rough kiss. The dry kiss of a dead man.

I fell onto the ground. The sun was rising.

The ground was red. It looked like the ground of the Maghreb, hard and reddish. We were off to one side, about three hundred feet from the church. I was breathing noisily and with fatigue. My chest was coming and going. Sonia was beside me. This time the sleeves of her jacket hid her hands. A full day's weight was upon me. Beside me was a beautiful woman by the light of dawn, who was standing up, giving me her hand, this time hidden inside her jacket.

"Come."

"Where?" I insisted.

Home.

I got up without much energy, cleaned the dirt from my ass. You could hear the roosters. Down below the lights of Puerto Píritu were tinkling.

"There's no time, let's run!" she cursed and squeezed my hand. She was pulling me up.

"There's no time for what?"

"Run, man!" she shouted at me. "It's about to become day-time."

We began to run through a small and irregular trail that opened a path by the southern side of the church, I felt the whips of a few branches against my face, a piece of my shirt was left on the thorns of a cactus, we crossed the Calvario Hill and left behind the twelve black crosses, I was running behind Sonia. I started to open my mouth a little, I felt exhaustion rising once again, the uselessness, I lacked the strength to stop, to not take another step, I was falling down the narrow trail, it bordered a cliff that displayed an aggressive and thorny vegetation, a liquid was flowing from my eyes, it was tears, they slid down my cheeks. I was falling down a trail at sunrise toward an unpronounceable place, trapped by fate. I had always been trapped by fate, I always thought I was setting a trap for it, but fate was taking me down through the foothills of some desert dunes. And that was my story. I could stop there and not tell anymore.

The clearing sky was passing, the last stars, the first clouds were passing, the final nocturnal birds, the third cries of the roosters and the drops of a paltry dew. The noise that was starting from a few of the doors of the port's colonial houses was passing; the remote siren, an isolated scream, the burnt green, the nonexistent green was passing. I was falling into the hole. I remembered the pit of the church. That running made no sense, unless I was dead, unless they had killed me twenty-four hours ago along with Silvestre, unless I myself had taken the gun he had used to kill himself and had blown my face off, or the commandos of the presidential guard had opened hundreds of holes in me. It was death. It was the well. The place. The inhospitable land and the dawn that never became daytime. The country taken over by the army, their checkpoints. Sonia was beautiful, thin death, sweet and serene running in front of me, she was the exhalation of the fall, of the end, she was a road through a tunnel with no light at the end, she was a beginning that would have no end which had been given the

name Puerto Píritu. Or Camaronera. I was dead. There was no
other explanation.

I thought I had fallen for hours. We finished edging
around the cliff, we began to go around another one. I
looked at the circular ruins of a church. I recalled having
read a story about a man who wakes up from a long dream,
a man who builds another man. The circular ruins were a
story, yes. But these circular ruins were real, they were the
ruins of the circular walls of the fishermen's town of Camaronera; the walls of the mission of Jesus, Mary and Manuel
murmured to me. When I thought I was about to kill the
president I saw that Caracas was burning and that Paris was
burning, I remembered Lourdes's voluptuous lips making
a ring around my glans, dampening it, I felt the erection
of he who dies in the gallows and Paris and Caracas were
burning and now the morning that never turned into morning stopped limpid, my eyes were crying, my lips began to
chap because remembering Lourdes was not my privilege, it
was simply a lie. A strange death ended in front of a medium-sized and dusty house, with windows and doors made
of old wood, a fall that suddenly stopped and gave us the
fracture, a crack, an entrance to the big house. We slid like
rats and it was dark. I remembered the pit. I remembered
Poe's story. I remembered that the story about the circular
ruins was by Borges, I remembered that when I was a child I
wanted to put together an impossible erector. That Poe was
a drunk and Borges was blind. Useless ruminations. I was
inside, in the dark, in the center. I sought out Sonia's hands,
she wasn't there. I sought her eyes and felt myself under the
glance of other eyes. The darkness was like a carousel, I was
going round my own burial, I was whirling in a definitive
vertigo, I was dead, I fell onto a woman's lap, the piety that
dried my sweat and my urges. I closed my eyes and let the
river flow once more, I let myself follow its meanders, I had
collapsed without honor or glory.

I was listening to the wind. It was beating outside. It was beating strongly. It couldn't reach me. I was listening to the leaves skim over the song or the earth or the asphalt. It was a rain of air and leaves, constant, painful. Over here a tenuous, loud, paused breathing—close by. I thought of Sonia. She was outside. Far from the darkness. I tried opening my eyes and remained inside. With the sound of the wind and breathing. It was the same thing, air that comes and goes. A tide that sounds. Warm breathing, the wind and breeze outside. My will was returning. The desire to belong to myself and incorporate myself in all senses. But my eyelids were heavy and so was my arm. I lifted one of my arms and felt it fall toward my face and hit it. I was dead. My will had lifted it. Will wasn't enough to keep it there. It wasn't enough to think of desire, of action, I felt that I was breathing beside the wind and breeze and the nearby breathing. I couldn't hear myself. I felt my chest expand and contract. I could sharpen my perception. I was lying at some place of wind and breeze. Stretched out to my full length. In the middle, to the side, in a corner, I myself was underneath, stretched out lengthwise... I focused my perception and my memory and I stared with closed eyes. A rifle in my hands, the telescopic sight precisely in my eye socket, the skin beneath my victim's ear, Silvestre, sprawled on the floor beside me, with his piss-stained pants, his face destroyed and the revolver in his lap like a strange doll. I felt a burning in my chest, the memory made me feel cold and there was an ache in my bones. High dawn, the sunrise that paints itself distant and mauve, the Greeks would call it aurora, I called it Sonia, who was running down the trail and taking found paths and climbing onto the back of a pick-up truck. Did we climb onto a pick-up truck? I only see myself falling like a rock with the certainty that I'm dead.

"Sonia!" I screamed.

I stood up and opened my eyes. It was dark. I tried to adjust my vision. A ray of light slipped through along the floor. Three feet of fine light. A light beyond the darkness, the light coming from where the wind razed. I was in a room on a small bed with a soft mattress. A room I presumed was tall and dry, warm. I had been sleeping. I couldn't say whether it had been for one or two days, a week or a month. I was bloated, slow. I thought slowly, bitterness moved in my mouth. I brought my hand to my face, touched it, my beard had been growing for days. Was I imprisoned? Where was Sonia? Beside me. No, not beside me. Someone was breathing next to me. I wasn't surprised to see a blurry silhouette. It had been beside me before I reacted. It extended its hand and placed it on my shoulder, which was when I realized that I was naked and the hand was a woman's. I didn't move. I brought my hands to my head, ran my fingers through my hair and rubbed my skull. It wasn't daytime yet, the light that leaked under the door was from an oil lamp. I wasn't imprisoned. The figure was feminine, she had her shirt off. Her outline was thin and her thick breasts rose from her chest like pears. Why was she naked? Why was she reaching out to me and stroking my back? Why was she moving closer and kissing my neck? I felt heat between my legs, the smell of that woman was penetrating. She stuck out her tongue and licked me. I didn't reject her. I didn't reject anything ever since I let myself flow with Abelardo or Heraclitus's river. She was exploring me like a mountain cat. She poked around my hair with her nose, she was clinging to my pectorals with her hands.

"Where am I?" I recognized my timid voice.

"In your house."

"This isn't my house," I affirmed.

"Mi casa es tu casa."

"Sonia?" I asked.

"Tu casa es mi casa."

"This place isn't my house. Am I in prison?"

She kept kissing my neck, my cheek, the corner of my lips. I felt that her tongue wanted to enter my mouth. My mouth tasted bitter. I felt an intense heat between my legs, a strong and painful erection, the impulse of life or death, the memory of the waist, made me avoid the chain of absurd events, the mysteries, I realized I was returning to the ineffable. I grabbed the woman with both hands and turned her around, she let the sheet that covered the lower half of her body slip off her, she was left naked and she got on all fours, I covered her with my body and fucked her clumsily and hard, I took her by the ass and penetrated her without any rhythm, like a dog, my will was gone to hell and memories and necessities converged in a red and shapeless amalgam, igneous and magnetized stone, a woman on all fours in front of me, a woman who was soaking my loins, she was breaking her waist and joining her chest with her thighs, from where she lifted her ass and offered it to me; woman who resisted the slovenly impulse, woman on all fours who screamed and cursed, who collapsed me. I ejaculated and fell. I came and it stung, inside her ass. I felt pain, I tossed out a breath or life itself. I think I vociferated, I didn't believe anything. I fell asleep and lost consciousness. Outside the breeze forcefully shook the branches of a tree that I presumed had medium-sized fronds. Everything remained outside and I was inside.

You wake up once again and the wind continues outside. It furiously drags the leaves that gather on the town's old sidewalks and embankments. It's a town with ten houses, almost all of them uninhabited. You are inert and fixed on a small bed with a soft mattress. You don't need to squint because there are several candles in the small candleholders that hang from the corners of the room. You try to remember and the word succubus comes to mind. An engraving seen in some dictionary from your grandfather's library comes to mind. Remember your grandfather? He has been left behind, further than Abelardo and the guerrillas you curse from your cot. In the dictionary there was an engraving that kept you awake for more than one evening. It was of a bird with thick claws that was clinging to a man's stomach, a bird with a woman's face that was kissing the man who was lying on a

Gothic stone. It was the incarnation of the devil in a woman. You think that Sonia is the devil and that the evil one has saved your life from an assassination adventure. The devil has transformed himself into a beautiful woman who has let herself be fucked in the ass on all fours, who has extracted your feverish sperm. You know there are incubi and succubi. The incubus spills the cold sperm and the succubus gathers the warm sperm of men. These fantastic stories, you tell yourself and you feel quite anguished. You see yourself mounting a thin woman who hits your lower parts with her posterior. It's the moment when you feel mortal terror and as you look around you notice they are present. Who are they? Three women and two men. You only recognize Sonia and they repeat that their house is your house and you curse and yell and scream shit, how long will it keep being your house in my house, your house my house. They remain impassive. They stare at you fixedly. Why did you abandon your grandfather. What happened to the library. His library had chimeras, all libraries hide chimeras. Chimeras are monstrous animals, grandpa, you hear yourself say, you justify yourself, I left your house, my house, grandpa, in search of a chimera. Your grandfather's house is small and green, it has two stories, it is aquamarine. Your grandfather searched for chimeras too and he was lost in a labyrinth, he would ask for your house which is my house, which belongs to you all, the one he left one day, to end up in a garden of withered hedges, of questions with no answers. Wasn't life like that, grandpa? You couldn't quite explain to your grandfather. You merely left the house, his house, your house, chasing after a chimera and now you recall his old library made of iron and crystal panels, a dictionary with an engraving of a succubus. Sonia is a succubus, you decide. Where did Sonia bring you? You're lying on a narrow bed, in a room with high ceilings and adobe walls, washed with lime, just like all the houses in this town, a town with few houses, almost all of them empty. The wind is perennial in the town. You can hear the sea behind the wind, a furious, open, oceanic sea. But it's there in a room out of several houses with high roofs, old houses, in ruins, your house. Sitting in front of you, five lecherous ghosts. You seek out Sonia's glance. She smiles at you. She continues to smile like all women smile. There's the thin woman who knew how to hit your

*sad pelvic bone with her ass. You recognize the succubus. There's a
small woman with generous breasts and shapely legs, who has a vulgar air, what you think is that you'd want to have her alone to spit
on her, piss on her, shit on her, harm her. You think that she's pretty
but she smells of poorly washed skin, of ignoble metals, you must
punish her. You realize your thoughts aren't clear, you'd like to ask.
Why have you come. Why has Sonia brought you to this unfortunate
town. Abelardo once spoke to you about fortuitous facts and about
Marxism-Leninism. Everything had its dialectic and emerged from
the conflict of contradictions. You should find an answer. You have a
revolutionary theory. You should also know that you were headed towards revolutionary practice with the intention of changing history,
of exacerbating the contradictions and creating a revolutionary state.
This reality can't be more complicated than your life. Look at yourself,
you're lying on your back, with your mouth closed, full of questions.
One of the men introduces himself. His name is Humberto, he is tall,
he has worked on his muscles, he keeps an exercise routine, he has the
glance of a slave. He asks if you would like some soup, if you want
to eat some grilled fish. Suddenly you feel hungry. And they place a
folkloric ceramic tray in front of you. Everything seems too folkloric
to you right now. You eat without pause. You let the thick broth move
down your throat, you carve the meat of the fish and lift it to your
mouth, it's soft and white. You see the small woman, she's sitting in
front of you, she smiles, uncrosses her legs, opens them and you notice
how she displays the entirety of her hairless genitals, you shouldn't
look at them, but you see and perceive that odor that doesn't end up
pleasing you, she laughs, not like Sonia or all the other women. She
expresses the laughter of power. Of what is imperishable. You're fa-
miliar with it. You remember Roca. He is there in the room, in the
apartment Lourdes has rented. He is well-dressed, his skin gives off
the aroma of a cologne you find repugnant, almost like the odors of
that woman who sits in front of you with her legs opened, she opens
and closes them, she closes and opens them like Roca's jaws, he tells
all of you, his comrades, that the Ministry of Internal Affairs is only
the beginning, that he has been called to the cabinet and will surely be
assigned projects of greater importance. You finish eating and Andrés*

presents himself, he is a tall, thin man with an earnest glance. He removes the tray and asks if you need anything else, shakes your hand. All of them are waiting on the small woman's glance. She brings her legs back together and stands up. She approaches you and stretches out one of her arms, her face is out of focus, her fist opens, she has long fingers and fingernails, the devil's subtle claws. She is the Venus Porneo, the owner of the house, her name is Carla, she has a Sicilian air. Very black hair, black and curly. Tiny eyes, almost Asian, she laughs like Roca, the laughter of powerful people, she has the white teeth of a rodent. She looks like a rabbit. She is a Sicilian rabbit, she caresses your face with her nails, giving you two affectionate slaps on the cheek.

"We're a family," she tells you, "we have this old house in town. There are only a few houses here. We keep ourselves away from the cities. We left them a long time ago. We live without any hurry and in peace."

"And what am I doing here?" you ask. Reality seems heavy, plastic, slow.

"You've come with our Sonia," Carla answers.

"And is that enough? Is it enough for Sonia to have picked me up in the city for you all to receive me in your house and keep telling me that mi casa es tu casa and those types of things?"

"It's enough" Carla affirms.

"I don't believe you," you say and get out of the bed. You're standing in front of her. Stretched out full length, just as long as you've been lying on the bed for days.

"You have to believe. Don't you see me? You're here with us, facing me." She approached Sergio, she leans over the tips of her fingers and blows into his eyes.

"Listen, miss, I learned, and I've been learning for years, that everything in the universe has an explanation. That everything is called to interpretation. That we have to understand reality in order to transform it." You're surprised by the petulance of your speech.

"You've put some effort into it," she replies and turns her back to you, she's about to leave the room, followed by both men, Sonia and Olga. Her name is Olga, Olga winks an eye at you. You feel affection

towards Olga. Olga has sat beside you while you've slept. She has taken care of you.

Carla stops before crossing the bedroom door. The entourage stops with her. A procession of shadows you still haven't assimilated. Sonia is no longer wearing the jacket, she isn't biting any sleeve with her hands, her arms are uncovered, she's wearing a white cotton t-shirt. God, you realize she's beautiful, that you should have stayed on the side of the road, at the church, that you should have kept fleeing toward the east and soaked your feet in the yellow sea.

"I hope you don't find too many explanations, they can be harmful, unpleasant and not necessarily true," she finishes crossing the inner corridor of the house and leaves her odor, which penetrates my nose with force. "The door to my house, your house, remains open and we gather at the end of the hall under a withered grapevine, in front of the cherry tree."

You're left alone with Olga's wink. You think you're dead. Your life is not this one that you are now living. You live in a stupor. You live through a shameful event. The breeze sweeps the patio. You realize that you're in an old house with inner courtyards. No one is thrown for such an unexpected turn in life, you think aloud. Alone and while you are dying you repeat the phrase and realize that you've been dying for days.

That phrase remains.

Alone and while you are dying. You think that he's dying and doesn't stop dying and that somehow you're passing through death. And when were you alive? You want to scream and say "Shit, this isn't possible, it's a fucking dream. Tomorrow I'll wake up and accomplish my fate. I will kill the president."

And what if you don't wake up? What if in a little while you get up and stick your face out the window and stare into the inner patio of the house with astonishment? You observe its few trees. Some geraniums in glass jars, the ferns hanging from the beams, a green that struggles with the breeze and the salt and despite that resistance it is intense, Lourdes's eyes, Sonia's eyes. This life you die is possible, you begin to accept it, you go back to the room and lie on your back. You close your eyes, your heart beats so strongly. You feel scared.

You think of the engravings in the dictionary at your grandfather's library.

And I'd been there for three days. I went out into the inner garden of the old house. Ferns hanging from high beams, scattered lemon trees, the star jasmine that grows on the columns and wooden sheds and the little cherry tree with twisted branches where the group gathers. The door to the house remained open, from there you could see the town. Ten or twelve houses. The houses had outdoor kitchens, all of them except ours. My house? Hell is a place that always keeps you warm. The fishermen always went out early and threw their boats into the river or the sea, above the town, above us reigned the fury of the perennial breeze, it never stopped. And that's why the fires were so enchanting and the whirlwinds danced like dervishes, prophetic blackberry bushes whirled around themselves, tumbleweeds that swept the only street, the only plaza, the ruins of a circular church.

I said our house. I didn't have any other. Only three days and I swore it was the truth. Because I woke up and followed the fishermen, they untangled their nets and talked about the catch. What else could a fisherman talk about? I kept quiet, they paid me no mind, I had always gone out with them at daybreak, from the beginning of time, this was a common occurrence even if all those mornings I never had were only three mornings. They tossed their boats into the river or headed to the beach, they let themselves be swallowed by furious waves and didn't come back until the afternoon. The herons crossed the sky with their nuptial feathers. I remained on the shore along the beach, I found the shade of a bush and laid down. Then I went back into town and ate something and drank, retraced my steps to the beach and slept under the chosen bush until late in the afternoon. The sunset brought Humberto, naked—he was running along the beach, he jumped, he was extravagant—he followed an exercise routine completely naked,

I think the Greeks did the same thing. I read that the Persians were surprised in Babylon when they saw Alexander and his general staff jump and wrestle with their naked bodies in the open air. Humberto came and went and when night arrived he was joined by Olga, then Sonia, they jumped into the sea and closed a circle, they laughed and kissed each other, caressed one another. I saw them and it had been a while since the herons had passed on towards the river and the frogs had begun to sing and the moon and stars came out and the sea was tinted silver and the foam burst in its whiteness. I got up from under the bush and ran to the sea, wet my feet and went back home.

Ever since Sonia brought me to her house, my house, since the night Olga loved me with hard slaps on the ass, since the conversation I sustained with Carla, I had wandered among them. I had been a shade that spied on them. Andrés slept with Carla and Carla with Sonia and Humberto gave his ass to Andrés and Olga gave her tits to Carla. I understood that the shades blended into each other, were promiscuous, Ulysses never said it. The whimpers from their games were blended into the breeze that moaned and irritated; it persisted in the night, moaning and breeze and games and conversation in the corner behind the cherry tree. The strange family that had set me aside, didn't see me, didn't feed me, didn't smile at me. They passed at night and disappeared into dark rooms with high ceilings at dawn. And I was in my house, their house. And I didn't feel I should ask anything. What's three days? A lifetime.

On one occasion after we had clashed with the police and escaped with the money we had robbed from a bank, I was wounded in the ass. My comrades put me into the car and mocked me. I had been shot in the ass. They took me to the safe house, where I was taken care of by a doctor who was friends with the party. Then they told us the shell wasn't safe and we had to abandon it, we had to disperse, I was told to go to the doctor's house. His family didn't know anything about me. He hid me in a wardrobe where he kept his old clothes, where I had to spend three days. They became a lifetime. I never left. I would shit and piss in a bucket inside the wardrobe, I ate once a day, the doctor wouldn't stay to talk, I never opened my mouth, I was beginning to go crazy. I didn't sleep. I thought I would spend the rest of my days inside a wardrobe, pissing and shitting in a corner, bloated by my odors, by the silence, by eternity. They took me out one night and I felt like I was drowning in the open air. Many months passed before I could take to open spaces with the joy that one supposes you should have in them.

Now I was outside, I came and went wherever I felt like going. But I was locked in my shadow, alone.

When we kidnapped the clothing executive, I stayed in a tiny, false room. I kept my routine there. I wouldn't speak to the victim, I would play games of chess with myself and lose. Seven months as a fucking nurse, I would clean his hair and teeth, bathe him, make him do exercises, check his heart rate, feed him, clothe him, the weapon at my side, I would put it together and take it apart, clean it again and again. When he got sick and was delirious from his fever I had to wipe his ass. That motherfucking old man, fucking kidnapping. I was his shadow.

In the desert, with Elmer, we were shadows preparing ourselves with arms. We would perform military exercises for shadows, we arrived in a strange country as shadows and got lost for six months in the Sahara. And all that for what? So that I wouldn't know how to pull the trigger with precision when I should have changed the course of history. We took apart landing strips, created false scenarios to confuse satellites, learned how to use C4, to slice throats and fire missiles and I couldn't fire a basic rifle, hit my objective just below the ear, I who destroyed weaklings, who had executed more than one traitor, who had faced off against soldiers and police, I wasn't able to hit him just below, at the base of his ear, the most important target of my life. Because that morning, on the day of the attempt, I was a shadow that wasn't reflected by reality. And Silvestre and Dominguín and Lourdes. The party and the revolution had been shadows from the very beginning. Ever since we didn't go through with the armed struggle, since the soldiers left us waiting because of an order that day in El Valle, ever since they invited us to be a part of the revolution they made.

And what might shadow me now?

Everything.

I let time pass in their house and in my house. Immersed in my doubts. Why Sonia? This end of the world? This town? Your house is my house, our house. Three days that seemed like a lifetime. The insertion into a reality that accepted me because it had nothing to accept. I was there from the beginning, since God created the rivers and seas.

I found out that the country had been put under a moderate martial law. Can one be moderate under such circumstances? The police delegation had been taken over by two soldiers: a sergeant and a corporal. They would show up at the little store in town and drink a soda or a beer, they said the counterrevolution had been thwarted and that the traitors would be sent to a trial by the people. I heard that the president's only party was his Armed Forces; all suspects were in jail, all those who conspired, even a few foreign journalists. But these were the rumors of ghostly officials.

I lived under lecherous shadows. I didn't understand their codes. I didn't want to make the attempt to understand why I was asking myself other things: why the hell had they arrested a few conspirators. I was the conspirator and was free and in my house our house, her house and your house, with no reflection by the light of day. The other one was Silvestre and he had shot himself in front of me.

Finally the president had enacted a coup and now governed the country under a state of permanent revolution, with the army and the dauntless Minister of Internal Affairs, comrade Manuel Roca. There would be military civilian courts to try the traitors to the process and the homeland; I found out through the sergeant about everything that was going on. So what was

I doing there in that place of sea breezes and herons and fish-ermen and ghost houses? Why didn't I just walk into town. No one was stopping me. I let myself be and let myself be with anger. I was dead.

One afternoon, on the third day, I awoke at sunset. I had dreamed of Lourdes. I saw her beautiful round face like an Italian Renaissance virgin, it was soaked in semen, she was moving her tongue and licking. Lourdes used to say that re-ceiving a man's cum on her face was humiliating. There was a gesture of power and submission behind it. Lourdes and her theories that always turned out to be hot air. When it came time to fuck she transgressed all of them. In the party we knew she was Roca's girl and by a fluke also Dominguín's. I say it with objectivity and without resentment. I dreamed of Lourdes's beautiful round face. I was woken up by a dark red sun that was sinking into the sea, the day's last herons were crossing the sky. Sonia was running toward the sea. She was naked, slender. I felt tenderness. My Sonia had changed so much in the last three days. Her tits were balancing in the air and with Lourdes's face still in front of mine, round like Sonia's ass as she dove into a choppy wave before it broke. I decided to leave the world of shadows and go toward the shadows. I ran af-ter her. I dove headfirst into the turquoise sea, I was throw-ing away Lourdes's round face and following Sonia's round ass. As my head emerged from the water I looked for her. She was a few strokes away from me. I swam furiously. I took her in my arms, pulled her close to me. Our bodies made of wa-ter gripped each other solidly in the crash. She was breathing with fatigue, I closed her mouth with a kiss, she flailed as if she were drowning, I took her by the waist despite the com-ing and going of the waves, looking for a place to step on the sand. I settled my feet and she lifted her legs, installing herself on my waist. She was kissing me. Now she was doing it hun-grily, swallowing my lips bathed in iodine, squeezing her tits against my chest, I sought out her nipples, sank underwater and drank from them, bit them, came up for air and went back to them. With a slight push, Sonia separated herself from me and went underwater, I didn't see her until I felt her hair between my legs, her mouth seeking my cock and swallowing it beneath the waves. She sucked once, twice, three times, came up for air; she took a breath and went back down, sucked and we were knocked over by a wave, I felt her lips moving, taking my cock into her mouth, making me double over, looking for the bottom, earth, swallowing water, I was drowning when she released me and floated to the surface and settled her feet on the ground, she ran slow like the sea allows and stopped. The water was up to our waist.

"Now it's your turn."

I filled my lungs with air and went down. I grabbed her by the thighs underwater. They were the legs of the Colossus of Rhodes, she was open and I sank my face there, I brusquely opened the first lips of her cunt, it was water flesh, weightless flesh, it was a great wounded jellyfish exposing a tiny head, a grain foreseen in the depths of the abyss, a snail's neck. I moved my tongue but had no air left. I was dizzy. I had to lick her. Above. Where the wound ends. Where the world begins. My lungs were bursting. My ears ringing. I clung, I held on with my mouth, I was a mollusk kissing a mollusk, pulling the water flesh, looking for air in the mollusk and licking it. I grimaced and desperately came up from the depths. Sonia fell back, I regained consciousness after two breaths of air, she was screaming. She set out for the shore: she laid down on the sand as though she was the incarnation of all the shipwrecked whores of the Caribbean and waited for the undercurrent to spit me out; I went to her: loot, lumber, sphinx, and I fucked her like a beast with no other desire than dying covered in foam and drool, swallowed by the plenitude and hit by the waves that cover us and drag us, annulled by the night. Eternal under a full moon, with dogs barking in the salt mines, frogs and a perennial breeze. Stupid life that returns, empty.

I lay beside Sonia for a long while. I was playing with her nipples. Tracing their outline with my index fingers.

"Who are you?" I asked.

"Who are you?" she said right back.

"The man who tried to kill the president." I pulled my fingers away and turned my back to her. I was claiming my act for the first time. She hugged me. She was collapsing against me, breathing me. Nothing surprised her.

"Is that what you do, kill people?"

"No," I answered and drew a sun on the sand.

"And what about the president?"

"What?"

"Isn't he a person?"

I wanted to explain to her that I'm not a killer. That the president isn't a person, that the people I had executed before weren't people. They were targets. Objectives.

I remembered when we had just come back from our desert training and Roca told us that Rubén was a spy. That he had information about the military coup. That he had probably already passed it along to the enemy. We set up the operation, intercepted his car and took him down the old highway to La Guaira, where we took him out and told him we were about to execute him. That he was a traitor. Rubén got on his knees and swore by his mother that he wasn't a traitor. That we were mistaken. We told him he was a motherfucker who was passing information along to the DIM. He swore again. Silvestre gave me a sign, I stepped aside and pointed at Rubén's head. He covered his ears, crying, and began to scream. Silvestre and I shot. I think that when we were leaving, Silvestre complained that we had waited too long to pull the trigger.

I stood up. I felt sick. Rubén was a person. *What the fuck?* I thought. *How many people have I killed?* I didn't want to remember anything. I felt nauseous, chills in my bones. Sonia stood up and said we should go to the house. Carla would be wondering where we were.

I straggled behind her. My whole life I had been straggling. The breeze was hitting against my naked body. We crossed the village and entered the garden, in the back by the cherry tree amid the columns where the star jasmine crawled, a light was shining.

"Wait," I took Sonia by one of her arms.

"What?"

"Don't say anything."

"About what?"

"About what I've told you."

"And if I do would you kill me?" She turned her back to me. I took a quick step and grabbed her arm again.

"I'm not a murderer," I said with a dull voice.

"And I'm not a president," she smiled and showed me an irregular, white set of teeth.

Her eyes were glowing. I hadn't seen them so dark and so green. I felt a great tenderness for her. I remembered her in the store. Her hands clamping down on the jacket, her hair a mess, balancing to the rhythm of the blues. It was like having found the real Lourdes, an everyday girl who might fall in love with me. I felt nostalgic. Nostalgic for three days ago, for my life, for the city full of smoke, police and soldiers.

We took a shortcut and zigzagged between the lemon trees in the patio. The breeze as always was breaking harshly and carried the aroma of star jasmine and brought the aromas of other bonfires and the laughter of other people. Distant laughter, made tense by the solitude. Laughter at night in a ghost town. Once again, in front of the cherry tree, while Carla looked at us from the back sitting on a wicker armchair, I stopped her.

"Wait."

"What?"

I brushed her still damp hair from her forehead. Her face was clean. Her eyes dark and green. My chest swollen. I kissed her eyelids, I kissed her on the mouth.

"Sometimes I think I'm a character in a novel," I told her, "I think we're in a novel and we've just become aware of it."

"You realized it," she declared and let out a laugh.

I was actually a character in a novel. A novel built with a waste of whimsy on the author's part. A novel that created a framework of its sequences with rude coincidences. Besides Humberto, who was smoking a cigar behind Carla's wicker armchair, Lourdes was smiling at me, Roca's woman, Dominguín's lover. My political enemy. My secret obsession.

And she smiles at you languidly, her lips smile at you, she, the schemer, the cheater, standing in front of you, behind the armchair with her hands flat on her lap, her dark green eyes, just like Sonia's, a serpent's eyes.

Fixed on you. You look for her hands. What are you looking for in her hands? They've found you, to find is a simple game for those who are starving, for the thirsty, to find is to hunt, they've hunted you down, she's in front of you. What does she have in her hands? You feel the weight of the night and it is dense, the nights are dense in Carla's house, the nicest house in a fishing village. How could they not find you in the nicest house in a fishing village? A novel is written and you think that your character will emerge from the plot and will reproach you for how bad you've handled things. Her hands, one on top of the other, on her lap, she is a Renaissance tracing. Her abundant hair falls in curls on her shoulders, her pale skin, Carla's smile, Olga's smile and the indifference of Andrés and Humberto. Do I actually have a house? You can hear someone saying, this house is not my house, you repeat it and think that the moon runs just above the cherry tree, the dry grape vines, the dead nettles, you in the center of the patio recall Lourdes in the middle of the desert, during a military exercise, you weren't going to be shooting at dummies, you weren't about to ambush supposed enemies, nor were you in trenches underground with surface-to-air missiles, it was just you and her. Being alone in the desert is like not being anywhere, it's a small room, devastated and dark. A room of light or darkness, or stars; we had to survive the desert. You had always needed to survive the desert, you recall that Abelardo told you that life for the revolutionary was an inhospitable desert, in that empty immensity you would have to find plenitude and sense. And that's what you did, until a few days ago your life was full of sense and purpose, you found yourself about to change the course of history, you were seeing history through the telescopic sight of your rifle, stilled, the desert you had migrated across since childhood finally stilled, reason was the skin behind the ear, the target that was giving a speech to the crowd and you failed. And she, who had wandered the desert with you and covered herself from the sun in the sand, the one who refused to give you a sip from her ration of water, she was looking at you and smiling. What was she waiting for, to pull out her weapon and fire?

So many questions filled your head. As always there were no satisfactory answers. Before, when you had comrades and parties, you received orders and, when you didn't understand them you would ask and they'd respond with rank, they left you with vague satisfactions, always vague, you never had a certainty that wasn't a dream. The dream of martyrdom, the dream of a vindicating historical event. Your certainty was the certainty of Abelardo, to create a new world. But here you are, look at yourself, in front of Lourdes, your hands are shaking and the color has left your face. You're as pale as Carla. And Carla? Why do you feel a hidden contempt for her yellow skin, her black eyes, her Moorish hair, for the undefined smell that becomes unpleasant, it smells like storage, like metal, sweat and metal, sweat is metallic and she smells like a drop of sweat, the drops on her upper lip, the ones she doesn't lick. And have you made a new world, Sergio? You feel like Lourdes is inquiring. Who is she to demand an answer? A seeker of answers just like you, a woman pissed on by fatality or by her lovers, which is the same thing, execrated by theorists. Did she have an answer? Why the delay? Shoot, already! You dare to think of the scream. We haven't achieved anything, you found me, do what you have to do, take me outside, with no witnesses. Then you burst out laughing. Are they actually witnesses? Look at them, they're here and not here, not even Sonia who offered you hearth and lava in her skin, she's not here, her presence is weightless, her presence is elevated and departs from the center of the patio to beyond the top of the grape vine, Sonia's ascension reveals a mystery, they have no weight, Olga *weighed on your pelvis, she hurt you, she was heavy, you can affirm that, but she's not here and she is beside Carla and the others move with pauses on the scene, they stop and continue like fatuous fires; except for Lourdes who keeps smiling, her smile has gone through variations, more than a person you think of a sequence that arrives and tells you not to worry about a thing, that you're safe, that you're safe because she's fleeing, that everything has gone to hell, that you're both victims of a move by Roca or by the government or by the government and Roca, that there's a state of emergency, a military and revolutionary democracy, that's how they plan on announcing the state if they haven't already, she doesn't know, because she hasn't read the papers, Sergio, life is built on strange events, don't be surprised, I'm here because of the same reasons as you and I've arrived here because of the same coincidences, if coincidences actually exist, we know that, we're materialists, despite the fact that everything is a consequence of the dialectic and of the contradictions it generates, what happens is that there's a second when an inflection is produced, a fracture in the system, and a spontaneous event is born. How do you think the universe was born? You answer, not knowing what tone you're using, you tell her to stop talking shit, to not justify anything else, to proceed, a dead man doesn't need any explanations, don't you see that I'm dead, that I was killed at one point, it could have been immediately after Silvestre blew his head off, it could have been before that. Silvestre shot at me in order to abort the change in history and my body fell but I continued to watch, someone said that you enter death with your eyes open and look, I've kept them open and that's why I saw miserable Silvestre go to a corner of the battlement from where he was supposed to shoot the president, the fucker put the barrel of his Magnum in his mouth as if he were biting a churro and he blew his head off, he made a mess with his brains, the son of a bitch had no sense of aesthetics, he shit and pissed in his pants, shit, piss and blood inundated everything from that point on and once I was dead I proceeded onwards. Did Silvestre have an order to kill me? Was Silvestre a perverse move by my comrades? I was dead. How if I wasn't able to escape the siege? How if I wasn't able to reach this place where reality is a shadow? And you're dead too. What other option is there? But you're not dead either. And everyone else? She comes out from behind the wicker armchair, extends her hand to you like a friend. She was never your friend, you and her were always adversaries, at a certain point she would brandish the weapon, she had it hidden, she'd use a method with strange resources that would be activated from one moment to the next, she'd pull out the dagger and would bring an end to your life in hand to hand combat. She had always beat you. When Elmer trained you in the desert you were never able to dominate the martial arts, you were clumsy, your body refused to obey and to protect itself or attack. In the hand to hand exercises you would struggle with Lourdes, you'd embrace her angrily, you'd try to grab her head and pull on it, separate it from the body, she would slip out of your arms, enfold you with hers, place herself behind you, you felt the pressure of her tits on your back, the firm breathing, the skin on her cheek and her hair, the drop of sweat, she would place you in the position that would let her break your neck, then she'd pull one of your arms, make you spin and nail you in the balls with her right knee. You'd fall and let yourself go, under the tents in the desert in the daydream of fainting. At any moment she'd let the dagger shine and cut your throat. But no, look Sergio, I escaped from Roca when I noticed he was about to apply his forced humanism on me, you'll find it obnoxious how I reacted when my turn came, but that's life and now I regret everything for all of us, everyone is dead except you and me. Are you sure you and I aren't the only dead ones in this stupid mess? You spit the words out at her. And she gasped and everyone else followed the little spectacle you were offering with seriousness. It's impossible for you to have merely arrived here just like that, you tell her, it's impossible for you to be here because you want to and she responds that it didn't happen that way, that it's incredible, but it didn't happen that way, she was fleeing from Roca and was protected by a rural doctor who helped her escape to the house of the doctor for the ambulatory clinic in Puerto Píritu, he would hide her, he had the means, and his means were Humberto and his Vespa, the doctor wasn't at his ambulatory clinic, he couldn't stay there without awakening suspicion, there were already national guardsmen at the police station, she went to the doctor's house and he wasn't there, that's where Humberto came into her story, it's an* outlandish and brief story she won't tell you about, the doctor was Humberto, what a bad plot, hardly believable anyway, and he brought her to this house which is safe. Why was she using the past tense, she thought, I'm fleeing, I'm still fleeing and I'll conjugate it in the future tense, I will flee and if you want to conjugate it in plural Sergio, we'll flee, we're stuck in a difficult situation, Sergio, we'll be in this house which is your house which is my house until we can move, reach Güiria and escape to Trinidad.

She reaches out to you, offers her open hands, you're alone despite the shadows, alone in the center of a devastated garden, in a house with walls that are peeling, under a useless grape vine. Who was the fool who planted the shoot to watch it diminish in a land where the grape vine will always whither? To flee, you give her one of your hands, barely graze her fingers, long, warm, beautiful. The cheater had beautiful fingers, the only people who have fingers like that are people who have taken the lives of another. How many lives has Lourdes taken? How many will she take? You graze her fingers and think it's not possible, such coincidences do not exist not even in the lottery, much less in your dreams. But there's Lourdes, tall, with her hair falling in red curls on her shoulders, she watches you with the dark glance of her green eyes. The dark green of Sonia now elevated, gone and absent, once again a shadow in the house that isn't your house, she remains on her verandah, I don't have a house, Lourdes, all that's left is the escape, to burn or escape, you can hear them, they're coming for you, you're together in a fishing village, in the house with the high ceilings, the only house and the only ruin, you're together because you don't know that the universe has cracks, time and space become horizontal planes, you can walk along them, so there you are and there she is, you're both looking for an explanation, you both suspect the other's intentions, you both think that one of you must die. Another death to nourish life? Whose? Lourdes I don't have a house and she, distant amid the scene watches the people going by, Carla winks and nods gravely. Olga hugs her, Humberto sits on the cement floor, Andrés lifts his hand to his mouth and lets loose a yawn, Sonia watches them

from the verandah, the moon reflected on her face. We're both outside,
Lourdes answers, let's flee. There's no alternative.

And your grandfather? He was abandoned far away and disappeared
like these shadows. He was a proper man who thought about doing the
proper thing at almost every instant. That's why he opened his library
and let the books out and always sought a land where he might plant
himself, he is not here and won't be anymore, you lost the link, his
hand, the journeys throughout the country in search of land, a place
to build a house with wide corridors where you all might survive.
Your house. What would you need to survive, you wondered? And
now the question is easy, all your efforts to understand are ridiculed
by the fluidity of the answers, now. To survive disillusion. What else
can man aspire to, no one survives death, some try to survive disillu-
sion, to set oneself apart from man, leave him outside. That's cynical.
No, it's a legitimate act of prudence. To flee, to flee to Trinidad. Your
grandfather's father was born in Trinidad, his father had also escaped
from one of so many petty tyrants in the century of revolutions, he
was raised there like an Englishman of the East Indies, his affect-
ed English and the colonial customs refined until he was ill, these
made him vulnerable. When he returned to Venezuela he felt rootless,
the natural thing would have been to go to London, to continue his
studies in a college, but his father had died broke, bankrupted by the
rebellions, his uncle was in Cumaná and his escape was in the oppo-
site direction. To flee to Trinidad, that's where Spain had gone after
the first insurrection against the peninsula, that's where the killer's
hand had reached, that's where destiny had reached the father of your
grandfather who would become an adventurer seeking gold in the
state of Guayana and who would hand over his soul while deep in a
hammock in the middle of a jungle and afflicted by unspeakable pains,
my father would complain, your grandfather said, I remember him,
he was pissing blood and complaining, he never stopped playing the
harmonica, deep in the hammock where he kept complaining until the
day death shut him up. Trinidad has the ocean, it's the place where
fate hits you in your gut and you, Spain, would come and drink the

poison, or you would banish yourself forever to die afflicted by the bites of an illness that prolongs itself in pain. No, no. Lourdes would be there, she would put you to death. Grandpa, and you, where are you. Gone. Your land doesn't exist, neither the dream nor the possibility of escaping disenchantment exist. Why don't I see you among us, the dead? The breeze creates whirlwinds in the center of the patio, the zinc rooftops rattle outside, the fishermen's houses creak, Carla is about to clap, they haven't said anything, haven't done anything, you are both poor actors, you deserve applause. And how will we leave. No one's threatening us here, you say, you think that only Lourdes threatens you, Roca will reach us, she answers. And why should both of us die, why now. It's a cursed fate I will try to conjure, she says. You don't believe her, you feel like crying, you think of your grandfather, you know he has died, that one day he ran out of air, that he won't free you from Lourdes as he did from Abelardo, he won't free you from revolution.

THE BLAISE PASCAL CITATION

Elmer was a meticulous man and he disliked having to do a subaltern's tasks. He knew he would accomplish his objectives within a reasonable time frame. That he'd give each one a shot to the head after humiliating them. Executing someone was easy. Protecting oneself from execution was a delicate matter. This last point took up most of his time.

Doing Roca's dirty work made a rash of hives break out on his forehead. He would wipe the red zone with a handkerchief and think that he had once worked for dignitaries during moments when the fate of the entire planet was at play. He knew how to provoke his adversary to the point of taking him to the edge of thermonuclear wars, he executed impossible targets and trained the best men and women for combat, who went on to fill the East and the West with uncertainty and assassinations.

Here he was, a man from the old school, at the service of Roca. He needed to drink something stronger than Evian water.

The smoke was a persistent presence. The city was illuminated by imposing lights, the light of the last day, Elmer thought, he stood up, left the easy chair from where he had dedicated himself to elaborating a plan, the plan wasn't appearing, he felt resentful, he kept looking over his shoulder, he understood that sooner or later he'd have to flee from a stupid hunter. He recalled Vladimiro Montesinos's oblique glance, staring into nothingness, into the paths of nothingness while he was picking his nose, he never imagined he would be felled by adversity planned by mortals in a lab. When Elmer met the ineffable one at the hacienda where they were keeping him, he was received by a small, thin, balding man, who was cold, he didn't mean to be cold, he wasn't trained to presume that condition, he carried it within, it was an innate feature. Roca was a resentful man, the resentful acquire coldness by means of a deaf passion, Vladimiro had never exerted himself. There he was, covered by the mantle of an attractive superiority, deaf; although he seemed to be attentive, he was autistic—*geniuses are said to be autistic,* he would repeat that over and over and Elmer evaluated him with the contempt of those who have formed themselves by means of pure effort. He understood himself as a professional, that encounter was enough to reach the conclusion that sooner or later they would have to eliminate Montesinos.

"In front of a blind Oedipus the only thing left to do is watch him fall down a precipice."

It had been a mistake to bring him, he was a man at the end of his road, with nothing to add to the process, he had sold his idea about the illogic of his methods to three or four sorcerer's apprentices. He was laughable. He presumed to be a persecuted man who had fallen due to the unfeasibility of his methods; domineering to the point of clumsiness, he found resonance among neophytes. The Nazis had the mania of recording everything the Reich did, both publicly and privately, honorable and horrific, they recorded the parades of the Hitler Youth, Eva Braun's gym routines, the perversions of the regime's dignitaries, they wouldn't stop, they recorded their concentration camps, the arbitrary trials, life in the Warsaw ghetto, Gestapo interrogations, SS oaths, torture sessions, executions, exterminations. In the end, thanks to the German leaders' scrupulous mania of saving moments for posterity, the victors had access to a detailed inventory for judging the men who would rule for

a thousand years, to hang them, blackmail them, force them
to work in their intelligence apparatuses. In the desert, Elmer
never allowed any type of register. Neither personal diaries,
nor photos or movies. Based on documentary evidence, Elmer
had never been in the deserts of North Africa. He buried himself under the sand, learned how to camouflage himself like
the Bedouins, he was nothing and no one, he wouldn't act, imperceptible to radars and satellites, he never made the mistake
of exhibition. But Vladimiro, the man who was so praised by
some who found his methods suitable for protecting the process from enemies, kept a detailed register of his life, he was
a man who hungered for documentation and planted pupils
in the heart of the political police; so everything began to be
recorded and registered, they would organize recordings with
the same meticulousness as in Hollywood, baptisms, first com-
munions, parties, CTN meetings, appointments in hotel rooms,
they began to permeate each one of the pores in the body of
power until they became unbearable. There are antibodies and
resistances; it is the moment when nosy individuals crumble
ostentatiously, that's what Elmer said to Roca in an argument
they had while jogging in a public park, he's a dead man, he
was saying, I noticed it in his glance, autistic people are insects
that fly towards the fire, they burn and laugh, I want to be the
one to execute that son of a bitch, Elmer said, I'll have to make
him turn off his cameras. He thought it was foolish to pretend
to erect a surveillance system in which everyone is filmed, this
condemned the movie's director and his pupils to death. Elmer, resentful for having been expelled from his arid paradise,
wanted to be the executioner, he hoped to find himself at the
end of the story with enough bullets in the cylinder of his Magnum .44 to blow the heads off these idiots. He recalled the eyes
and the arrogance of a finished man who was running his last
100 meters without any obstacles in a country too folkloric to
understand that you have to break a few eggs to make an omelet, much less a revolution that doesn't even have the most basic sense of self. Before he asked them to serve him a rum and

ice, he thought it had been a shame to hand over Vladimiro, it angered him, they should have called him, he wouldn't have left a trace, he would have put an end to the pretensions of the crazy video—ridiculous videocracy—with a beautiful gunshot, one of those taken without warning, from a prudent distance, that leave a tiny trace of entry, an orifice with an aura from the dark iridescence of gunpowder on the forehead, accurate and discreet shots, barely, in the nape of the neck, a balloon, a ripe oval tomato that explodes and stains. But they were clumsy. Despite having felt the odor of trash clog their noses, they let themselves be blackmailed by operators who kept two or three irrelevant videos, they didn't know how to cut the head of the Turk, they lacked the balls, their pulse was unsteady, this is what Elmer thought, it could have all been so simple, Roca understood it, to execute in secret, disappear, no one is free from the excesses, unless he wants to expose himself. To create fear, damn it, create fear, he shouted, as he jogged in the park alongside Roca, they needed to learn once and for all that fear is the only thing that paralyzes and they didn't learn it.

The rum and ice arrived, he let it sit for a while, he walked to the large hotel window and contemplated without surprise a landscape hidden in folds of smoke, there are several types of smoke in this country, several mountains are on fire, and he had a task, a small and irrelevant one, he had to suppress two insignificant, minor pustules. They had let the big ones burst a while ago.

Where would he begin? They had already raided Sergio's hideouts. He never appeared around his safe houses. No one had seen him, his old companions were no longer among the living, Roca had taken care of that, his family was interrogated and hadn't heard anything. He had to wait, remain alert, no one completely disappears unless they're dead, he would eventually give signs of life. Caracas was big, but it easily exposed those who tried to hide there, people couldn't blend into the city, they stood out, Sergio would make himself seen, he was clumsy, fanatical, hurried, Elmer knew him, he had evaluated him in the desert.

Lourdes was a dedicated student. They couldn't wait for her. She wouldn't go to her hideouts either, she already knew that her companions were martyrs and she wouldn't knock on her mother's door. She was a cold woman, with the capacity to stop and think, to make unhurried decisions. He would start with her.

How did she escape from the hotel? They had seen her get lost in the kitchen. The kitchen had few exits and all of them were blocked. That left the duct they used to throw out the trash. She had escaped through there. The man who ran after her wasn't mistaken. But he had acted like an imbecile, Elmer thought, he should have stopped the truck, pulled the drivers out and made them empty all the trash from the back. And what if she was dead in the trash? What if he had hit her? The man swore he had emptied a clip with ten rounds. Lourdes was a well-trained woman, she surely knew how to bury herself, avoid the vulnerable points of space and throw enough cardboard and paper over herself to cushion the impact of the bullets that might have reached her. He was sure she had fled. That's why he ordered Lorca, his assistant, to begin at the dump.

Lorca spent the whole day amid detritus. He studied the place, the sanitary landfill was an immensity of compacted shit inhabited by beings from another world whom he interviewed fruitlessly. They looked at him like a great human mass dressed in black, that was displaying a bright badge and the photo of a woman, but they wouldn't stop to look at the badge or the woman in the photo, they were looking at the wrists, the fingers, the earlobe of the man who was interrogating them. They were looking at his rings, the watch, the gold earring. They were looking at his hair in a ponytail, he was walking amid the groups of homeless people and repeating the question, he would offer money and everyone would start to say yes, that they'd definitely seen that woman, that she had gone that way, or that way, that she left in a rich man's car, that she was taken by some hoodlums, that she was a hoodlum and had taken away their bottles and cans.

Then he looked at a group of uniformed men that were walking around the edge of the trash plain, he headed over to them and asked what they were doing there.

"This is where the guy who shot an officer must have escaped, it'll be impossible to get him out of there." The man in the uniform pointed to a shantytown built out of tin and wood panels.

"It doesn't matter, hunt down anyone, I want anyone these people might identify as a hoodlum, make sure they point him out to you, and you bring him," answered the group's commander.

Two of the uniformed men climbed down to the tin city. A filthy air was floating over the plain on which the dump was planted, it pulled up the sediment, cartons, papers, a smell of gauze and dead things. A pile of dead leaves like shit. Lorca might have thought that Lourdes could be there, buried in any particular spot. It's a good place to bury someone. In such a rotting place anyone might disappear. The searchers were dispersed alongside the vultures, infected emanations emerged from the landfill, the birds were fighting with children and adults for pieces of organic trash. The uniformed men didn't take long, they were coming up the hill with two skinny men, with naked torsos, they were handcuffed, as the rules mandated. The functionaries reached the commander with short breath, Lorca stepped aside slightly, the prisoners were forced to their knees.

"Which one of you shot him?"

"No man, no. None of us shot anyone, it was a chick."

The leader of the commando kicked the one who spoke in the chest.

"Was it your mom, you fucking son of a bitch?" He hit him in the face with the butt of the gun before he fell to the stamped-on trash. The other man began to scream, to beg, they hadn't done anything, he swore by his mother, it had been a chick.

"It was a chick, mister commissary, it was a chick, a well-dressed lady who shot the officer, I swear by my mother, mister commissary, I swear, it wasn't us."

He hit him flat on the nose with his fist.

"Yeah, we believe you. Stand up!" he yelled at the man he had knocked over with a kick. "Turn around, you bastards, I'm going to do you a favor, you kill one of my colleagues and I'm supposed to give you a prize." He approached them and spoke. "I'm going to free you from your miserable lives."

He immediately fired a shot into the nape of one of their necks, the other one was crying, lifting his hands to his face, speaking things that made no sense. The commander of the uniformed men pointed at his parietal.

"Wait!" Lorca shouted.

The officer was sweating, he looked at him disconcerted, he was looking for something in Lorca's face.

"You're not about to read him his rights now," he attempted a smile, "I have to execute them, I have to maintain discipline in this chaos, this isn't the city, they killed an officer, there aren't any rights here, there are no humans. See, just trash."

Lorca walked up to the detained man.

"Which way did the woman run?" he pulled him by his filthy hair.

"That way, boss, she went through the shantytown and onto the road, she hit the road, she went that way." He was pointing toward an imprecise location.

Lorca turned his back to them and descended into the tin shantytown where his immense figure became blurry. A shot was heard, the motors of the trucks sounded as they noisily emptied their loads.

"Lourdes isn't in Caracas," Elmer said to Roca. They were sitting on the terrace of the café at the Intercontinental.

"Not even from here can you see the city clearly, " complained the minister.

"Sergio seems to have been swallowed by the earth." He took out a handkerchief and wiped his forehead, wide and reddish.

"You should resolve the matter quickly, Elmer, we need you in the palace." Elmer felt like his mouth was filling up with bile, his saliva tasted bitter, his eyes were shining.

"You know very well that Lorca can handle this minor affair."

Roca took a sip from his cup of coffee, he wasn't looking at his interlocutor.

"It's the perfect name for a killer."

Elmer got up from the table and got ready to leave. The sky had turned dense, the clouds and the smoke were offering a spectacle for the end of the world, fine bolts of lightning were crossing the sky that afternoon, you could hear the uproar of a dry storm, the sirens wouldn't stop sounding in the distance.

"Wait."

"There's nothing more for me to add."

"You've got to understand I can't leave this in the hands of a killer."

"You've lived in the hands of killers your whole life." Elmer turned around, he felt ridiculous, offended, interpreting a scene of indignation in a bad soap opera. It was unforgivable.

"Don't pressure me, Elmer. I have the whole country on the edge of rebellion, the press won't stay quiet, the labor unions are defying us, we're being accused of having installed a camouflaged dictatorship, of being a military democracy. Don't you understand that the fate of the process is being played out here?"

"What's being played out is your own job, that's what you really should say. You, better than anyone else, know you're a fucking wage laborer and if they take away your salary they'll give you a shot to the head as your severance pay."

"You insist on saying stupid things. You get offended by the stupidest things. You don't seem to understand that this is a delicate matter, that I don't trust anyone."

"Have you ever trusted anyone in your life?"

Roca threw the napkin on the tablecloth, the flash from a lightning bolt crossed his face, the thunder was quickly heard.

"When will they be dead?"

"I can't tell you."

"Look Elmer, you and I are fucked, no matter what happens, whether this thing becomes consolidated or not, we're fucked, you with less room to maneuver than me. Ever since the Vladimiro thing, they mistrust all intelligence men, they don't forget your resentment for not having been placed at the head of the security project. Everyone knows you boycotted Vladimiro, some even think you filtered the information."

"Don't fuck with me, Roca."

"Bring me some good news and I'll get you out of here to Buenos Aires."

"Why Buenos Aires and not Prague?"

"There's no place for you in Europe. There's no place for us.'

"And what's in Buenos Aires?"

"Big opportunities," Roca smiled. "Argentina is a country that's been collapsing for a century now. Is there a better setting?"

Elmer walked down the steps of the terrace at the Intercontinental and passed through the lobby. He couldn't erase the mocking grimace from his face, he was a common and imperceptible figure. He exited towards the hotel entrance and waited for them to bring his car. There was nothing else to do, he had to find Lourdes as soon as possible. He took off, looking in his rearview mirror, again and again as he connected with the avenue and crossed toward a street and turned around at a small plaza. He noticed he was being followed. He accelerated his car and connected once again with another one of the avenues, he made several turns, he knew he didn't have a single car following him now, he glided into the parking lot of a mall and without a word handed his keys over to the man in the booth, set off the alarm and created a traffic jam. He walked through the crowds of people and didn't enter the galleries, he took a passageway that led toward the street, he got on a bus, took it for two blocks and jumped onto the zebra crossing under a stoplight that was on red, there were people on the street, everyone was running, a fine rain was falling on the city. It was then he took a taxi.

Buenos Aires, he said to himself. *Roca thinks I'm an idiot.* His cell phone rang, Lorca was calling him from a small town, he was in Oriente in front of a walk-in clinic, waiting for the doctor.

He had to think. He knew it was crucial to think very insightfully. If he found Lourdes and Sergio, if he executed them, he would be executed at the same time. Without any pause. He more than anyone knew how these spirals of execution worked. Could he trust Lorca? No, he didn't trust anyone, he had to go to Oriente, he had to put together a plan B.

He got out of the taxi and went into a workingman's restaurant in an industrial zone.

"So Manuel, who's the favorite in the fifth?" He extended his hand and received the set of keys for the warehouse.

"Scarecrow can't lose," the other one answered naturally.

In the warehouse he changed his clothes, losing no time. He left the restaurant transformed into a worker. Instead of his impeccable suit, he was wearing khaki pants, a striped shirt and a tan leather jacket with fringes. He pulled a key out of his bag and after unlocking the chain that guarded a motorcycle, he climbed on, fastened the helmet and drove onto the avenue in the industrial district, he was lost among the cars through the density of the smoke, the hills continued to burn, night was already here, he would have to drive for a long time to a town in Oriente without forgetting Roca's promise of his bones ending up in Buenos Aires, maybe at the bottom of the River Plate, which was another way of saying nowhere.

Doing investigative journalism isn't easy. People always mis-understand the purpose. Manuela sits down at the counter of the usual bar and orders a scotch. She's under pressure, she has to speed up her work on the conspiracies. She has interviewed union leaders and businessmen; all of them say the same thing, their opposition stance hadn't contemplated the assassination of anyone, much less the president. Why should she believe them? Many people want to see the presi-dent dead, a representative from the National Assembly had told her. She thought that many people wanted to see her dead. There was proof of the attempt, the bullet embedded in the tree behind the stage where speeches were given, the dead in the nearby building. "Did that justify the declaration of a state of emergency?" she asked in one of the first reports. She had to go little by little, there was a state of emergency and she could easily be silenced. This wasn't the story of the Vladimiro case, where she was able to act without any prohi-bitions despite the phone calls, the disqualifications from the high spheres of power and pressures from within the news-paper. She was well informed by her sources, even a sector from inside the government gave her tips, they had an inter-est in the case being uncovered. This was definitely anoth-er scenario. Today everyone watches out for themselves, the informants don't manifest themselves or if they do it's with a great deal of fear, doubts and ambiguity. This wasn't the first time she had dealt with those factors, but it was the first time she did research and published under a state of emergency or in a military democracy.

She wasn't clear about the identity of the men who were killed on the day of the attempt. She had been denied access to the files. A frightened little bird had told her that one of the dead was an old school guerrilla fighter, who had even partic-ipated in the coup attempts back in the nineties. She couldn't send out trial balloons, any piece of information had to be corroborated over and over again. At one point, when she had been researching the case of some fishermen murdered by the army and who were said to be Colombian guerrillas, she received names of police officers and commissioners, she exposed them, took a personal risk, was threatened with a lawsuit that would have taken her to jail for propagating defamatory information, and received death threats that corroborated for her that she was following the true facts. The informants continued to reveal more, and gave her motives: behind the massacre there was extortion, they needed to create a climate of insecurity for the ranchers of the region so as to justify a group of "professionals" who could provide assistance and protection in exchange for a certain amount of dollars. From there to a paramilitary and mercenary group there was a magical and invisible line. This is what she affirmed. She was accused of advocating in favor of the Colombian guerrillas, they pulled out images of soldiers killed by insurgents from the other country, they systematically attacked her. Despite that, she had friends in the Attorney General's office, in the congress, in the army and within the State's security apparatus. She was supported by human rights organizations and was able to expose without any consequences the cause of the massacre and who was the perpetrator.

She had always arrived at the end game, she never took up a case if her instinct didn't tell her something was there. This limited her to a monkish lifestyle, she didn't have any outside interests. "There's no room for Plutarch in the business of investigative and denunciatory journalism," she would tell her friends, outside interests are weaknesses, pieces that the accused can light on fire, she would repeat, it's not easy being on this path, you have to forget about any gratification besides the research itself, it's very similar to religious work. She allowed herself to drink alone, never accompanied, unless by one of her informants, never a romance or flirtation, inappropriateness didn't fit in a job that finds and denounces inappropriate acts. I'll save them for my old age, she would tell her students, I'll save them for another life. In this one I'm a type of Dominican inquisitor, a flat being with one ambition.

She is feeling sad and empty by her third whisky, the cell phone rings, she hears a man's rough voice, he tells her he corroborated the information about the guerrilla fighter. She tells him she needs more facts, he was an assistant to a minister, he tells her and hangs up. The government's cabinet was miscellaneous, not all the ministers had the same interests or came from the same places. There were moderate men and extremists, extremists who opposed each of the others and didn't follow the same objectives. Who was his minister? By process of elimination, it was Roca, a guy from the Jurassic extreme far left, a man who knew how to handle himself in the medium of power, cold, dark, sparing in his declarations; suddenly, as though she'd been touched by grace a question came to her. *Where are the minister's colleagues from the party?* In a recent interview he had mentioned that he had separated himself from all party ties to give himself fully to the process, that the process was the only political party he recognized. But the process has many angles, there are those who want to take it towards a conservative and right-wing militarism, while others hope to make the process a revolutionary trigger of universal proportions, some dream of a Soviet situation in the backyard of the United States. The moderates hope to consolidate a few changes in actors and institutions while continuing with a constitutional and democratic regime. Those groups were in constant struggle and those in the know said that this served the president. Who was the president aligned with? With himself, Manuela was thinking when Marcos arrived.

Marquitos was Manuela's closest collaborator, a journalist from the society pages of one of the big newspapers, he was the man of the parties, places where the truth of the country gets overheard, as he would say. Everyone close to Manuela was under surveillance, but Marquitos went unnoticed, he was frivolous, gay and disaffected with politics, his reason for being against the regime, he had to have one, was his frivolous-ness. It didn't go beyond jokes. He was the contact for the best government and opposition informants. After kissing her four times, twice on each cheek, as if they were in Paris, he complemented her dress combination, always impeccable, the best of Margarita Zingg, discreet and exquisite.

"Darling, and all that for nothing," Marquitos stammered.

"Let's not start."

"I'll tell you something, I'd save the dollars, the reason anyone gets dressed is for someone else to undress them." He ordered a margarita.

"One dresses to feel good about oneself."

"And why would you want to feel good about yourself, all alone," he responded. "By the way, last night I was at Nena Bastidas's wedding, a lot of riffraff there, my friend, people who throw rags on themselves as if they were cologne, such poor taste!" The bartender placed the napkin, then the drink. Marcos received the margarita and brushed the tip of his index finger on the edge of the glass, carried it covered in salt to his lips and gave it a timid suck. "The general commentary was that you have to read the history of the Third Reich to understand this situation."

"I don't understand," Manuela interrupted, as soon as she took a sip from her whisky a teenager pulled at the sleeve of her blazer asking her to buy a set of tools.

"Leave us alone kid, don't be so rude. What's she going to do with those horrible mechanic's tools?" He sipped his margarita. "This is impossible, with the street hawkers, the smoke and the sidewalk vendors, darling, it's Caracas/Calcutta instead of Paris/Texas. So as I was saying," he rolled his eyes, "everyone was there, some people said nothing would happen, that they'd reinstate constitutional guarantees, that it wasn't the first time they were suspended, that the army would return to their barracks. But the skeptics, you know I love those killjoys, so romantic, they were talking about the Nazification of the process."

Since the beginning of the regime, the president had spoken about a conspiracy to kill him. It was said this was part of his strategy of confrontation. He kept repeating it over and over, until the assassination attempt.

"So this is the burning of the Reichstag," Marcos told her that Juanito Perdomo said, "it's been a laboratory attempt and guess who's behind all this."

The teenager showed Manuela the tool set once again, insistent, he was a dark skinned and sickly boy, with a face stained by the sun, his glance fixed and brilliant, the fuzz on his upper lip dampened by drops of sweat. Outside a loud noise was heard, an explosion, Manuela thought it might be one of those bombs they'd been setting off in churches. The people from the bar went out into the street, the journalist thought the situation had reached a breaking point—that the contention dikes are beginning to burst, the boy insisted—in the tool box she saw a revolver instead of ratchets, she froze, people crowding around the entrance to the bar, the light from the smoke entered through the door, from the sunset of the afternoon that Manuela began to understand as a final afternoon. The drama occurred quickly, it happened in such a way as to not be understood, the teenager let the box fall, grabbed the weapon and pushed Marquitos, he yanked his wristwatch off and shot him in the face twice, he turned around and looked at Manuela, he aimed at her. The weapon spat out two more shots, the bullets broke the bottles on the shelves behind the bar, the street vendor made his way through the crowd, pointed at them, shot towards one of the windows, threatened them and rushed out into the city, he was lost in the smoke and sunset, Manuela was leaning over Marquitos, trying to revive him but she didn't know how, his face was destroyed, he'd lost his wry gestures, they would never exist again. Marquitos, the most trustworthy friend, under the least amount of surveillance; his mouth was leaking blood, coughs and his life.

Manuela's cell phone rang, she stood up like an automaton, looked for her purse, brought the phone to her ear, and heard the rough voice again.

"The question, Manuela, where are Roca's comrades?" She cut the call, the journalist returned to her seat and stared at a dark point in the bar, and she sat like that until the paramedics and police arrived.

She came and went. She was sitting on the swing, her father taking pictures of her. They were in the park at the hotel where they'd spent their vacation, her cheeks burning, she was more sunburned than she expected, that was why she'd exerted herself so much, she bent her legs and swung herself with force, her face finding the breeze, it hit her straight on and she felt some relief, the day was blue and it remained fixed in the family's memory, the father snapped the picture, she smiled, her smile frozen forever, she smiled at her father, smiled at the breeze, smiled as she came and went, at the vertigo, at the world moving up and down, the clouds passing by. Then she was no longer swinging, she was inside a car, her cheeks burning, her back and arms too, her mother put cold cream on her and she continued to feel the burn, it was inside her, they started the return trip home, but she was burning, she felt like she was burning and so they stopped at a hospital half way there, she had a fever, Manuela sweated and shook, barely covered by a sheet, she remembered how her fevers always alarmed her family, they were disproportionate, with convulsions, baths in tubs full of ice, her father going out at midnight to find an open pharmacy, they called the doctor, they put a homemade poultice on, gave her enemas, took her to emergency rooms, she sweated and shook in the hospital. She remembered nights at her grandmother's house in Barcelona, a city with old, elegant houses, on an arid and cracked earth, immense city of four ancient houses. She would spend some of her vacations there with her grandmother, she would escape the afternoon heat in the library, she remembered long sessions reading, her father had read the *Iliad* to her in bed, before she went to sleep, *it's ludicrous,* her mother would say, *but she was enchanted by the rhapsodies of that story that had endured in the memory of humanity forever,* Achilles watching his horses cry, Hector dead, dragged by his cart and his horses around the walls of Troy, cheating Odysseus. Tangible victory belonged to the cheaters, the enjoyment of the spoils, although they might have to wander for twenty years, they will rejoice in their achievements and intrigues. Who was Odysseus, then? Which one of the ministers was elated? It was hot at her grandmother's house in Barcelona. Barcelona had four houses, it hadn't changed much, now it had more houses, more people, people from outside, people who gave scandalous colors to their houses, who went out and built markets and sold, it had big avenues that led to the Morro, but Barcelona wasn't always like that. Inhospitable. The Neverí River was shaded by a few bushes, that still river where the corpses of notable aristocrats of the republic had once floated, murdered by the caudillo, lanced by the people in arms that didn't accept the republic. Bolívar fled on horseback, and reached Cumaná by donkey or mule, on board a brigantine he was expelled from by his uncle, shelled with canons by his own, on board a brigantine he would go into his second exile. Barcelona had four houses when she was little, she thought, she liked to watch the Neverí flow toward the sea, she would walk under the sun on the barren land toward the sea or toward death, all rivers die in the sea, all of them account for their sweet water to the stormy plasma, blue, roaring. The turquoise sea is far from Barcelona, you have to drive for a while by car, not now, now it's a pleasant drive, now you arrive in a few minutes, back then, on small roads, not back then and a long time ago, when the Morro was a miserable fishing village. Occasionally she remembers her grandmother's library, where she found Blaise Pascal and the precept that would mark her life: "Whoever doubts and fails to investigate becomes not only unhappy but unjust." It was the phrase, each person has a phrase that will change their life, these are destiny phrases, she thought, she was too young to read Pascal, but libraries back then didn't have any room for light reading, they were sanctu-

aries, places to leave untouched unless you wanted to be initi-
ated in a mad obsession of abstruse knowledge. What a phrase,
what a fever, she felt a fever and knew that the Morro was a
fishermen's village, that she convulsed with fever ever since
she was a child, she heard a dirty, raspy voice. The question:
Where are Roca's comrades? The houses were made of wattle and
daub, of adobe, of sticks and zinc, the houses of the fishermen
at the Morro weren't miserable, they were taking her there, beyond was Lechería, where Professor Lovera's corpse one day
appeared floating, she couldn't forget that image, deformed,
eaten by fish, it was a piece of flesh or a sponge, he had escaped
from his restraints, a chain, a pick for working the earth served
as an anchor, the prisoner had freed himself, the tortured man,
professor Lovera's deformed body, she remembers, someone
had to investigate the circumstances of that death, someone
who might think like Blaise Pascal: "Whoever doubts and fails
to investigate becomes not only unhappy but unjust." That
moved a journalist, he opened the case and found the guilty
parties, they were charged. It was brave to do what he did, it
was moving, the young journalist told the world that in a democracy the political police were behind disappearances and
torture was an institutional policy, that's why she believed in
him when they named him minister, he was different from the
rest, he had ideals, a past that made him committed, an ethics,
he was not obsessive or adventurous like Roca, no, he had been
there, denouncing, but now he accused her, he mocked her in-
vestigations, he was a man of power and he justified the State's
reasons, he denied and endorsed, forgot that not only had he
become unhappy but also unjust. She was thirsty, she looked at
Barcelona, solitary, hardly any bushes grew, La Casa Fuerte
that General Freites would defend until his immolation was a
symbol, a pile of devastated adobe, there they stood, they recalled an effort, one died in the name of such efforts in order to
not be "merely unhappy, nor unjust." Of what use was Pascal's
citation, she heard the voice that asked: *Where are Roca's comrades?* She was paralyzed, sweating, enveloped by fevers—fevers

devastated Venezuela, malaria was planted in the soul of her ancestors, now she was shaking like them, her paralysis was translated as malaria. She was in a house, it was tall and big like her grandmother's, it was an old house with wide corridors and a great central patio, a house that was silent during the day, surrounded by fishermen's shacks. What house was that? It wasn't part of the Morro, no. The fishermen's houses had burners outside the fence, they were more elaborate, the nets were drying in the calmness, the breeze was whipping around, during the daytime everything was violence and serenity, the sun's glare and assault, which explained the solitary house where the shadows (ghosts?) slept. The women covered their bodies with veils, the men walked naked down the corridors, they wandered at night and whistled, they gathered under a tree and looked at each other with excessive sensuality, she remembered that her uncle went to visit her grandmother once, her uncle was a beautiful man, he would comb his hair back and fix it with gel, he wore white suits and black ties, he smelled of aftershave, her uncle barely paid attention to her, he would occasionally pat her on the head, he would smile when he saw her in the library, her uncle was elegant, people told many stories about his romantic adventures, of girlfriends who had killed themselves because of sadness and abandonment. One very hot night she felt her uncle's body in her bed, she remained frozen, in silence, she heard his suffocated breathing, that breathing was clipped in the vapors of a breath that smelled of liquor, he spoke to her softly, it was hard for him to move his tongue, his hand touched her shoulder, went down to her breasts which were barely appearing for the first time, she felt pain when that panting trapped her breasts with its big hands and she whimpered, began to cry, he was calming her, telling her he wasn't going to do anything to her, that he only wanted to be nice to her, to let him do it, her uncle's hand was moving now along her body, it was moving behind her, it came and went with anguish, clumsy and hurried, came and went, she was crying, barely whimpering, frozen with fear, the blows of a viscous dampness reached her back, the beginning of her ass, something hot was growing cold there, something that had been emitted with force against her body, she remained frozen by fear, she felt she was about to burst into flame, that she was being taken over by fever, she became delirious, calling her father, asking for help, she felt scared, she wanted to be saved by the man who had told her about Hector's greatness. That's how she remained, amid dust and battles for days, taken over by the fever, drenched in orange blossom water, with warm damp washcloths, in the heat of her grandmother's house. She awoke, coming back from the dream, she awoke and sought her grandmother's eyes; her grandmother asked her what was wrong and she told her that her uncle had climbed into her bed, her grandmother slapped her, told her to shut up, told her she shouldn't tell lies, that two brothers can kill themselves because of a lie like that, she had suffered a fever, she'd been delirious, that she shouldn't say foolish things, that she couldn't tell her father about what she had dreamed, she kept repeating that two brothers can kill each other because of lies like that, that she must forget. But she didn't forget, she kept quiet but she didn't forget, she left her grandmother's house and never went back, she refused to, they would go elsewhere on vacation, she would go with her father, she would keep quiet, she took the Blaise Pascal book with her, and she felt unhappy and unjust. She had fevers each time she felt the ring of pressure tighten, and now she flew, rode around on a little horse in a carousel and she saw the old house, it wasn't her grandmother's, she wasn't in Barcelona. *Where are Roca's comrades?* The question.

In an old house in a fishing village. He answered. She opened her eyes. The sun was rising, the light was filtering through the blinds of the room at the clinic, she needed to stand up, she had a headline, she had the newspaper article, she had to get to the offices, Marquitos had been murdered, they were scared, she had to get out of bed, calm her fever and keep working: She had an idea.

And the headline appeared... "Who are Roca's comrades?"

A big black stain on the paper, a photograph of the minister and an inscription that read:

> The Minister of Internal Affairs, Manuel Roca, has had a long career. He fought against the dictatorship of Marcos Pérez Jiménez and was an activist in the Young Communists. Later, as a party member, he was a leader of the armed struggle. An old conspirator, he didn't abide by the peace of the Tactical Retreat and along with other comrades kept up the struggle. Roca is a party man. He created the party when he was left without it, he maintained it despite the change in situation and, along with his cadres, he incorporated himself into the process that the army officers began at that new time. Today he is at the head of affairs for the State. He appears to be alone, without his old comrades. Who are Manuel Roca's men?

She didn't add anything else. The next day another photo, Manuel Roca in the mountains, or in a botanical garden, with a rifle leaning on his shoulder and a mug in his hand, in front of a fire, beside other combatants.

"Are these Roca's comrades?"

A circle trapped a man's face. It wasn't Roca, the name was left in suspense.

In successive installments:

A passport photo of Joaquín. The inscription read: "Labor leader, president of the Workers Federation at the end of the sixties, a companion in studies and in activism of Manuel Roca, during the dictatorship." Immediately afterwards came the photo of a man's corpse thrown in a trash heap, hands tied behind his back, hours after being executed. The inscription: "Joaquín Toledo, executed by a dissident cell of the Communist Party." Then Manuel Roca in Havana. "Anyone who hands over the workers' movement to the democratic peace of the bourgeois government will pass into history as a traitor to the revolution and to the working class."

A forty-year-old man with bad hair; he wore an Angela Davis-style afro. "Darío José Terán. His comrades in the 23 de Enero neighborhood call him Loco-Motive. In the party he's known as Dominguín. A veteran of the seventies, an apparatchik, an organizer. He was trusted with tasks of agitation and other contingencies, he was involved in a massive escape of political prisoners. Right hand of Manuel Roca in the PLP." Then the journalist asked herself: Does the PLP exist? Is Loco-Motive pulling the strings of the revolution in the shadows?

The man beside Roca in the photo where the minister appeared with a rifle and a coffee mug was highlighted with a red circle, it was the front page of the newspaper, then, he appeared in a full length photo, he seemed to be a key figure: "Ramón Danilo Perdomo, Commander Lucas, a leader of the communist youth and guerrilla commander in the western fronts of the country, a man of action, the hijacking of a plane to Havana and the bombing of a radio station are attributed to him, he planned a massive escape of political prisoners. Along with Loco-Motive or Dominguín and Manuel Roca, he is a founder of the PLP, he is also known as Silvestre. One of the dead men in the location where an assassination attempt was made against the president.

"Where are Roca's comrades?"

The smoke was filling up spaces. Visibility was minimal, the hills continued to burn, people spoke of a conspiracy, of criminal hands, of foreign agents commissioned to create chaos. The National Guard was on the street. Their men set up checkpoints, they did their rounds pulled by dogs, something up to that point known only in airports, they watched from their patrol cars on the avenues, the streets, the corners. They stopped, checked, asked for documents, detained people. They had never been so active before, in conjunction with the army, omnipresent, uniformed among civilians, wearing camouflage, they suffered through the smoke, their eyes irritated, their noses congested.

The president arrived at the Institute of Sports early in the morning. He didn't spend much time giving long speeches, as he usually did, he greeted and welcomed the new authorities, with a few words and a cup of coffee, he posed for the cameras and eluded the rounds of questions. He was tired. He didn't display the restless glance of other moments, he didn't struggle with conflicts or provoke journalists with his phrases, let himself be seen, gave his hand to those who needed him, he continued to be the leader, it suited him well, the leader must maintain masks, a poet would say; a novelist's voice, roles; a playwright, he couldn't present himself like he did the other night, hard and hopeful and calling the people to join together in their struggle. His eyes no longer leaped, they were still, with traces of melancholy, he must find a lyrical glance, he thought, he had tried to, this was how he would display himself during some gatherings when he would recite a verse by Whitman from memory, a sonnet by Neruda, he would let fly from his soul whatever he saw, he would let it go beyond the multitudes, relax his facial muscles, arriving at the place where the auditorium expected to be taken, and yet he felt that he wasn't lyrical, he must study drama, learn from dramatic orators, express the epic nature of his deeds, his ambitions, to be the epic with his gestures and glance—Cicero, why hadn't they insisted he read Cicero? That's what he was thinking, he needed to take more time, but now his glance should have reflected the emptiness of statues or the exhaustion of heroes. What would Achilles' glance have looked like? Heroes don't have glances, they possess the glances of others and they look within themselves and beyond, they possess the glance of a god or a destiny. Was he not destined? So then, what glance? He was anguished, he didn't know how to ask his closest advisors, the aesthetes, the historians, the knowledgeable men, if that glance was already being drawn in him, the one that is absorbed in the other and in the glance of the god, the glance that doesn't see or express, the glance that dictates. That was the glance. How to dictate with a glance? Only fate dictates, so how does one become a dictation once and for all, a sentence, a history. He wasn't among the people, he was outside them, his thoughts must remain distant and uncorrupted, he couldn't contrast them without receiving the fawning response, no, no. To fawn was to corrupt, but how would he find an answer? A pleasing and objective one. All of them, even the ones that affirmed him, were unpleasant interactions, he was alone and he governed in solitude, this is what he said in his historic letter to the old Supreme Court. That was the glance, the glance that doesn't look because it's alone, in front of an abstract painting, exactly in the center of nothingness, creator of the forms and modes of governing wisely. This is what he was thinking, feeling, but his government was something else, the details, the mundaneness, the interests of his avid collaborators, the mistakes of the vulgar.

Roca was waiting for them in the VIP room of the Institute of Sports. Thin, well-dressed, without any tic that might denote feelings, distant, as always. He had a carnivorous glance, predatory, it was a feline's glance. The president thought, he didn't know why a columnist had compared his glance to Roca's. There he was. What would he do with that man? They were in the midst of the stage for consolidating revolutionary power and they couldn't get off the ground because the feline and ridiculous Roca had let a few undesirable threads come undone. He thought he was a veteran, the necessary animal for executing hard plans. So far he had the sensation of having made a mistake, but he didn't have to do everything. How far would Roca get. He sat down in front of his minister and ordered a small cup of coffee that was soon on the little plate in his hands, he took a sip and made a brusque movement to avoid staining his shirt with a few drops that fell from his mouth.

"I can't even drink coffee anymore," he made a gesture that indicated the discomfort of his bulletproof vest.

"So Manuel, am I going to be able to make this revolution in peace and with decorum?"

"You've made it in peace, that's your virtue."

"And what about decorum? Do you think we can afford the luxury of making this process indecorous? That we should show some bloodstains?" the president asked.

"On some occasions it's inevitable. It's a reason of State, we have to defend the revolution at any cost."

"Even at the cost of my image?"

"No sir, your image is intact. No one would suppose that you..."

"They can't suppose what isn't me," he interrupted.

"Of course."

"And what about your image? I put you in charge of a ministry so you would lead it day and night, so that you'd stop those damn leaks from the press."

"I'm working on that," he answered, "but you have to consider that we've entered a non-conventional phase, at least that's what I thought."

"You thought?"

"Can I be honest with you?" he asked.

"Aren't you always honest?"

Roca cleared his throat, stood up, took a few steps around the small room, stopped in front of a kinetic sculpture, sought out the words, one by one.

"We can't continue under the previous legal system. If we forced this situation it was in order to create a new constitution after we passed through the purging stage. You have to suspend civil rights, silence the press! A statesman doesn't fear repression when reasons of State require it."

The president placed the cup of coffee on a little table in the middle and leaned back, he sank as much as he could into the easy chair and from that reclined position answered almost with a "do" from his chest.

"You can't drag me into an unmanageable situation in order to cover your mistakes, Roca!"

The minister stopped wandering around the room, stood still, with his back to the president, he thought that the most sensible thing would have been to rid themselves of the lunatic, now they would have had clearer definitions, he sighed and let his response emerge dispassionately.

"I'm not dragging you anywhere that history isn't already leading you. We can't say we're making a revolution if we keep the forms of the old order."

The president stood up from the easy chair, stood face to face with his minister and thought about history, he was a great car, a beautiful racing car.

"Who the hell are you to interpret history? You're at my service, at the service of this revolution that isn't dragged along, the revolution and me, myself, we set up history. If it runs you over, I'll leave you with those that have been run over, I'm sorry brother." He approached Roca and put his arms on his shoulder, brought his face in closer, he spat out at him: "You who interpret everything with that orthodox head, don't you see that the century passed by in front of me? Shit, Roca, don't you realize that if I skip over the laws I'm done? The opposition won't topple me, they *are* me, I've made them to my measure. No, they won't, not even the army will, they're my party, that's what I intend, not even a foreign power, reality will do it, you and your stupid form of taking power. We're not Bolsheviks, you idiot. We're Bolivarians. Maintaining forms, most definitely, we have to keep them, we should make the moves we have to make right now, detain those people you have to detain, get rid of those people you have to, you can do all that, blame our enemies, put them on a list of undesirables and persecute them or make them be persecuted by the people, try them, sanction them for evasion, asphyxiate them, now, during this brief lapse" —he grabbed him by the cheek, pinched him like he would a child—"this lapse is brief and it will end, if you can't manage it I assure you history will run you over. Muffle the scandal, create another scandal, invent something, if you don't invent you err, remember?"

He pulled back his arms from his shoulders and turned suddenly on his heels and prepared to leave the room, then stopped at the door.

"Ah, that girl, Manuela, not even with a rose petal. Understand? You figure out something, make an agreement with the press, but don't touch her."

He left. Roca was now alone in the room immersed in confusion for the first time in his life. A mountain was falling down on him, he asked himself what everything was for, he, a pragmatic man, with no existential doubts. He saw himself at the heights of power, on his tiptoes on the edge of a blade, he felt vertigo and thought he had to readjust himself in the scene, he had to find a way to be given a position in an embassy, but before that he had to finish what he'd started.

A small town in a humid and tropical zone was the same as any other town in a humid and tropical zone. Wattle and daub houses, some of them leaning forward, others leaning to the side, none of them balanced, drunk and victimized by the rain or garish from the heat, they formed double lines on the narrow streets, each one had its backyard, the animals weren't there, there were bushes in the backyards, the corral birds moved around unhindered and the pig was another one that enjoyed free transit. There were plantains in the backyard, chili pepper bushes, a lemon or mango tree, a shade tree. The earth hadn't been planted and there were puddles, wildflowers, medicinal herbs; it was a chaotic Eden where the afternoon heat was attenuated.

Small towns in humid and tropical zones had, as they all did, a center. Where a plaza extended two steps above street level, the bust of an illustrious man on a marble pedestal, bushes and trees, worn out benches, with rust in their metal parts. Diagonally, it always depended on the perspective, it could have been at the front, the church closed its doors to the dead hours, almost all hours; the sanctity of the place didn't exempt it from intoxication in its equilibrium. It leaned just the same. It opened its doors when the priest came, on Sundays or when there was a vigil for a dead person, you had to pay attention in order to see the church open. Attention was the first thing one lost in a town in a humid and tropical zone.

Those towns had walk-in clinics, there the doctor who did his residency kept busy giving vaccinations, curing the fevers the shaman couldn't cure, the dysenteries. He was a much busier man than the priest, in general he lived and consulted in a tin trailer.

The figure of Lorca was born from the fog, he was a figure dressed in black, with a ponytail, his hair pulled back, shiny and greasy. A cigarette hung from his lips, he stomped on the floor, walked hard, was disorganized as he moved, every now and then he put his hands on his waist, stopped, oriented himself, hooked his thumbs in his belt, in the style of the wild west shooters, he was repulsed, he couldn't stand seeing mud stains on his shoes. The fog rolled down the mountain, the sweat of morning, the breeze came and dampened the nose, throat, bronchi. Lorca coughed before he pushed the door to the walk-in clinic.

The morning wouldn't be busy, the doctor thought, he had a moment to lie on his back in the well-made, narrow bed. His space was orderly, his friends told him he was like a girl, neat, obsessive, meticulous. Now he was far from his friends. His friends from adolescence and from college. He had closed a cycle. New friends would come, distant, measured relationships in affection, adult ones. His marriage to Irma would come. It was a matter of doing the rural residency and returning, organizing his affairs to begin graduate school, he didn't want to wait. He loved Irma very much, they would lose the best years amid books and the sick internal organs of patients. They would live together joined by reluctance. When reluctance reaches you, a friend would say, you're screwed, the salt is spilled and everything begins to lose its flavor. He was nostalgic for barroom philosophy. And it was true, consummation as a couple would happen with the burdens of maturity, those burdens can't be thrown off or lightened, they're tied tightly. That's why, when he returned from the rural residency, he would go to the courthouse, to the church, he would get married and look for a house. He remembered Irma's big lips, she knew how to kiss, she knew how to stick her tongue in his mouth, she caressed with her lips, she would descend from his mouth to his neck, from there to his chest, she licked around the belly button, bit the skin, looked up at him with those brown eyes. He stopped thinking about Irma, remembered the woman who knocked on his door, she was fleeing, she had bruises on her skin, she was tall and slender, that's how Irma was, beautiful and strong, sure of herself. Maybe his friends were right, he thought, maybe he had a strong feminine trait in his personality. He was seduced by confident women, with inalienable initiative. Irma, the fleeing woman, Irma.

The door opened suddenly. The doctor looked at Lorca, felt the world was upside down, the sky at his feet and city men lost in a town of the humid zone. Lorca didn't speak. Lorca didn't greet him, he didn't ask for permission and sat down beside him, he slapped him in the middle of his chest, it was a friendly slap, he let loose a smile, he released his fatigue in a snort through his nose. *That's how dogs laugh,* he thought. And the man in a black suit and white shirt, tarnished by the sweat of a long trip, asked him about the weather, the guest houses in town, the food, the endemic diseases. Leishmania was endemic, Lorca remembered the comrades who arrived with their skin eaten away by the parasite, many of the men who were fighting in the Bachiller mountains could be recognized by the trace of mountain leprosy, the upper part of the ear perforated by the bite of the parasites, the nose, a finger.

His trigger finger, that's where the mosquito left its corrosive charge. That's where Lorca carried it, he left his hand for a while on the doctor's chest, he saw himself in the middle of the thick jungle, fleeing, he wasn't alone, he was with part of his column, they'd split up, whoever didn't follow orders was summarily executed, the order was to hand over the weapons to the party, they'd decided to not hand over the weapons, they didn't belong to the party, and it was a golden rule of any uprising in any century, the weapons belonged to those who carried them, it was a golden rule, only cowards put down their weapons. In any case, the weapons were buried, were hidden, so that they might be taken up again when the circumstances called for them. He was fleeing from the party and fleeing from the government, they would meet up with Abelardo somewhere in the mountain, sea mountain, mountain that rots and envelops there, somewhere, Abelardo's group and Lorca's, they found each other and rebuilt a column, they knew nothing about the city, they were isolated and the army was performing air raids. The moment came when the bombs took up the entire sound of the jungle, they had to mobilize, break the siege, they set up an ambush, a blow was necessary to concentrate the army's attention in one place, they had to cause a few casualties for the enemy, demoralize him, disconcert him in his search. That was when he noticed his swollen, tumescent finger, with tiny, pustulous blisters, his trigger finger. They ambushed an army patrol, it was a convoy, a jeep, a van with soldiers, they weren't alert, they trusted in these zones being clean, they had bombed the night before and Abelardo stepped out in front of them, as always, he exposed himself and shot by shot gave the first sweep with his assault rifle, one of the three soldiers up front fell; Lorca mobilized his stiff finger, swept the rearguard, the comrades from the column hidden in the vegetation, they tossed their grenades and opened fire at their discretion. The army responded to the firing taken over by confusion, they couldn't hit anything, Abelardo had crossed their path striking repeatedly with the bullets from his rifle, then he was lost in the scrub, this was his art. Lorca wasn't working well in the rearguard, his movements were clumsy, he was thinking about his finger, about the gangrene, about the venom, but he wasn't thinking about combat. Then he found himself surrounded by men who were shooting at him, he responded, but without the effectiveness of other battles, he decided to run, he was turning his back to the enemy, he would die with a bullet in his back because of that damned swollen finger, suddenly three, four, six, a hundred assault rifles sounded, there was an explosion, Lorca fell headfirst onto the ground, he was looking at his finger. The only thing he could hear was the noise of the flames, the shooting ceased, Abelardo, smiling, was looking at Lorca laid out on the ground, they fled and left behind four dead, he told him, but he kept staring at the finger throughout the retreat, the hard march to the sea, the burial of the weapons and the return to the city. His finger remained like that until they treated it in Havana, he hadn't lost it, but a shadow of dead skin distinguished it from the others.

The doctor tried to sit up.

"Wait a second, buddy, there's something I'd like to talk to you about," Lorca let out. He was looking for a cigarette among his things, he took the box, offered one to the doctor and placed one in his mouth, shrugging his shoulders in response to the refusal of the man spread out on the bed.

"This is a quiet town, you don't see anyone, no one sees you. You pass the time nicely here, you put on mosquito repellent, you've got to avoid the damn Leishmania. Look," he showed him the finger, "I'm scarred for life. As I was saying," he roughly inhaled the smoke from his cigarette, all at once, "it's an ideal place to be alone with your books." He picked up Stendhal's *The Red and the Black* from the bedside table. "You can read in peace, take notes, you can even write long love letters to all those girls you left behind in Caracas. You're from Caracas, right? I can tell. A place where nothing happens, but one day someone knocks on your door. A girl or boy?" his eyes moved from side to side, "And asks you for help, for medicine, that you check a wound. Asks you for money, for an address, they have nowhere to go, if it's a girl she sleeps with you, she'll put her city girl nipples in your mouth. How long has it been since you sucked such nice ones?" He let loose a cackle. "If it's a boy you'll drink a bottle of rum and remember stories you could have lived through together had you been friends, but which you shared just the same because guys always do the same things. If both of them show up, he'll play dumb and go walk around the plaza, carefully, he shouldn't let himself be seen by the people in town, you know, they're being chased, while she opens her legs for you, shows you the inner portion of her nicely shaped thighs and you do her," he finished his cigarette and lit another, "but you don't just cure their ailments, you feel a sense of solidarity with them, you drink together and sleep with the girl a few more times, you're not easily sated, you've spent a long summer in this godforsaken town. You give them some money, you suggest places and write a friend's address on a piece of paper. Another rural doctor? Well, you'll tell me that later." He smiled at him, displaying his nicotine stained teeth, smoked again. "I want to propose something to you. Let's keep a secret, between you and me, before it's too late. I'll explain what I mean by late. Late because you might have found out about things you shouldn't know or because you might assume them. Before any of that happens, before I start to think that I shouldn't leave a trace of anyone with an active mouth and thoughts, you tell me where they went." From the bedside table he grabbed the handle of a scalpel, he pulled out its blade, took the doctor's arm, held him by the wrist until he opened his fist and cut the palm of his hand, leaving a clean, painful and deep canal.

"You're crazy!"

"Completely."

Outside, the impertinent sound of a motorcycle was heard.

GREEN HAIR DREAMING Of THE BITTER SEA

I spent most of my life fleeing. When I lived with Abelardo, I assumed his clandestine condition. People are supposed to have a sense of belonging, roots. I didn't remember being from anywhere in particular. I barely recalled having been from my grandparents' home, but I was from a town in Portuguesa, I was in Maturín or I spent a few months among fishermen in Santa Fe de Mochima. I could say that I was from Caracas, I could try to identify myself in one of its neighborhoods; I recalled my childhood, it was a narrow street where we would create spaces to organize stick ball games and think we were playing baseball, where I would spend hours watching the shadows move: they would begin on the eastern wall of the passage and finish at the western end, an entire world, the sun would go from one sidewalk to another across the street, at any moment, a figure would stand at the side street and send a whistle down the avenue, I would get up from the landing in front of the door to my grandparents' house, I'd run to his arms; my father would barely stop to pet my head, say things I don't remember, promise a weekend road trip to a house on the beach, talk about a new collection of toy cars, smiling, it was a beautiful and distant smile, the bolero coming from a car radio, a car as big as a house, full of light, comfortable, the closest thing to a stupid movie of mediocre men in a model town in the American Midwest. It was the melody of a normal life that became more and more sporadic until it eventually disappeared. That childhood was erased at night, in games of hide-and-go-seek, in the stars seen from my grandfather's car, in the serenades men would bring to my aunts, in the corner conversations of the old people, in the eyes of Aída. Where could she be? Many people can say what happened to their first girlfriend, many can say that she'd gotten married, that she's still single, that she died in an accident, that she lives up north. I couldn't say anything about that girl from the María Auxiliadora School, it was a vague and warm memory that remained in another world. Improbable. In another life I left behind friends, schools, the goal of being a petroleum engineer or of going to Anaco. Everything was swallowed up by the other life that never was. Whirlwind or disorder. I can't say I belonged to that neighborhood, maybe I was a sketch of that life, from that point on, my personal history becomes fragmented.

I could say that I belonged to the escape. Belonging to the escape is to stop belonging to a country, a city or a people. I was talking about those things with Abelardo, who always had a moment to reflect, *escape is a condition,* I was saying, I later thought about how one might inhabit a condition; how do you walk its streets, establish customs and affections? Abelardo used to say that people who lived in a ghetto or a neighborhood did so in their condition as inhabitants, it was a condition, but I was never able to give shape to his conclusions, it wasn't the same thing to belong to a city or a neighborhood one lived in and to inhabit escape and be clandestine as a condition. Escape is all the possible neighborhoods, I think Abelardo ended up saying, I never considered Abelardo to be cynical, his answers were strange: Zen Marxism or the definition of socialism as fascism of the left. Up to what point was he being serious? I took him seriously. That's why I had inhabited as many feelings as possible and I had become a parasitic plant, I had inhabited the necessary neighborhoods and cities and had become a fugitive. It was a condition. I belonged to a life project that would not be possible until after my death. Was there a more Christian idea?

If I stopped to think about these things I got depressed and I couldn't afford that luxury as I was undertaking a strange escape, an escape from another escape. Impossible, I thought, no one escapes the ineffable. I never felt I was out in the open air. Not so exposed.

I had to decide on something. Handle concrete things. I should have taken advantage of everyone's absence, or nearly everyone. Lourdes. She was sleeping in a corner of the room curled up on a rug. I didn't understand. She couldn't have arrived by coincidence, those coincidences in life belonged to my aunts or to my grandmother; there are no coincidences in life, there are consequences. And Lourdes was here because they had found me. No matter how many times she told me she was fleeing from Roca, that they wanted to kill her, no matter how much I pretended I was delirious or with fever. How could she sleep if absurdity was hanging over her? What else could it be than the absurd, were it true? No, it wasn't, she escaped from a hotel in the back of a garbage truck, made her way at gunpoint among the homeless, slipped into a city of tin shacks and was taken care of and treated by a rural doctor who sent her to another doctor in the port, someone who was able to give you better safety, he told her, according to what she'd said, and the doctor wasn't there, or he was, a guy on a motorcycle who stopped to talk with her, they smoked one, two cigarettes, Lourdes enjoyed the chat like a fifteen-year-old, she had all the time in the world ahead of her; it didn't fit, she asked him what he did, he told her that he was the doctor, but that he wouldn't be the town doctor anymore, he'd finished his rural residency, he'd paid his debt to the world, he was closing the house and retiring to the shadows, she became desperate, asked for another cigarette, she thought she might be able to subdue him and take his Vespa, flee on it, get further away, but where to? The guy told her he lived nearby, in a fishing village, at the shrimper, he lived with some other girls, they shared interests, you know, a community, they lived in a big house in a fishermen's village, his name was Humberto, she could come, he recognized her and knew she would sign any document that might take her out of the world, no problem, we were beyond everything.

"Who are you?" she asked.

"Humberto and I just closed my office. I've gone out for a ride, you always forget things. You know." What if she went with him, if she arrived somewhere she could rest and think. "Isn't that what you're looking for? You have to sleep, catch your breath, think—", so then she climbed onto the back of the Vespa and came and found everyone gathered under the cherry tree, surrounded by six columns covered with star jasmines; in the garden, in the center of a house nearly in ruins. Where else could people like that live?

What did she feel when she saw me come back from the beach with Sonia? Commotion, fear; she looked at my hand to see if I was carrying a weapon, she thought she had reached the end, she hid behind Carla, behind her transparency, her metallic odors. She realized that I was only wearing some fishermen's pants, that I was shirtless, that my hair was sticky and yellow from the sea, the sun. *How long could he have been here?* she asked herself. Time became a breeze for her. He couldn't be armed, she thought. And what if the others...? She didn't know, she should have given me her hand, stood in front of me, it was a dream and she saw me reflected, I saw her and we merged our realities.

The plot was so stupid, it was almost a plot from a bad movie. Who would have believed her plot? Did it matter? What mattered? I looked at her, there she was, curled up on the cot, now that she was there I realized they only let us use the room for sleeping, that the others were absent during the day, that they didn't exist, that the other doors in the old house were always closed. Did they sleep in them? There were three bedrooms and we occupied one of them. When the light occupied everything, where did the shadows hide? I walked out into the inner courtyard of the house, looked at the sky, it was blue, always cloudless, in the early hours a less persistent breeze blew. It merely ran, gently. It moved my hair, touched my skin, it was the breeze of the world that moved with us inside. I wanted to go out, walk around the village, a solitary village, founded on lumps of mud and salt boulders, the landscape was sepia, maybe orange, despite the blue sky or the red laths of the houses. Lourdes was still curled up, in a deep sleep, she was sleeping a good wife's sleep. I always thought she was beautiful, she always did whatever she wanted to, but she was such a pain in the ass. Now, defenseless, on that rug, I could finish her off, not believe her poor story, hit her with a stick at the base of her skull and bury her under some bushes, it wouldn't cost me anything, but I wasn't a murderer, I said so to Sonia, *I'm a soldier. You're a killer,* Sonia told me, I shut her up with a kiss to the mouth. She was Lourdes on the other side of the mirror. And if I killed her and remained at the mercy of Roca's plans? This could all be planned by Roca or by demons. What was convenient right then, I concluded, was to let the river flow.

The ball uncurled, came to life, stretched, turned around and looked up at the ceiling, it was tall, so tall one might think it was a rusted sky; Lourdes was bathed by the dark light of the room, she was beautiful, I thought. She was lost, she had put up a front, we were trained by Elmer for combat and ambushes, for sabotage and even for escapes, we were trained for fraud. Whoever commited fraud was an actor. I thought Lourdes was a good actor, she seemed defenseless. We talked until the lights of dawn appeared, dawn in the fishing village was slow, it lasted an eternity, life happened beyond there. It never passed. The inhabitants of the house retired, one never knew exactly what rooms they used. It didn't surprise her to hear the moans, nor the laments, or the whispers and snorts of the shadows, it seemed like we had been trained to admit the sensual ululation of the ineffable. In any case, she was used to the extravagances of communes, she had lived among squatters and homeless in Paris; there was a trace of occupiers in the shadows.

We weren't from the village, the village didn't resent our presence; the village was a reflection beneath the sun, the men would set off on their boats to the sea and would get lost in the fickle waves, while the women, from early on they would light the stoves at the doors to their houses, everyone else would sew and repair nets, everyone doing their own thing.

We passed the dawn. It became daytime while we were talking. Lourdes didn't convince me at all and I didn't have to convince her about anything. That was when she curled up, brought her knees to her forehead and stayed there. I couldn't sleep, I wasn't tired. And Sonia, where had Sonia been? I couldn't hear her on the other side, nor her anguish, or the whispers of her voice, she had crawled up to the lintel and covered herself with dead leaves. Where might she have been now, I needed to be with her on this side; it was so bitter to think that it was Lourdes curled up on this side and that she wouldn't appear beneath a palm tree, or in a fishing shed, to lean her head on my chest, she would listen to it and affirm that I could do something, flee to Trinidad, cross the Antilles swimming and get lost in Guadalupe or Martinique. Where would she go without breaking the mirror? At what moment would she cut Lourdes's throat?

The day rose. That's what my grandfather would say. He was a man of ideas. His ideas were fixed. He was anticlerical, believed in a metaphysical communism, something like the lunacies of Victor Hugo.

"Life is eternal and continuous," he would tell me, "we are not this life nor will we be another, life is a single thing through time, one dies and is reincarnated and the mission does not belong to man, it belongs to the spirit that works in harmony with its creator, in this manner, there is a meaning in each element, nothing is fortuitous, the strength of coincidence is a tall tale, coincidence exists, it's something else, men are missionary spirits, some of them lie once they are incarnated, others support the work of the father creator which is none other than to communize the earth, the earth is nothing more than another grain in a supportive universe, it's the black sheep mentioned by Jesus, the teacher, when he named man he named the earth, the flesh is the earth, the earth is the gathering of the spirits that commune in the idea of equality."

He believed in all of this down to the tiniest detail, Victor Hugo also believed it, he lived in permanent contact with the spiritual masters and received council through his medium, the writer's daughter was also a spiritualist, but my grandfather went even further, he committed himself to the real communists. He conspired because he thought the spiritualist commune would be materialized on earth—he believed in other worlds—after the Marxist experience, he was a heretic, none of his brothers in the faith accompanied him in his adventures, he believed that a hundred years of forced communization must pass before the advent of a commune of universal love. Victor Hugo didn't even come close to believing this, nor did my old man's collaborators, which is why, along with a few unconditional collaborators, he started a newspaper, then he chose a plot of land and founded a communal project among the Indians, at certain moments the communal project was merely logistics for the party or the guerrillas, my grandfather was always concerned with logistics, he would lend out his cars, his money, he himself would transport the comrades from one place to another and he never felt any contradictions, he was a father, that was his spirit mission on those occasions, that's why Abelardo came into our lives, that's why my mother could believe deep down that she was impelled by the spirit of Rosa Luxemburg and she was crazier than Victor Hugo's daughter, more confused, she never stopped to think about the consequences, and always just beyond, in this or that project, in the projects that were definitely Abelardo's projects, but she didn't end up with arsenic in her bowels, nor with a shot to her head, nor with her face bloated by the gallows, her soul or her faults in an oven, inhaling gas. No, she had the qualities of a dancer, leaping and moving forward, she didn't know quite where but saving herself from her panic or from madness. She was good at surviving. I didn't know if I should wish for her luck. I'd never had it, here I was inside a novel, in a gothic fiction, I spent my days in the heat and the iodine made me old in this village that each day seemed more like a mirage to me. I didn't know if I should cry for a disappeared Abelardo, buried in a pit somewhere in the desert. I was overwhelmed by Lourdes's questions, standing in front of me, with barely any clothes on, I could glimpse her round, medium-sized breasts, and she looked at me like Sonia did, from her dark green eyes. I made breakfast for her. Two arepas and fish. Water. It was what I could find in the hamlet. It wasn't a continental breakfast. But who said Lourdes was used to this type of breakfast? Well, I'd imagine she would eat cheese, bread and wine in Paris, although I had no doubts about it, she would have lunch and dinner at one of those restaurants in the Place de la Concorde or in Montmartre. She knew how to order good French food, during the breaks from PLP meetings, she and Roca would remember certain dishes. She would eat unleavened bread with sardines in the desert, filthy herring; but when Elmer would invite her to his tent, I imagine they knew how to carve a pheasant and uncork a bottle of good champagne. Scrambled eggs with chopped tomatoes and onions with Dominguín, refried canned meat, she was omnivorous, that's what you learned in comrade Elmer's training camp. Two arepas and fish were actually quite good. It wasn't technically a breakfast, they would have to make do with it for the day. I didn't know what her days in the future would be like, but this one she would spend with me, I had planned for us to go to a fisherman's shack, we would be alone, no matter what we would be alone in the village. From there I would have a perfect view in order to control any possible prowlers. She could be waiting for an accomplice, they didn't want me dead and she wouldn't dare subdue me. It was better to go to that shack, where we could spend the day comfortably without worrying about intruders. She spoke to

me about the intruders in her life, I imagined she must have
had a thousand and one intruders, her life invited intruders, I
couldn't help remembering my mother. She invited intruders,
I concluded one night as I was taking one last drag off a cigarette. What the fuck did my mother have to do with Lourdes?
Nothing.

We began to walk, the village was passing by alongside
us; it's a cinematographic trick when you make landscapes
pass by you instead of you passing through them. And it's a
life trick. There we were, standing still, as though we weren't
walking. And in the background, in a hamlet of impoverished
constructions, sheds set up with stoves outside, a place without
a church, without vegetation, without plazas, without a single
court where you might play something, anything, only sheds
and demolished houses, all of them abandoned, even ours.

Ours was an abandoned house and was inhabited by those
people. I wanted to ask Lourdes what she thought about
our hosts, but I kept quiet on our way to the bodega where
we bought cigarettes and soft drinks, water; we passed the
police checkpoint, it was manned by National Guardsmen,
Lourdes grabbed me by the waist and leaned her head on my
shoulder, she was setting up a farce, it wasn't necessary, the
two soldiers were trapped in their uniforms by the sweat,
the drowsiness and the heat, they chewed on toothpicks and
placed their rifles between their legs with the barrel under
their chins, if they let off a shot by mistake, one of them would
end up without a head. The soldiers were used to seeing me, I
was just another shade in town, they never asked about anyone, they installed themselves to shoo flies and mosquitoes,
to fatten their bellies with beer. We continued to be caught by
the use of a technique: fixed, the landscape continued, both
our glances looked over the place, finding things and losing
track of them, she sighed, tried to say something, I was paying close attention, very close, I relaxed more and more as the
beach passed by us and brought us closer to the cabin, at the
far end of the inlet. We threw ourselves onto the sand and

looked at the sea, indecipherable for the Greeks and for us, at each moment closer to being the happy cave dwellers in a good short story. How about this, I thought, we went from the noble revolutionary to the noble savage. I didn't want to comment about anything with my companion, nor could I. At each moment my distrust was growing.

"Do you have a plan?" she said to me. The breeze began to gain strength, to hit us insistently, it was the same breeze as always, the one that doesn't caress you, that the elements breathe.

"I'd like to get rid of plans. I could spend the rest of my life here."

"You know that's not possible," she smiled, she was beautiful. I had always recognized her beauty, it was a plague.

"I've started to think that everything is possible here, in this place, and that everything else is impossible." I shrugged.

Lourdes furrowed her brow. She seemed to want to interpret my play of words. It wasn't a game, it was a random maxim. The wind was moaning over the inlet, in the distance you could see the blurry shacks, they seemed like figures coming out of a mouth of shadows. We were witnessing the blurring of matter in the landscape.

I pointed toward the void.

"Nothing exists."

"We exist, Sergio, and we should plan on keeping ourselves alive."

The force with which the breeze whipped the sand made matter an intermittent phenomenon. The sea existed, it was chaos. Was it not solid? If I had learned how to paint, I could have made a painting and registered the loss of bodies; they weren't lost, they were erased and that's how we ourselves were erased; so, if I was a great painter I could paint death, Lourdes's, my own, I could develop a technique on canvas and blur things like the moment that superimposes itself on another moment displaced by the breeze, the brightness and the sand blurs. It would be easy.

"Does any of it make sense?"

"What?" Lourdes asked, she was moving her red curls out of her face.

"What we've been, what we will be if we escape. Look, right now things make sense, we're outside, the world doesn't exist, we're spectators. Had you noticed before how the world is erased?" I stretched out my arm toward the sea. "It doesn't exist, in this case, only we who watch it disappear exist."

The hamlet had been swallowed by the breeze and the sand, by the light, the sun was high above, a focal point of the breeze. The breeze comes from sunspots, from its storms, I thought, thus the miracle of the hour, the blinded landscape was excluding itself, the sea was becoming transparent, then it would leave, it wasn't there, it disappeared and light remained in its pure state, the light was neither white nor yellow, it was a cold fire, a bundle of darkness that dissolves matter.

"We actually do make sense after all this." I looked into Lourdes's eyes, they were no longer green nor black, they were the color of the sea that had disappeared, she had a compassionate, human glance, a new type of glance. She stretched out her arm and made me touch her face with my hand, it was a caress.

"You're depressed, Sergio."

"No, I've given myself over to the moment. Here you live moments in a different manner." I took her hand. "I've been thinking that nothing else can happen to us anymore. Don't you realize what's happened? We're dead!"

"Don't be absurd. We'll be dead in a few hours. I assure you they'll make us suffer before they kill us. If we don't move our asses we'll get to know Roca's extreme humanism."

"And what do you think of Roca?"

"He's a monster."

"Isn't that right? I suppose you've realized it now, after he's given the order for you to be killed."

"And you, when did you realize it? Don't fuck with me! I always knew he was cold, ruthless, necessary."

"Just like Silvestre and I were necessary," I said with a sense of estrangement. I wasn't yelling at the world. I wasn't yelling at a living being.

"It's likely. All of us are necessary in some way."

"So then, why are you surprised? All of us can be assassinated or executed. Why don't you give it a name?" I picked up a fistful of sand in my cupped fingers and let it fall into the void.

"I feel bad, Sergio, but I want to get out of here, I want another chance. I'm not about to die right now because I don't feel like it."

"All we do is die."

"Whatever you want. Don't get all transcendent on me. Let's get out of here. Let's give ourselves a chance. Help me at least."

"Am I necessary?"

Lourdes stopped speaking and turned around, she threw herself face down onto the sand. I could see her face, there were tears streaming down her cheek. The moment was passing and the sea and the hamlet would be visible again: and yet, they wouldn't be visible until early afternoon. Those intermittencies were the famous holes in time. On what side of time was Sonia to be found? Probably on the same side as Carla and the others. On what side of time was I? Right now in none. I couldn't integrate myself without losing Sonia. I couldn't. But I was faced with the necessity of saving Lourdes, maybe I was beginning to fall into her trap, but there she was, alive, she wanted to keep living, so I wouldn't give myself over to the shadows quite yet. I could break the mirror.

The light of day was blinding. The world had been erased outside. Lourdes and I didn't have anything to talk about. I continued doubting. I would continue to believe until the end, if I gave myself over to believing, that they'd found me and she'd come to kill me. She was waiting for the right moment, she stalked and acted. But she would be in for a big disappointment because I was dead.

The wind was blowing from west to east, I didn't know what it could mean, I would like to have been a sailor. When I was a child I read a great deal about sailors, later on when I was able to, I did it. I sailed. All sailors were renegades, I was born to be a renegade, I had been one on land, which justified my clumsiness. I was an albatross. When would the hour come for me to commit suicide? Life was easy in purgatory, I always resolved my affairs. Time to eat? As always, ever since I was there my eating habits were not very elaborate. I walked down to the hamlet and looked for something, fish with side dishes, yucca or yautia. My grandfather was always happy to see his table served well, he demanded to be served like a sheikh, I think that despite his stumbles with reality, he accomplished a few things, he tried to live in communes that were based on the idea of returning to ingenuousness and to the natural world of the 18th century. He had 18th century vices, my grandfather, that mania of calling himself a rationalist despite his belief in spirits was a direct result of them. Karl Marx did the same thing, I discussed it several times with Abelardo, it gave his utopias a scientific nature, and he "discovered" laws that ruled his system. On one occasion I heard a colleague from the party talk about the third law of the dialectic, a cancer was eating away his colon and he shat through his stomach into a little plastic bag, he wasn't responding to chemotherapy, and yet, he never lost his beliefs, scientific materialism was an indisputable truth, that was very 18th century, to speak of the third law of the dialectic as if he were speaking about the laws of thermodynamics, it was coherent for my colleague, for any Marxist, and thus for Karl Marx. I heard a friend say that Joseph Stalin in the name of historical materialism condemned Mendel's laws of inheritance. I now felt as if I were out of time, I was taking Lourdes the only thing there was to eat, fish and yucca bread. Why did I remember my grandfather amidst the exile that I was living? I looked at him sitting at the table, he would talk and eat, he was compulsive, he never stopped expressing himself. I felt like I never participated in his banquet, I would mock his ingenuity, the difference between us was that I was aggressively ingenuous. I had his eyes and he no longer existed.

I had no guarantee of my existence.

We ate at the end of the afternoon. The sunset came together, that was how the afternoon appeared and retired. Sunsets were different from dawns, obviously. But I didn't feel nostalgic at sunset. The sun announced darkness with the exaggeration of the reds and oranges, it drifted away, became a fire, announced death, its cold heat caressed our skin, Lourdes immersed in her terrible thoughts, watched Humberto appear, he ran along the beach, naked like a Greek soldier, he leapt over the waves and plunged in, Sonia arrived gorgeous and full, she leapt over the spray and plunged in. I had never seen Carla or Andrés swim at the beach, they seemed older, more relaxed, more timid and perverse.

Lourdes was probably asking herself who they were. She must have known more than I did, she didn't go there blindly. She looked at them and folded up on herself, gathered her legs and wrapped her arms around them. The day was burning above us, the light became a form in the color but we, below, were shades.

"I'll see you at the house," I told her, taking off my shirt. As I ran, I took off the rest. I leapt over the salty clouds and plunged in, underneath everything was bubbles and blue, I came up to the surface behind Olga, I hugged her, her back was firm, her shoulders blunt, she barely shook, turned around and grazed my lips with a kiss, smiling, Humberto and Sonia arrived, they splashed us with water, she was bronze-colored like the armor of the ancient Greeks, she knew how to laugh, it was something she must have studied, now I looked at her chin and noticed a detail, an imperceptible line gave shape to a tiny bump, something the others didn't have, not even Lourdes at the other end of the mirror; the detail made her unique, she kept hitting the water, she splashed me, laughing, I grabbed her by the arms, I pulled her close to me and stuck out my tongue, I passed it along her neck, I went down to her breasts, I licked her nipples and moved up to her cheek, I licked it, put it in my mouth and had that cursed feeling, that burning in my stomach, the bewilderment of love that is born and dies, I hugged her. I couldn't abandon Lourdes. We embraced and the night closed over the group, at a specific point in the darkness, the red dot of a cigarette was accentuated. Lourdes walked toward the house. On the other side, she waited.

How long did we spend there? I started tabulating. Lourdes must have been doing the same thing. Why hadn't she killed me yet? I didn't know. She insisted on leaving, that we still had a chance. *But I'm not fleeing,* I told her. *And what else can we do? What is Carla doing? I don't know.* It was as though we were repeating a routine. Beforehand, when I was outside, I would also do it. I had seen Lourdes spying. She avoided us, smoked and watched us. She didn't mix with us at all. I did the same thing, I thought I was excluding myself but I was inside, being observed. Where was she taking this routine? It repeated itself. Under the cherry tree. The same scenes, the breeze that didn't ease up. Carla opened her legs, her smell was not human, I couldn't establish a relationship between what she smelled like and what I'd smelled in my life. At first I found it unpleasant, then I missed the presence of her aroma in those languid hours. What were they? I have thought. What weren't they? What was Lourdes thinking? They didn't tell any stories, they had no past, they moved about at night. During the daytime I'd been close to opening their rooms, but I'd been paralyzed by an unspeakable terror. I'd fought in guerrilla fronts, participated in more than one assassination attempt, I'd trained in African deserts, and I was paralyzed in front of these rooms. And Lourdes. Had she tried to find out something? How did they make a living? I could shrug my shoulders, time had passed and I had the impression that when I retraced my steps I would be in another country, another time. In some way Lourdes and I had crossed through a fissure. I used to mock my grandfather and his metaphysical superstitions. That day I asked myself in what plane was I living. It's ironic that other worlds, so as not to say other dimensions, offered me refuge. Maybe I was wounded on the day of the attempt, a head wound? Could I have been in a coma, living in a vegetative state? Was this the vegetative life, a coma? Each person gets the vegetative life he deserves. Mine was lecherous, my penis burned and I felt sharp pains behind my balls. No one loses their prostate in a life like this one, I consoled myself. This meant Lourdes must have been injured as well. Somehow we created a bridge, established contacts. Those who live a vegetative life can make contact with each other. This was how Carla, Humberto, Andrés, Olga and Sonia all dreamed on the bed where they vegetated in hospitals anywhere in the world. I asked Sonia about it. She was my confidant, she had no reason to be one, she surely told Carla everything. I was certain that Carla was perverse. *But Carla is an ancient one,* Sonia said to me. What did that mean? I didn't know, it must have been that she was the first one in the group, or maybe she inherited the leadership from another one who was no longer around. And she would laugh at my conjectures but wouldn't deny or add anything.

We ate frugally. We were frugal in everything except sex. That was where we would exceed ourselves. The house would fill with the sounds of love over and over, we were never enervated by the practice. We were machines that only stopped minutes before sunrise. My love for Sonia. That was evaporating. All loves evaporate. I merely felt tenderness for memories of yesterday, for a month or a century. I wanted to ask Sonia: What are you? But Lourdes stopped me. Or was it Sonia?

"Leave it at that. Listen, I have a plan."

"I don't like your plans."

"Are you going to stay in this limbo?" she spat out.

Carla was walking toward her wicker easy chair, making signs at me with her index finger. She was smiling, she was moved to change things somehow, she stood up from her armchair and went to her room. I was thinking about what Lourdes had said to me. I didn't like the fact that she had plans.

"So?"

"Tell me later," I turned around and headed towards the room, after Carla.

"We don't have time, you bastard."

I went into the room. It was illuminated by tall candles. In front, to one side of my bed, there she was. Her eyes were small, she had the face of a rodent. She stuck her tongue out and showed me the tip. She moved it like a snake. With another woman it would have been a pathetic gesture. But with her it figured as an ancestral movement. She was unknown. As ever. I felt this. Pale. Terse. Delicate despite her fragrance. How to define that fragrance if I had no measure, no element of comparison. She smelled and it was strange. Despite having smelled her for days, she was strange. She was squinting even more and lifting her skirt, she didn't use panties, I saw the end of her thighs, the smile, the same smile as the Gioconda. I then realized the greatness of Da Vinci consisted in placing the genital smile on a woman's face. She undid a knot that tied her hair and she let it fall over her back. She made no other gesture. Not even when I took off her clothes and sank into her breasts. Generous, disproportionate like those of the first Venus must have been; completeness offered by the firstborn woman. She who wounded me with her nails and opened furrows in my back, she who left me with bruises and teared my skin, the sinister one, for being the first and the last, I remembered Apocalypse, Alpha and Omega, I felt terror in her flesh, and inside her flesh I didn't want to understand anything, I left myself in death, in the smells of plagues and wars, the sweat of the years, she was passing through me, Carla, the pious one, with my body in her lap. I wet myself in all women and I was bathed by the moods of the earth, that was how I was left, lying still in bed. Carla lifted her index finger to her mouth and asked me to be quiet, to let myself go, she was on top of me and was licking me, her breath was neither sweet nor bitter, it was cold; it was the breath of swords when they kiss to death the bodies they charge, it was her and she made me sleep in an absolute faint. Neither Sonia, nor Olga, nor Andrés fucking Humberto up the ass, nor myself receiving a caress from Humberto on the beach, none of us had any importance. They would pass on, I would not remain. Carla would be outside under Lourdes's glance: God, it couldn't be. It became daytime and I felt bare, alone. The evil one was right there. The one who came to take my life. I felt certain that we wouldn't have another night in the big old house in the fishermen's village.

Morning arrived and I was in the room. I didn't want to go out. I had a conviction, if I went out, I wouldn't return. That was what I would have put in my diary, if I had the habit of keeping one. We imitated Che in many things, but few of us kept diaries. He had the mania of writing about the small events in his day, of writing his life. We had a bad habit, not following the best examples of the men we admire.

Lourdes brought me arepas and fish. She remained sitting in front of me, watching me. I wouldn't have known how to say in what manner she watched me, she just did. Nor did that glance deserve an adjective, I couldn't have said it was inscrutable. I knew exactly what she wanted. To kill me. And if that was the case, why didn't she do it when I was asleep? No, that would have been a murder. Those who are brought to justice need to be conscious at the hour of assuming their destiny.

"You should get up, Sergio. We can't spend all our lives here."

"And why not?"

"Because they'll catch us. Because sooner or later they'll reach us."

"How?"

"Passivity, our passivity works in their favor."

"I thought it worked in ours. I don't act, I don't make mistakes."

"You're acting, every day the soldiers at the checkpoint see you, the people in town, the fishermen, there must be people asking about us around there."

"No one talks about the dead."

"These people aren't dead."

"I'm staying. Give me a reason why I should go with you."

"I need you. We need each other." She took out a cigarette, lit it, inhaled deeply. "Before you came here, what did you do?"

"I tried to kill the president."

"Why?"

"That was the original party line. To create revolutionary conditions. He has strayed from the path and takes for revolution what translates into personal power. Something had to be done. To stop him and move and create an insurrection."

"Did you really believe in that?"

"Yes." I realized the witch was setting me up for a trap. "But now I don't want to believe in anything. These days have meant a lot to me."

"For me too!" Lourdes yelled at me.

"I don't want to save myself for the revolution. I don't want to transform anything. It's all so banal."

"We're in agreement. But Roca's men, this government, definitely Elmer, do you remember Elmer? They're all coming after us in order to kill us." He remembered Elmer in the desert. A man everyone liked very much. Cold, I saw him shoot an actual target, a spy. He hadn't touched the prisoner but he subdued him under so much psychological pressure that he was trembling, he had pissed and shit himself. A shot to the nape of the neck that had been announced so many times, suggested in so many ways, lived through over and over until it detonated, I think the prisoner never knew if it had been an actual shot. Tidy and inscrutable Elmer. I remembered he had been Lourdes's lover, or at least he'd brought her to his tent. She couldn't move beyond men of power.

"Why you? You're the worst one of them all," I said to her. I was challenging her with my eyes. "I think you failed, you should have climbed into bed with the president."

"Are you going to help me?" She pretended not to hear my words. "I have a plan and I have some money."

On the other side of the avenue, in front of a house on the corner of the port's embankment, there was the son of a bitch. He opened the door to the black Toyota, stretched and looked at his suit; Lorca searched in his pockets, pulled out a box of cigarettes, it was empty. He crumpled it and tossed it into a trash can, he made the basket, feinted like a basketball player, tall and clumsy, dressed in a black suit. He walked diagonally, crossed the avenue, didn't look to the sides, barely stopped on the island to wipe his shoe. He gave a little kick, disgusted, reached the other corner, dragged his leg, scraped the sole of his shoe repeatedly on the edge of the sidewalk, I felt like telling him that it was good luck to step on dog shit, he probably knew this, of course, and he thought he'd finish us off that, but he was unhappy, he was waiting; then the motorcycle appeared, on the motorcycle sat Elmer, it passed in front of the house, disappeared down a side street and reappeared. If he saw us we were done for, and we knew it. Up to what point was I not lost already? And what if Lourdes had brought me here to turn me in? Trials were no longer in fashion. There was a time when they would give you a quick trial and then shoot you in the nape of the neck, but by then, if anything, they would just shoot you.

We were heading toward the walk-in clinic, where Lourdes had left her bag with the money hidden. They were waiting for the doctor. Humberto would never come. We had to forget about the bag. If they saw us they'd catch us. Lourdes let Humberto's Vespa run, she turned the handlebars and we did a U-turn on the avenue. We were moving along attentively, the morning was warm, the sky clear, there was very little traffic, the only thing you could hear was the sea crashing its waves on the other side of the embankment. We didn't hear Elmer's motorcycle, nor Lorca's car, we'd left them behind but we hadn't lost them. It was a matter of hours before they found us, the two of them were enough to surround us.

"We should go back," I told Lourdes.

"It's impossible, they're going to hunt us down, even into hell, it's a matter of hours. We have to get out of here."

We headed towards a neighborhood near the port and saw a policeman. Lourdes brought the Vespa close to the officer, stopped a few feet in front of him, got off, went up to him and started to ask him directions for a hotel, I approached them, we looked like tourists, we overwhelmed him with questions, we grabbed him by the chest, immobilized him, broke his neck, took his weapon, he was left lying on the sidewalk, no one saw us, it was a solitary street lost on a slope. We went back to the motorcycle and took off, now the sun had risen, the day began, we had a weapon.

We couldn't keep running around on the Vespa all over the port, we'd expose ourselves to being seen by Elmer and Lorca. I would've liked to go back, I was sure that nothing would happen to us if we were with Carla, we were safe, it was a fishing village lost to the world. In any case, all they had was Humberto the doctor's address, nothing else. They would get tired and leave. We would detain Humberto, he wouldn't go back. Lourdes stopped the Vespa under a leafy bush near the beach, we sat on the edge of the sidewalk, she explained to me about action, we had already acted, we had a weapon, action generates consequences, it's not Buddhism, it's dialectics. I was tired of thinking. Of classifying and naming. I was tired of everything. I was returning to the world with the distaste of those who have nothing to seek in it. I once wanted to change it. At that moment it meant nothing to me. To go back, why not? It was paradise. Why should I listen to Lourdes? I was still submitting myself to discipline. For what? We wouldn't be able to break through the blockade. It was impossible to go against those two without ending up with a body full of bullet holes. I decided to go back.

"Listen to me, you bastard," Lourdes said. She was squeezing her jaw but speaking strongly. "If you turn your back on me I'll kill you and if you leave facing me I'll kill you. I don't have any options."

"Do whatever you want," I answered and began to walk, I didn't turn my back to her, I was walking backwards, then I turned around. "Ever since the day I shot at the president and missed, I've been dead."

"Sergio, someone has to do it." I felt her pulling the trigger.

"Do it, then."

She fired.

A man in a black suit was running toward us, he had a pistol in his hand and he returned fire. The shot hit the tree where Lourdes was standing, she responded, I began to run. I took off down a dirt road, the sun was at its peak and it fell on me like a flaming stone. I heard another exchange of gunshots, the Vespa was making noise and approaching me, at my back.

"Get on, asshole!" I jumped onto the motorcycle, Lourdes didn't take off, she put the barrel of the gun in my face, the sun and the barrel were burning me.

"Listen carefully, I have two bullets left, I can bust your head open and with the other one do something desperate that'll take me out of this fucking town. Are you coming or will I make you stay?"

I shrugged and we took off. We left a cloud of dust behind us, along with the midday heat. How the fuck had Lorca reached us? Where was he when he recognized us without us noticing him?

"I told you," her words were being fired back towards me but the wind didn't take them away without me being able to hear them. "Small town... now they know we're here, they won't leave town, they'll search all the hamlets until they find us."

You're stuck to her back, you ride as a passenger on the motorcycle, she lets loose words and you only pay attention to those that interest you. You will put together a commando, not for a political purpose but as a task for national salvation. People live by saving themselves, look at alcoholics, smokers or cocaine users, who on certain occasions, when they hit bottom say they'll leave their vices behind, that they'll go somewhere far away or will start a new life. Others join groups where they save each other. You were a group. You two. An anonymous commando. You talked about it with her, you were anonymous killers. It doesn't matter who you kill for, a life is always taken. Homeland, revolution, cartel, band, a piece of bread; it doesn't matter, you've deprived someone of their most valued possession, the only one. Everyone has plans and lives and suddenly the homeland arrives, the revolution or a crackhead's needs and everything goes to hell. They take away your memory, they take away your present, take away your hope. You're moralizing, you don't like morals, you have your life and the life that awaits you is to take away others. But everyone is on the road, in the middle of the way, everyone avoids someone from passing by and running them over. Nothing defends you, not the State, nor institutions, nor international organizations or letters guaranteeing your rights, regardless things happen to you with all their bad luck, they take away your house, profession, future; any day, after having escaped from men, you see yourself in a spot right there, just below your nipple, it's an innocent shadow that has dispersed hundreds of sick cells to the lymph nodes, you've imploded, cancer is simply an implosion, now the future is over, your plans, pending affairs, the realizations to come, you're fucked. Who has fucked you over then? A terrorist who's placed C-4 in a car bomb? A man who wants your wristwatch or your wallet? No, you escape from them and the calls of the homeland, of God and of revolutions, and they take it from you just the same, but you have to save it, you have to fight, it's an order planted in the genes. An illogical order. An absurdity. To pick up a sword with a luminous edge and let it plunge into the belly, stick it in, to grab a gun and open a piercing in the sky of the mouth, to finish one's self off before they do is coherent. You have to live, cling to Lourdes's back and live, reach Trinidad, allow streams of air to enter your nostrils, your lungs to burst with air and iodine. You no longer hold tight to the motorcycle's frame, you cling to the driver's body, you're one with her, your arms fall when you cross dirt roads, you hug her, breathe in her smell, she smells good, she is sweating, her hair smells like smoke, like straw, you hug her and let your face fall into her neck, you close your eyes and remember Sonia. Who was she? You grew tired of asking them. They lived there in those houses, they lived without any fears, liberated. And who are you? Carla has that strange smell, that unknown metal, that metallic amber in the skin, in her breath, there with her, with generous tits, her tits with large and erect nipples like halos, your mouth tasted of that, of her. Who was she? And she answered you with another question. What am I? What were Carla, Sonia, Olga? What were they and which one was their house, she remains on the verandah, green flesh, green hair dreaming of the bitter sea, of her house, in that demolished house they resist against the breeze, the sand, the salt and at night they come and I want to tell them. Don't you see this wound of mine, from my chest to my throat? Carla knows it and thinks you're dead, here I am amid shadows and her painful hugs give you bruises and she tastes like that when you kiss her. What is she? You won't see them again. What is she? A moon icicle holds her over the water, black hair, fresh face, and you tangled up with your bitter girl. Where is she, tell me? In front of you, you cling tighter, you've passed through several neighborhoods, you stop at a gas station, we get off the motorcycle; Lourdes walks toward the store, you see her pull out the gun from her jacket, she threatens the men behind the counter, asks them to open the cash register, she grabs canned foods and soft drinks off the shelves, you have to do something, you tell yourself, the attendant at the gas pump has noticed what's happening, the attendant on the next island tries to run and warn someone and you tell him to stand still because if you pull out your gun you'll kill him on the spot, you won't hesitate at all

and his sisters the whores and the whore that gave birth to him will
have to go from door to door to pay for his funeral, they should stand
still. Lourdes moves and pushes a uniformed man who's standing
outside, beside the soft drink machine, the guy falls on his face, she
leaves without turning around, you pull out the hose from the Vespa's
gasoline tank and turn it on, step back, you yell, not one move or
you're heading to the morgue, you scream at them, Lourdes arrives
and tosses an object toward you that shines in the reflection of that
afternoon that's just beginning and leaves a glare over the world, it's
a sawed-off shotgun, you grab it, move the bolt and load it, you climb
onto the back of the motorcycle and without holding onto anything
you cling to Lourdes's back, she is Atlas and sustains you, you cross
the roads of the earth, you kick the dogs out of your way, the inopppor-
tune goats, the children walking with their belly buttons sticking out.
They burst onto a street and glide on the pavement, out of sheer iner-
tia you point the rifle at a man driving a van, you yell at him to stop,
you shove the barrel in his face, the man brakes, if you don't let me see
your hands I'll blow your face off, you yell again, you get off, shove
the man out of the truck, he had a .44 at his side, fuck, you laugh, we
won the daily double, little by little you're becoming an army, before
you take off, this time it's you at the wheel, you fire at the Vespa's gas
tank, you let the wheels screech, it's as though the sun had exploded
in everyone's face, it was hell at mid-afternoon, no matter how far you
got, no matter how much you rolled up the windows, you felt hot, you
were inside, under the skin. You cross from the narrow street towards
an avenue, you'll have to drive along the embankment, leave town
and get on the highway. You do this and Lourdes moves closer to you,
clings to you, her dark green eyes are shining, she smiles and gives
you a kiss on the cheek, very close to your mouth.

We began the escape towards Trinidad. The fishing village and
the old big house remained in another life. We were lucky. We
were able to break through the barricade set up by Elmer and
Lorca. We had left them in a town that was looking at itself,
shaken by the radical disarming of a police officer, the robbery

of a gas station and shootouts, car robberies and explosions. It hadn't experienced so much turmoil since the war of independence.

We were headed towards Oriente province. But we couldn't continue in the van we were driving. At the first crossroads I turned toward the plains, then I got off the main road. I wasn't very clear about the route, but we had to avoid any police checkpoints. We continued along a road that took us to a small town, we wouldn't pass unnoticed in small towns. Lourdes was counting our artillery. We had two revolvers and seven bullets. The shotgun only had three cartridges left. It wasn't enough artillery to earn a living. We had to procure cartridges for the shotgun and more ammunition, the weapons were fine.

We crossed a bridge over a creek. I left the road towards a narrower one, we entered a low hill, typical of the plains, the trees were slashing the mid-afternoon rays of the sun. The route became rugged, almost non-existent. We climbed an incline, where the trail took a detour, Lourdes told me to stop. We got out of the van, picked up our scant belongings, hid the weapons, not much, just enough, in our coats. Then we pushed the vehicle down the cliff. It took off bouncing toward the river, the current dragged it into a small pool, it sank headlong to the bottom, first the roof stayed on the surface, Lourdes launched a stone at the van, she looked like a little girl, with her blue lace dress that clung to her body, a black denim jacket, high heel boots and a Stetson hat. The clothes she had borrowed from Sonia's trunk. It seemed impossible for her to have driven a motorcycle, overpowered a policeman and held up a gas station dressed that way. But that was Lourdes. I was tempted to think that this was my girl, she was at least Sonia on this side of the mirror; at certain moments, when she forgot about the weight of the weapons inside the coat, she made a gesture, a movement as though she were about to bite the sleeves of her jacket with her hands. I remembered the kiss on my cheek, it wasn't damp, it was intimate. After so many years of political activism, we had become comrades. I remembered that comrades were those who shared the same bed. The roof of the van finally sank.

"Perfect," she smiled at me with her intense green eyes, with her big teeth.

"Perfect? You're crazy. We're lost in the plains. We don't have the slightest clue as to where exactly. The National Guard, police, Intelligence and the men from Roca's apparatus are all probably looking for us."

"Don't you see?" She pointed toward the van. "We've erased our tracks."

"But how are we going to get out of here?"

She began to walk.

"Traveler, there is no path, only trails across the sea."

I thought we were walking in circles, we had a couple of cigarettes left. We decided to move away from the river and follow its course from afar, we found shortcuts and trails, the sun was starting to decline, there was a slight breeze blowing. A hamlet should have appeared, a highway route. It was a matter of patience. We found a piece of land set apart by fences, we crossed over the barbed wire, I pulled out the shotgun, we were advancing cautiously. Night was falling, we managed to see some ruins, it was an old temple with adobe walls, destroyed many centuries ago. It was on a hill, from there we made out a dirt road and a hamlet. We decided not to go down at that hour, it would be suspicious. We would spend the night in the ruins. Up to that point they had been favorable to us.

Lourdes took off her jacket. Her back was wide, her shoulders firm, athletic. She walked around the ruins, without any weapons, just a stick, I lost sight of her in some bushes. I thought to myself, "She should have taken one of the guns with her." In any case, she knew more about this than I did. After a while she returned carrying a rabbit by its ears, she looked like a prestidigitator in the middle of that hill. She was able to find a den. We gathered leaves and dry branches. We improvised a campfire. She skinned the animal, buried the fur and placed it in the fire. Another problem solved.

The afternoon fell slowly. The sky seemed like an oval filled with hydrogen. The immense sun was devoured by the savannah, a tumult of mauve appeared over us. We would live through different afternoons together, we would live forever, I thought. We were dead and together, a way of living forever.

We ate the grilled rabbit with a rough day's hunger. Night appeared, we put out the campfire. The breeze began to blow strongly, the sky cleared and filled up with stars. I recalled my grandfather and his worlds beyond this world, he believed that many of those stars and planets were inhabited by superior spirits. It was madness to believe that, I said, and Abelardo burst out with one of his phrases: "If they believe it in Hollywood, why not let your grandfather believe it?" We set ourselves up in a corner where two walls met amid the rubble of that ruined mission.

"Tomorrow we'll find someone to give us a lift heading north," Lourdes commented. "We have to find a way to reach Puerto La Cruz, it's a big city, we can find some money and go unnoticed."

"No one who robs a bank goes unnoticed."

"We won't rob any banks. We'll do everything like we did today. There are lots of tourists in the port, we'll be selective pickpockets. They're expecting us to pull off a big heist."

She came up to me. She sat down beside me. Shoulder to shoulder. Then she let her head fall on my chest, she hid it there. She clung to it. She turned and looked at me. The night was complete above us. And why not, I said to myself. I kissed her. We smelled of tallow, of earth, of dried blood, of filth. We then became two indigents, we ate each other's flesh, we were the dregs of the earth and we loved each other until we collapsed exhausted.

I fell asleep and thought about things that stop making sense. I thought that everything was supported by scientific bases. That's what scientific materialism was about. I wasn't a good student,

but we had read Marx, Althusser, we never stopped comment-
ing on the classics and trying to interpret any event in the light
of their teachings. We knew it was better to be orthodox than
informal revisionists when it came to matters of revolutionary
theories and principles. That's why we never thought we had
attained revolutionary power by winning elections and having
a president with an activist's rhetoric. In our discussions we
talked about the electoral process, we never believed it to be
a point of origin, much less revolutionary, the political actors
changed but, despite media scandals, bourgeois legality was
never transgressed nor was the old order ever demolished.
Roca was always in agreement that we back a few nationalist
officers as a tactical move that would destroy the old power
structures and provide a motor for a revolution, a radical and
violent change. That was the party line.

After joining my body with Lourdes's, I fell asleep with
those ideas. The line. The immensity of the universe was falling
upon us, the night air was dampening us, the open air stripped
us of any meaning. We were nothing in a corner of the ruins of
a church. No one. What use had lines or convictions been, we
were lying there naked. This was life. A camp site. A herd of
animals, the instinct to not lose track of her. And why should I
hold on to her, I thought I saw Carla's tiny figure, for a few moments I saw her rodent eyes, intermittent, beside the fireflies.
What had happened to them? Where, when were the ghosts?

I was grieved by nostalgia, I gave myself over to the embrace shivering, to the peace of my woman. *That's what we are*, I
thought, *a man and a woman thrown from the order of things, we're
looking after ourselves, moved by primitive mandates.* My love for
woman was being born, tenderness, the responsibility of being
a couple, of fucking her with the urgency of animals facing the
death that stalks them, that never steps back. Sex is the ease of
the ephemeral, of the person who is going to die. Man in his
pretensions had separated life from death, he distanced them,
condemned one and praised the other. Like a God he separated
light from darkness, but God had never separated light from

darkness, the darkness was in the light in the same way that life was in death.

I had lived within vertigo and I had not always fallen. There were moments of no gravity, of elevation even. It was always a spiral, intoxicated by circumstances, then abandonment was falling. And I was thinking of the line, of history, of its upsets that are not as they seem. The deep night and its sleep arrived; conquered, I slept.

We woke up soaked to the bone, but it wasn't the dew that awakened us. Nor the buzzing of insects. We were in a deep sleep. It was voices, screams, laughter. We got up without much of a notion about our surroundings, for a while now we had lost track of basic notions. We looked for our jackets, bags and weapons, we peeked out from amid the ruins, we sought remnants that would sufficiently hide us. A boy dressed in blue jeans, a checkered shirt and cowboy boots was throwing stones at us and laughing, calling other children, all of them wore red berets on their heads, they began to occupy the spaces, the tables and awnings, flags were waving everywhere and trucks arrived full of people singing hymns or climbing down to the rhythm of the *joropo* music that was starting to sound.

Lourdes didn't pause, she ran up to the children and grabbed their hands, she proposed a race and went down with them to where the people were gathered, I had to hurry to do the same, before we reached the kiosks we found a group that was getting off a little bus, we grabbed each other by the waist, we blended in with the delegation from El Tigre, present, Anauco, present, Clarines, present and everyone to the revolutionary fair, we assumed responsibilities, carried boxes of beer, victuals, electrical components, we joined the outing. And in that way we had something to eat, we joined the audience at discussion panels about land laws, we booed at the moderates, sang Viglietti's song "A Desalambrar," we were volunteers in a food stand, we ate as much as we could and spent the rest of the day there.

For a moment the idea crossed my mind that the president would attend the party and I told myself I couldn't fail this time: I knew very well how the security rings were organized around him on these occasions, its weaker flanks. I felt that history made sense and I was facing an opportunity, but only the mayors and regional party bosses from the government party were dancing to the song "Seis por Derecho," intoning patriotic slogans and songs by Alí Primera. We left the group from El Tigre and went with the one from Puerto La Cruz.

"Not even if we'd had it made to order. Not even if we'd asked our angels before we went to sleep," said Lourdes.

"It's too bad the president didn't come," I whispered.

"And what would you have done?" she smiled. "They would have recognized us and we'd be dead."

"Who knows."

"Don't be silly."

"Lourdes," I said to her before climbing onto the flatbed of a big truck, "I'm convinced our life depends on the president's death."

She moved closer to me, grabbed me by the waist, she was sweating, dirty and enchanting. She was laughing.

"Won't you ever stop being an idiot?" She silenced me with a kiss. The truck started moving, I was crumbling inside. One more afternoon, one more sunset and we headed toward Puerto La Cruz with a drunk and revolutionary multitude.

MANUELA'S
METAMORPHOSIS

Manuela knew that if she touched the sensitive points of power they would begin to make erratic declarations, the spokesmen would retract themselves and, finally, her articles would gain form and veracity. An action is reaffirmed in the one that follows and one mistake leads to another and one lie to another and things proceed in that manner until arriving at the truth, it is a dynamic that doesn't stop once it is set in motion. She wanted to know what was happening. She was under pressure. Her editor at the newspaper was demanding that she be precise, that she attack once and for all, that she denounce the plan. He was also under pressure and couldn't move any further, unless they had some news.

She maintained what her sources told her, that behind the assassination attempt there was a movement in play by the radical sectors of the regime who were trying to take power. A president threatened and in the midst of conspiracies could declare a State of Emergency. In fact, he had suspended some guarantees. The plan was made evident by the bombs and explosive artifacts that went off in universities and churches, the land expropriations, the mobilized crowds that harassed dissidents, the other crowd that confronted the crowd, the threats of those in power to protect the process with the weapons of the Armed Forces. In actuality there were few facts, only bewilderment and danger could be named as tangible phenomena.

The regime was nourished by a dull anarchy. The sensation of the abyss and of civil war. And yet, somehow there was a sense of governability. Nothing happened, but the climate was tense, groups for the defense of the revolution were organized and the official discourse was ranting more and more aggressively. But that wasn't enough. They needed to set fire to the Reichstag, Manuela told her editor, a self-inflicted aggression. But how would it be done? Who would be used so as to leave no loose ends? Who needed to make a commitment during this phase of the revolution? The key was to be found among Roca's colleagues, in the men of the Popular Liberation Party. Where were the men of Minister Manuel Roca's party?

The PLP was a party that had survived the dismantling of the armed struggle of the sixties, it had always positioned itself on the far left, in their time they believed in the proposals of Pol Pot. Its leaders, including Manuel Roca, had travelled to Cambodia, and they continued with low-profile military activities. Many of their cadres died. Among them José Ruedas, Commander Abelardo. There were those who thought he had fled to Cuba with other comrades who distanced themselves from the party line, but his bullet-ridden body appeared in a ditch in the outskirts of Caracas. It was then maintained that he was assassinated by the political police, but it was filtered to the media that he was the victim of a purge, a power struggle in the heart of his organization. During those days there was a wave of executions; informers, infiltrators, police officers who had participated in the fight against subversives were shot. Manuela published a few investigative pieces. And she published a report by a military intelligence officer in which he admitted to having passed along information to a cadre from the organization about undesirable figures within the counterinsurgency; the officer made himself pass as an ally; this was what some sources said, others claimed that the party cadre was a counterintelligence man. Those agents and informers who were considered undesirable by the leaders of the political police were shot in plain daylight. José Ruedas,

Commander Abelardo, pointed out the executions, he said in a meeting of the Party directorate that he had a feeling they were doing the government's dirty work. He was opposed to "bringing to justice"—he underlined the phrase with irony— informants and police officers. That was not the movement's task. He denounced the military intelligence official and refused to continue being manipulated by him. He repudiated the organization's policies. Later on he was found dead. Manuela put together a file and mapped out the PLP's organizational chart, substituted dead leaders with living ones, and followed the readjustments, a fallen cadre for a cadre won over, little by little, the top of the pyramid was occupied by the ineffable Manuel Roca. Had Manuel Roca been the contact between the military intelligence officer and the PLP? Who killed Commander Abelardo?

Manuela had investigated the minister's history, his role in the Tricontinental in Cuba, his connections with liberation fronts in North Africa, she found out, through her source, about the training of a special group in the deserts of the Maghreb. She had followed the revolutionary's sinuous career from the cold and foul-smelling classroom in a school in the Andes to the Ministry of Internal Affairs. It was evident that he gave weight to Wilde's phrase: "each man kills the thing he loves." At least, each person who in one way or another established emotional ties with the former guerrilla commander and today minister was not to be found among the living.

I have him by the balls, Manuela thought; she was drinking coffee in the newsroom. *It's a matter of opening the manhole cover, Marcos, we just have to be patient.* Dearest Marcos, the only man in her life, the queen from the social pages. The journalist killed by a thief in a bar. A victim of the violence with a thousand faces and none. A violence that diluted everything in the country. It wasn't social, nor political, nor religious, it was a violence without adjectives. Behind the violence there were always operators of a sinister plan positioning themselves, there was always a plan; the revolution will be born out of confusion, it will be read between the lines, its coherence will emerge from anarchy, it will eventually impose an inevitable and different order. She thought she could hear the operators of history, very serious men, cold theorists, opportunists and cynics; they were elaborating the revelatory and perfect equations of the process.

"It's already gone to print," said the editor bluntly.

"So then I'll go home and sleep."

"Don't you want one of the security guards to accompany you?" the editor asked.

"No. It's not necessary."

"Things are about to become difficult for us. There's a state of emergency. This might be the last thing we're able to publish. At least we've left a record in the newspaper."

"Things will become difficult but they won't shut down the newspaper. We're not alone anymore, my articles have been published abroad," Manuela sighed. "I wonder if Manuel Roca will be able to continue with his plan."

"We shouldn't be naïve, Manuela. Of what use is it that you've been published abroad? They'll always claim it's a right wing campaign. Manuel Roca remains in power and anything can happen," the editor said. "This is a small newspaper, my affairs are in order. I feel as if I've put together my testament, Manuela, we're betting everything with this case, we're defying those people's plan, those people are dangerous."

"Don't worry, I'd even say that each day there are fewer of them. Roca is a man on his own, his influence isn't growing, we just have to apply some pressure and see what happens."

"Do you think something will happen?" the editor asked inquisitively. "Will they take you to court? Will they force you to reveal your sources? Will they shut me up? Will they shut down the newspaper? Will you find out that tomorrow there isn't any space for your articles? Will they become radicalized and establish a truly harsh regime? If that's the case, we're collaborating so that everything goes to hell, Manuela. History no longer has room for left-wing or right-wing dictatorships, we'll simply have a dictatorship, of an unprecedented kind as these people like to say."

"Dictatorships have always been like that," the journalist interrupted. "In any case, they won't be unprecedented, Fujimori is the paradigm."

"For now." The editor was left with the expression still on his lips. His best journalist had turned her back on him.

Manuela went to the parking garage and got into her small Fiesta. Before turning on the ignition she felt a drop of sweat running down her back. She always thought that after ignition everything would turn off, a great big red would appear, a reddish blackness, a silent sound, a muffled, eternal commotion. Everything would suddenly be over and the infamies of power would no longer be important, neither the country nor the revolution, everything would end, it would suffer an eternal fever, eternal night in Barcelona; her uncle sighing from behind her, her grandmother's finger on her lips, silence. Outside, the smoke. The city was smoke, the buildings were blurry ashes behind the smoke, the fire continued, the hills were being consumed. Far away, behind her, outside the city, the trash dumps were burning. The plague was falling on the city and it was thick, grey and suffocating. Caracas was burning and Manuela was driving through its avenues in her small Fiesta, crossing streets and looking in her rearview mirror, she didn't get scared when she noticed the car following her, the guardian angel, its lights were winking at her amid the smoke, she had to speak with her source, he was waiting for his call; she would change her cell phone every day, she had set up a plan with her associates of buying new lines on a daily basis, but still she didn't dare establish contact through the phone. No one in the newspaper came up to her to give her a message, she didn't open her e-mail. She proposed to use simple methods, less sophisticated ones, this is what the man who passed along information to her requested. Her information came through less expected channels, inserted as just another page in her cable provider's magazine, in a bottle of aspirin; they used third-party cell phones; she was anguished, a hand was stealing oxygen from her, a meeting was unavoidable, she was watching her job go to hell.

She had published Silvestre's identity, she had tied him to Roca's party. She had tied Dominguín to Roca's party and she continued to ask what was happening with the minister's comrades. Her source protected themself, she was sure it was someone close to the minister, she had to guard the exclusivity of what was being revealed to her. To relate the seemingly unconnected events in the case of the minister's comrades had been her strategy. The news items that had been printed yesterday in the crime section were a cyphered message, a wink of complicity: "A day of fury in Puerto Píritu. One police officer dead, a gas station robbed, a van stolen and a motorcycle exploded, have turned the peaceful tourist and fishing port into a Wild West town. Witnesses attest that professional gunmen have perpetrated this escalation of violence. The question asked by the town, frightened by the recent assassination attempt and conspiracies, is if these are actions of everyday criminals or, on the contrary, the work of experts skilled in destabilization. What is your response, minister?"

The informer recommended that she follow the case in the crime section of the newspapers.

Manuel Roca was dressed in casual clothes. A light yellow sports shirt and impeccable white pants. He looked like a golf player. He was waiting for Elmer, drinking a vodka and orange juice on the terrace of the hotel where he was staying. Meanwhile, he was thinking that a range of possible moves was opening up. More than one colleague from the cabinet was playing his own parallel game. When he arrived at the ministry he thought he would be able to control the holders of power. Power was not homogenous. It was a weakness in itself, the weakness that played into his hands. The president was the one who decided. His particular vision of revolution imposed itself. Until when? The president's whims were predictable for a man like Roca. To consolidate his position, to make himself an emblem that was beyond discussion. But after Manuela's newspaper articles, he was nervous, he wouldn't receive his Minister of Internal Affairs, he sent him messages via third parties, the cabinet meetings were a circle of listeners who assented to or applauded the leader's monologue. The leader made his decisions without the cabinet. Far outside. This was his strategy. Roca hadn't gone there since the journalist's accusations began to appear. One by one the ministers filed by and welcomed the plans; some, the ones who had the privilege, debated with and advised the statesman without any major incidences. The real advisors, the men with whom the president made his decisions, were behind a heavy curtain, they were masks of masks; they lacked any facial expression. For each Roca that fell to the side, ten rose up.

Manuel Roca had organized the assassination attempt and the state of exception in a biased manner among those anonymous groups. *This is how true men of power work,* he told himself. You would be behind the president, silent, glancing at the ground, resolving practical matters, were it not for those loose ends and that bad luck with the journalist. Manuel Roca wasn't the only one who was conspiring; he knew it, one survives amid masks only by being creative with new plans for the regime's consolidation of power. The minister thought he was going to be able to manipulate the other factions, which were in any case much weaker. His palate tasted bitter, an uncommon state of anxiety had risen inside him. He was starting to feel that not a single means of power remained in his hands. He was there to hunt down Sergio and Lourdes, to annihilate his party and whatever was left of the figures that had become renegades. Once they were annihilated, he would face an uncertain fate. How to escape?

Elmer sat down at the table and ordered a mineral water, he remained silent for a moment and asked about the president's health. The minister made a gesture of annoyance with his hand, the morning was beginning, he had one of the newspapers in his hands, he took out a handkerchief and wiped his forehead, he confronted his colleague, stared back at him, they sat facing each other. He felt screwed over by circumstances, they had never overwhelmed him before, the Minister of Defense had met with the military leadership and they had agreed to ask the president for his resignation. The minister—a goddamn fascist, he thought—was about to stage a coup, I saw expression in his mask, he'd take power from us, somehow he had to abort the movements of those interests that were acting to displace him, and why not eliminate him? If they had had an apparatus, a true party, they would have gotten rid of the president and the high command, once the vacuum of power was created, the revolutionary vanguard would take charge of the matter and then he would be secretary general, consistent with the orthodoxy.

"It's pretty early for a drink," Elmer let out.

"Why the hell aren't they dead?"

"It's not easy to kill a man in revolutionary times."

"Are you sure?" he smiled.

"We do what's necessary, within the revolution, for the death of... whoever needs to die." Elmer kept smiling.

Manuel Roca shook the newspaper in front of Elmer's face.

"How does this bitch know that Sergio and Lourdes are behind this garbage in Puerto Píritu? Why can't you do your job well, is the climate affecting you?"

Elmer shrugged.

"Someone's filtering information to the press."

"There's no doubt about that."

"Do you trust Lorca?"

"Are you sure you aren't talking in your sleep?"

"I don't sleep."

"That's bad for your health."

"You shouldn't have come back here."

"Why? Where should your men have planted me?" He made a calming gesture. "Don't worry. Lorca's on their trail."

"Don't give me that nonsense," Roca spat out. "You know I don't have any men. I trust you completely."

"And I trust you." The trainer lowered his gaze.

"The men from the Ministry of Defense must have followed you, they're the ones who leaked the information."

"Why don't you eliminate the Minister of Defense?"

"That's not possible."

"In a country without institutions, everything is possible."

"So, do what you have to do with Sergio and Lourdes. Confuse the people from the ministry. Plant them and don't leave a trace for the journalist. Once this is all over, I'll present you and Lorca as my comrades, we'll get rid of any doubts, we'll be able to shut that woman's mouth, I already shut down the newspaper."

The morning was rising, the light of the sun was competing with the smoke.

"And then what, Manuel?"

The minister shrugged.

"Every process generates expectations. Nothing is certain."

"This is the end."

"Don't be ridiculous."

"This is the end." Elmer stood up from his chair, turned his back to him and walked away. The minister drank his vodka and leaned back, spread out the newspaper and proceeded to figure out the crossword puzzle.

The messenger crossed the newsroom. He was looking back and forth uneasily. He wasn't carrying the day's envelopes or correspondence. He sought Manuela's cubicle and blurted out, "Last night I was kidnapped. They kept me until just now. I was in a damp, dark room, with my face covered by a flour sack the whole time." The man was shaking. "I thought they were going to kill me," —he looked at the journalist with rage— "and all because of you. Who's going to take care of my children if they kill me? They wanted me to tell you to not forget about Puerto La Cruz, that things are happening, that you should read the crime section, that they'll soon try to finish what they started." The man spoke with his eyes bulging. "Are you going to publish this, are you going to make them kill me?"

Manuela stood up and put her arm on his shoulder. She pulled him closer. The microphones planted in the office had already recorded the message, this meant that the informant didn't care if he was identified. Why didn't he call her? Why frighten this poor man? Could it be her source or were they playing at counter-information? Whoever was recording her would be asking the same question. Who would finish what? What had started? Would they start a coup? Were they at the doors to a national commotion? She pulled the man out of her cubicle and took him to the cafeteria. She calmed him down with a few words, using a compassionate caress, a hug. She didn't want to talk, they might be listening to her.

"Jorge, don't worry. I'll talk with my boss so that he gives you a few days off. Anyways, the newspaper is about to close. You can take your vacation. We're not going to make this a news item. We'll keep it a secret. You should do the same. Do you understand?"

She spent the rest of the morning thinking about the message. About its uselessness. About the means of transmitting it. This message was meant for someone else. She felt like something serious might be about to happen. But why? A coup? She didn't want to give herself an answer, she was scared they might hear her thoughts. They were using her. One sector against another. Should this surprise her? The same thing happened with the Vladimiro Montesinos case. Marco had been assassinated. She was being hunted, there were pressures on the newspaper like never before; they had forged documents, they were accusing the editorial group of tax evasion. They were asking for her to be fired. She didn't know to what point her editor would stand by her. They had already suggested to her that she spend less time on the Roca case. One shouldn't provoke the use of force via the media, which was a comfortable, cowardly warning. She had to push the limits. She remembered a phrase used frequently by politicians in power. "Either we invent or we err." She would have to invent. Events? Who was she providing with clues through her information in the crime section? She decided to disinform. She had the names of Lourdes and Sergio on her desk. When the messenger arrived, she was about to write her article, she was going to mention the minister's friends as suspects in the events in Puerto Píritu; but because of the situation she was facing, she kept quiet, it was what they expected of her, so she took a risk with an article that dealt with the serious confrontations between the Minister of Internal Affairs and the Minister of Defense. Both of them had different versions of the assassination attempt against the president. Both of them had identified guilty parties, and they didn't coincide. She knew about the struggles within the heart of the government and she decided to emphasize them. She was pretending not to have understood what was being communicated through the kidnapped messenger.

She checked the schedule of activities for the President of the Republic. She gave her resignation to the newspaper, her editor was astonished. She told him she had reached a breaking point, Jorge's kidnapping was overwhelming her. As far as she was concerned, the matter ended with her latest article. The newspaper could continue the investigation. That same afternoon she left for Miami.

She didn't stay a day in Miami. She changed the color of her hair and cut it all off, she changed the color of her eyes and had an Argentine passport made for herself, she then took a flight to Toronto and from there she took a direct flight to Margarita. She didn't have a plan, but she would be in Oriente province, with a few contacts and her eyes wide open.

Manuela was moving through Porlamar like a tourist. She was tall, pale, and the reddish color of her hair, now very short, her clear and varying eyes, blue and aquamarine, made her pass for just another Canadian out shopping with a camera in her hand. It was easy to imitate one, she would spend the mornings sitting at the terrace of a cafe, looking at maps and along with them the regional newspapers, she would stop at any event, a bank robbery, the death of a policeman, open and inexplicable cases, she was looking for the trail of the minister's comrades, but without contacts she'd get nowhere. She had reached a dead point. She was investigating without any tools. She couldn't do it any other way, using her tools would mean placing herself in the open, being found, and if they found her the pressure would begin. There was no way she'd be able to get anything out in the open. She started to feel despondent. She was beginning to feel her undertaking was insane. It made no sense to do what she was doing. With Vladimiro Montesino's case everything was easier. The informants were men who were "close" to the government, who thought that by manipulating the press and journalists they could get rid of their burden, confuse and attack those people whom they would use in the future as scapegoats. You can't get information unless you place yourself in the middle of a war of interests, she thought. In the case of Manuel Roca's comrades, she had perceived that the information flowed from one sector confronting another, from the enemies of the minister in the cabinet, placing her in a classic position, in the middle of a power struggle. But her informants didn't reach her as she would have liked, they encrypted information, made it hermetic, they were spasmodic, acting much too cautiously. They had put her on the trail and on the case, and yet they never gave her conclusive elements so that she might follow a specific trail.

She was alone, without her editor's support, and she was no longer the key journalist who needed to be manipulated in the conflict. She wasn't living through a conventional situation. And what if she managed to detect something? How would she approach it? She decided to call Rigoberto Marquina, a fellow journalism student who had gone on to work in the provinces. He could help her, they could share the credit. But how would she motivate Rigoberto? He had given up on having a career in the city in order to avoid getting caught up in big cases. He willingly accepted a mediocre situation that, according to him, brought him closer to happiness. Working at the *Clarín de Oriente* he had built a quiet life for himself, he was in charge of different sections, he was an adviser to the editors, a type of wise man who gave opportune advice. He didn't get into any problems. How would she involve him?

The afternoon was clear and luminous. She didn't miss the opalescent sky of Caracas that was burning on all sides. The city was burning and the blues that contrasted with the greens of Mount Ávila were gone, the Ávila had been scorched, it revealed hills of ashes and withered vegetation, suffocated by the smoke. In Porlamar the days were a festival of lights, she remembered the paintings of Armando Reverón and looked around her, forms were surging from the light, life was being summoned by the whites and blues, a bronze life adhering to the reality of the island. Manuela sat at a hotel bar with her shopping bags. She was trying to be a tourist, playing in the casinos, staring at the islanders who would lasciviously serve travelers. She was a mature, exuberant and enchanting woman. Rigoberto walked up to the bar, he was a tall man who used baggy, flowered shirts, loose pants, a Panama hat. A ruddy, festive man with a generous belly. Despite his neglect, he was attractive, with a two-day beard, with small glasses and an intellectual air. Things were going pretty well for him and he had his charms among the native fauna and even among the tourists; he was the man of contacts and he didn't stand out. In reality, no one stood out on the island. The island wasn't a boring place, many things were moving in and out of the hotels, including mafias, gaming, trafficking of drugs and prostitutes, fundamental components for a dangerous cocktail. However, an unspoken truce that existed between the parts, the territories clearly outlined, the complacent functionaries, and that new management rule of highly successful businessmen, win-win, was the reason peace reigned in Venezuela's largest tourist center. Traditionally, Margarita always had the lowest crime rate, now it had the lowest number of conflicts between criminals, and the jails were only filled with everyday people, thieves, people looking for a fight who never managed to come to their senses. The criminals, the real transgressors, reigned above legality or illegality.

Manuela smiled at Rigoberto, revealing a big and beautiful smile, she seemed like a happy woman. He opened his arms and extended them towards her, hugged her and filled her with kisses.

"Darling, darling, my God, you're looking so beautiful... The island air, the vacation, it's all done you really well." He was shouting, emphasizing his words, he seemed like a character out of a movie about the Italian mafia in New York. "You're so bad, you've been here several days and haven't called Uncle Rigoberto. I should punish you for that. I should, just for that, I shouldn't show you the dark side of this marvelous island. If you don't know it, you don't know anything."

"I went to Silguero," Manuela answered, without responding to his excessive affection.

"Don't be vulgar, woman. What do you think, that just because you go to a street with whores, fags and transvestites, with cheap dives, that turns you into someone who knows about a good night on the Island? Please, Manuela, you're displaying the naiveté I can't stand about you."

Manuela grabbed Rigoberto's hands and took him to a table under a thatched roof. The waiter brought them two whiskies, she didn't stop staring at his ass. Then she turned her glance, lit up by mischief, toward Rigoberto.

"The men on this island have better asses than the women."

She briefly explained her intentions to Rigoberto. He had followed her in the press, she laid out her conclusions about the whole matter for him and asked for his help.

"My dear, you're working alone," the advisor for *Clarín de Oriente* told her. "You've turned into a kind of solitary heroine. That only works in the movies."

"I can't work any other way. There's almost a state of emergency. They're already talking about a military democracy, without bothering to keep up appearances, it doesn't make sense, but public opinion has already been fixed. They've put pressure on me at the newspaper and my sources have been more cautious. They sent me a message. And I can't help but follow my instincts. Something's happening in Oriente. The minister's comrades, according to my count there aren't many of them left, are about to wage their final battle in Puerto La Cruz, in Cumaná, or here. Two of them are out of control, I'm assuming they're the ones that made the attempt on the president's life, my hypothesis is that the attempt was a laboratory move made by Manuel Roca, after which he decided to dismantle his party and eliminate his military command, which was minimal but effective. In fact the majority of his men have already died, I wrote about it all for the newspaper."

The afternoon was fading away, the night was falling with shades of pink. It was an absurd and sticky afternoon, a ridiculous afternoon, Manuela was thinking, while Rigoberto continued to smile, his smile revealing his intention of remaining on the margins, he was trying to figure out how to discourage Manuela.

"Darling, darling, don't complicate your life," he murmured. "No one in this country complicates their life more than they need to. Where's the opposition? Nowhere, and it won't be appearing any time soon. Don't you understand? Everyone wins now with that man, everyone is that man who talks to us and leads us, we're watching a country that's readjusting itself and what's coming is a civilian-military democracy, or simply military, despite the fact that it's, what do you call it, an oxymoron! No one's going to notice that and if they do it will be to let out a few hysterical howls or to ponder the originality of the event. What do you hope to find, Manuela?"

"The truth."

"You're surprising me, darling. You chose to make your career in Caracas, you've had some good cases, you have the National Prize for Journalism, we know you're a go-getter, that you're objective, that no one's about to catch you being naïve. The truth, Manuela?" He squealed when he asked this. "You're talking like the worst provincial journalist. Remember that I'm the worst provincial journalist and I'm not going after the truth. I'm going after the news."

"The news is an expression of the truth or it's the truth expressed, in the raw."

"Darling, darling," he put his arms around her, he took her by the shoulders, he looked at her eyes that weren't green but blue, too clear, albino. "Take all this as a vacation, look for the nice things in life, that's the only possible truth. A good lay? Fall in love? The news expresses a part of life, life is already pretty distorted on its own, it's no longer truth, it's a consequence of unspeakable manipulations."

"Don't start talking like such a sophist, you little piece of shit."

The journalist stuck his tongue out at her.

Manuela ordered more drinks and remained quiet. She was thinking the hour had come to retire, her career had ended on the day they erased Marquitos's face, on the day she wasn't able to connect with the phrase that marked her life: "Whoever doubts and fails to investigate becomes not only unhappy but unjust." And if truth didn't exist in journalism, she told herself, and if truth didn't exist, certainty did exist, certainty is the closest thing to truth.

"But it's not the truth, " Rigoberto squealed again.

"Listen to me closely, you little shit," she pinched his cheek. "I didn't come here to the island to resolve a matter of semantics, I haven't lived for something like that. If the truth isn't outside, it's right here," she hit her chest with her closed fist, "my truth, and my truth motivates me."

"That's just arbitrary."

"It could be. And what isn't arbitrary, the choice of life you've made? That's a crude case of arbitrariness."

"I love you. Did you know that?" Rigoberto smiled slyly. "I was always in love with you. I would have married you, that was my truth for a while."

"Will you help me or not? That's the dilemma." She summoned him.

"You don't leave me any alternative." He brought his face close to hers and gave her a clean, fleeting and noncommittal kiss on her thick red lips.

Manuela didn't get a room at the five star hotel. She rented a room at a modest inn near Pampatar. There she received the material to begin her research. Rigoberto would visit her each afternoon, they would have a drink together and she would go back to her work. She was gathering the elements. She was exhausted and nothing was clear. She knew about Manuel Roca and the comrades who had died, Silvestre, Dominguín, the others, even Abelardo himself. She knew everything about several versions of the minister's life, she was looking for coincidences and with them she was putting together an unofficial biography of him and a history of the party. At what moment did Roca's project coincide with that of the president, how had he been useful to the process or the regime? His participation in the Tricontinental. That was one point. The minister had been committed to national liberation fronts from other countries and he trained his men in the deserts of North Africa; Manuela recalled a legend; a Venezuelan who was training contingents of important organizations in terrorist camps; ineffable and ubiquitous, another comrade? It was said this Venezuelan was the best. And she asked herself if he wasn't involved in the knot surrounding the attempt or in that silent war of deaths and disappearances. Alba Rosa González (Lourdes), where was she hiding, where had she gone? Roberto Díaz (Sergio, many say he was Abelardo's pupil), what was he up to? He would be the third man who was present at the attempt and escaped, if this was true, or he was still fleeing or he was planted somewhere underground. Alba and Roberto, together, in life and death the sacrament of fatality.

Manuela would go out immediately after sunset and jump in the water. There she felt the blows of the waves, the pulse of a brute life beyond her, she would let that feeling caress her, her skin giving itself over to a voluptuous game, she felt arousal and pleasure when she lay on her back in the sea, on a blue, green, crystalline sheet, keeping the rhythm as she swam, it was breathing and movement like sex, she felt a tingling inside, the fullness of well-being, annulling her thoughts, she let herself be possessed by images and she saw an old house with a big patio flanked by columns covered by star jasmine, a withered vine and a cherry tree, in a fishing village. It didn't mean anything, the shadows collided there, they were lives in the background of an arid landscape, inside a mirror; a bonfire, the breeze that cuts, the unleashed elements, lights in the darkness, shadows that loved each other, that ate and licked each other, penetrating and leaving their shadows; shadows that took refuge in the night, in an old house, in a fishermen's village, there three figures, real and tormented, three figures that were superimposed on the shadows and danced with them, three figures that suddenly left and came back, that pulled her while she swam and the truth is one and undivided: the image of the old house with wide corridors, the ululating and voluptuous shadows, she sensed the odor of iodine and salt and the strange smell of the figures, a smell of metal, of silver, bronze, acrimony; there's goodness in the smell. Why did I see this recurring image?

She got out, dried herself and sat for a while on the shell of a boat that was resting on the sand of the beach, near the fishermen's nets; she was a tourist lost in her thoughts. Suddenly she became aware of the distance. Suddenly she felt she had intervened and was superimposed on the lives of Sergio and Lourdes; life in death, she was outside and the image of the shadows, or fishermen's houses insisted; the conviction that Sergio and Lourdes were protected by shadows beneath giant eaves became stronger. Pure Image. She was near a voluptuous universe of flexible bodies.

Nonsense, this wasn't a novel, this wasn't about giving space to the aesthetics of the author of a novel, this was reality, it wasn't a story put together by a novelist, it was reality, she remembered her fevers as a child, the awkwardness of the fevers, of Blaise Pascal's sentence, of the final shadows. She was startled by having worked in solitude. She had conceived her labor as a solitary exercise, a mystical activity, even though she was always surrounded by people who, without doing what she was, did similar things or worked toward their goals. Alone, now she was alone.

She returned to the inn. She had a frugal dinner, barely tried the crab salad and a cup of white wine. She went to her room and started to contrast events: the ones that had a source, the crimes that had been perpetrated by a band, an organization or a cartel. Crime has its web, it is a phenomenon that organizes itself; a type of ID exists for those who move within that web, they acquire it when they begin to commit crimes and the organizations recognize each other; the independents, the professionals, the police. Each crime has a name, a signature. No one can act outside of this web. Independence is a romantic notion, the solitary man ends up with a bullet to the head.

Thus, the minister's comrades have their IDs. Manuela understood them as she did everything that happened spontaneously. The acts without signatures are the acts of Sergio and Lourdes; only minor crimes could have no mark. Manuela checked the statistics of minor crimes and it was in Puerto La Cruz that they had increased, with robberies committed against small businesses and tourists, policemen disarmed, cars stolen.

After a week of having gone clandestine, Manuela reached a conclusion. Her instinct and her investigation, the handling of statistics, the vague conversations with Rigoberto, these were all leading her to an improbable place. While the crimes without a signature could very well be the acts of Roca's comrades, the possibility also existed that they were simply minor crimes committed by thieves, budding criminals, undocumented people. This is what Rigoberto told her.

"My dear, you're delirious." He touched her forehead. They were having breakfast at the inn.

"I'm not an amateur. I'm following a pattern. It's a constant that can be corroborated ever since the events at Puerto Píritu." She took a roll from a basket and put jelly on it.

"You astonish me!" It was too early to deal with Rigoberto's squeals, the other guests turned around to look at the table with the journalists.

"Try not to call attention to us, dear."

"You're paranoid, Manuela," Rigoberto put on an affected voice. He was talking in whispers. The waitress kept looking back at them. "You'd have to find paternity for all the minor crimes that are committed in this country. This is a country with an informal economy, of informal crimes, of Bedouin criminals."

"I'm not basing my analysis on the informality of the crimes. If you study the pattern of these events," she handed him a jumble of documents and notes, "they have a characteristic in common, they're erratic, no one recognizes the thieves, some of the witnesses point out a couple, a couple in the narrowest sense of the word, a couple that moves with haste, omnipresent, attacking all over the place in Puerto La Cruz."

"You're making me tired." He made a gesture of annoyance with his hand and drank a glass of pineapple juice, finishing half of it. "What do you want from me?"

"For you to hire me."

"You're crazy!"

"Don't hire Manuela, hire an intern, an independent journalist who'll be your correspondent for current events on the mainland."

"You want it and I'll do it. But it's the last thing I'm doing for you and I won't take any responsibility. You're about to be locked up in a madhouse, I don't want to be responsible for the aggressive treatments you'll have to undergo."

Manuela sat up straight in her chair and put her arms around Rigoberto's neck from across the table. She brought her cheek close to the journalist's face. She was performing acrobatic stunts so as to not lose her balance and fall on their breakfast. She gave him a kiss.

"And you actually kiss, woman?"

The sun fell vertically on the tropics. From dawn the sun was in its zenith. The light was invasive, total. It swept reality, the sand on the beaches, the streets and avenues, the docks and towns, the containers, the cumulus clouds, it swept the embankment where people strolled, came with the breeze, with the entire morning that would become day; several acts in one, the light that swept vertically from dawn to dusk, the surface of an equinoctial world. Manuela kept up her routine in the port. She stayed in a room at a small inn, in an upper story; a room on the terrace of an old house, from where she had a privileged view of Colón Boulevard. She showed up at the offices of *Clarín de Oriente* and went to the police precinct to gather data about the latest crimes. The visit to the police added nothing to her investigation. A robbery at a bodega, an assault against a couple of solitary tourists, the inopportune visits to gas stations, these were all routine for them. In her notebook she underlined the couple's actions, she individualized them, she knew who they were, they weren't the crimes of a couple, they weren't men or women, they were the couple, Sergio and Lourdes.

Who were Sergio and Lourdes? She remembered her fevers; the abandoned house that kept appearing in her dreams; inhabited by shadows; she had counted them, there were five shadows. But the ghosts were not alone, the ghosts would gather at the end of a hallway under a cherry tree and a withered grape vine, around a woman wearing a small dress; her skin was white and her eyes big and black, a naked woman, of metallic odors, surrounded by sexual avatars, ready at her command, who executed their moves like circus numbers.

The shadows were not alone. Who was with the shadows? You. You ask the little bed directly, the bed is hard and comfortable, nicely dressed with very clean, white sheets. The question comes and goes like the waves of an oceanic beach, repeats itself forcefully, this dream is an obsession, this recurring image that becomes reality, on your bad nights, nights when your temperature rises, in which you're overwhelmed by anguish, you know you're moving in the right direction, that whatever needs to be known will somehow be known, but you don't know anything, you're in the middle of that sun that embraces you, that doesn't let you go, not even in the darkness of the nights, when the warm breeze blows and makes your room a welcoming and melancholy place; you sit there, looking at the windows; they're old windows with wooden blinds, framed in wide rectangles, and through them the luminous points of the night enter, the wind blows, the aromas of the sea move around outside, the aromas of the woman who is sitting under the cherry tree and a withered grape vine, the aroma of those who are observing her. You feel as though you're involved. You see a young woman wearing green bell bottomed pants, a jacket with long sleeves that she bites with her fingers like pincers, she's wearing nothing underneath, her breasts are outlined and they are beautiful, breasts that stand out, in a harmonious way, breasts that transmit calm, she herself is calm, the beautiful, melancholic shadow, and everyone arrives with the night, Lourdes and Sergio arrive with the ghosts, what relationship could they have with the ghosts. You realize that you're also there. You've always been there. That it's not very professional to believe in ghosts and in Sergio and Lourdes. They're together, you know the house exists, the ghosts are not a lie and Lourdes and Sergio are a couple who are spreading those small stories that become legendary throughout the Oriente region of the country. The night passes and you go into the streets and will work on your journalism, your source is the street, the sun that falls vertically from birth to sunset, the sun that doesn't disappear at night, the angel of morning, midday and nighttime, perennial and tropical, that comes with the breeze and the aroma of waters stirred with salt. You go into that street, that crowd, and you blend in with the people, you go to the markets and look at the vendors' eyes and look for the news in their eyes and you search in the eyes of those who visit the market and you search among that night's catch for the couple that has become a heroic figure in Oriente, comrades on the run, a piece by Bach, harmonious, perfect and immortal and their eyes could encounter yours in the market, at a stall where they sell empanadas or the soup of the day, the corn tamales, the cachapas, it's so picturesque, you think and breathe deeply, you feel ridiculous amid a landscape that seems baroque to you, but their eyes could be there, four fixed eyes that freeze the immense passion of those who are fleeing. You visit the places where they've committed their crimes, people speak of them with sympathy, they stand there, they are hard and they threaten with firmness, they don't hesitate, they know what they're doing, they present themselves suddenly like strange and impossible figures and impose themselves violently, they don't need to threaten anyone for cash registers or pockets to be emptied, money goes toward them like fate, cars are handed over to them like an offering, they curse and barely draw a grimace on their faces, they express an unprecedented and senseless confidence. The others were born to be robbed and stripped of their belongings, that's life and they're the executors. It's them, the colleagues of the shadows, the lovers of the shadows, the dead that move about with life and resist the reality that pursues them in the form of a government or of mercenaries. You know you were born for this, you understand that people are born for other people and that you were not born to reveal the arrangements of the Montesinos case nor to tell the world how some fishermen murdered on the banks of a river were not guerrillas but rather victims of a macabre extortion stunt. No, all of that had been important and was now subordinate, you were attracted to the shadows that watched the shadows in the big house of a fishing village, that irrational empathy that was being built in your fevers and dreams. You're born for something and not just for death. You're born to find figures at the margin who reaffirm an unknown condition that keeps itself alive in people's souls, they aren't heroes, they are the anonymous springs of history, you like to think of them as that, as the losers who make the real history. You should ask yourself if history in all its rigor actually exists, but you don't, you're not interested. The eyes, their mouths, the gestures. You'd give your life for an interview with Sergio and Lourdes. And you see your days and nights immersed in your fevers that are thoughts, you wander the streets and blend in with the tourists, they could be among tourists, you just have to find one clue, the police don't give you one, you lack sources, you wait for the miracle and reduce yourself to your fevers at night in your room at the inn and the fear comes, you won't be able to meet the challenge and what use is living then, you're in danger, you know that no one is in more danger than those who disappoint the expectations of an incomprehensible but accurate design.

In the middle of the night the stars are up high, it rains, the rain is a rain of marine elements, the strong rain of the open sea, the water bangs against the wooden blinds. The lightning flashes on your fevers and the inn surrenders to the routine sounds of the evening. You are fixed like a thought. Fixed like a butterfly on a cork, you're sitting still with bags under your eyes, your body clothed in panties and a thin white t-shirt, white on white, the sheets in the blue of the evening and your body on the white sheets, in perspective, in the background, one can see from the room's high ceiling, the door opens and a man walks in, the darkness and the black suit, a human mass that subdues you, silences you, climbs on top of you and smells you, smells your nearly naked body, smells your sweat and the fever, the shadows, he wants to rob the shadows and the shadows resist, his face is yellow, his eyes fixed, he's big, you feel you're being suffocated by the tallest man in the world and it's your uncle and your grandmother is looking at you and puts her finger to her mouth so you'll be quiet, it's not your uncle, he closes your mouth, he says he'll take his hand off your mouth if you promise not to scream, that he won't harm you; and yet, he passes his hands over your bare legs, he turns you over and says he's about to take his hand away from your mouth, that he wants you to get dressed, to accompany him on an errand. You both have interests in common, you're both on the same road, he tells you, he whispers, you won't regret it, it's not death or the end of life, get dressed, I'm not going to do anything to you, we'll talk about your friends, about my friends. He takes his hand away from your mouth and you think you should scream loudly, with more pain than panic, you're on the edge of painful situations, life is painful and the scream that stops comes from your lungs, your eyes look at the hand that was gagging you, a finger stops you from screaming, it's not your grandmother's finger that asks you to keep quiet, it's a dead finger, with withered ulcers. Later on you'll find out that it's Lorca's finger.

Elmer was in the center of the room. Not Manuela's room. Elmer smoked a Cuban cigar, his mocking grimace never varied. They'd crossed Puerto La Cruz in the rain. The neon lights of the hotels were blue and red and the lightning blue and red, green. It rained, the fleeting rains by the sea smell of the sea, they'd crossed the entire city and they hadn't gone to a hotel or inn, they'd gone to a house on the cliffs, a large ostentatious house, without any furniture, in a neighborhood under construction; a model house. The atmosphere was serious, Lorca and Manuela burst into the room, there were two easy chairs, they sat Manuela down in one of them. Lorca remained standing, at her side, they didn't turn on the lights, you could barely see Elmer's baldness, you could barely see the sinuosity of the face from the glow of the cigar when it was smoked, his mocking grimace; there was a light on somewhere in the house, it could have come from a small room, a bathroom. The silence extended, outside it continued to rain.

"So," he puffed on the cigar, "you're Manuela."

She was sitting still, serene. She neither affirmed nor denied it.

"Admired Manuela. The president likes you. He's looking after your safety."

She thought they were playing at creating an atmosphere of complicity and trust.

"That makes me proud."

"It puts you in danger, Manuela."

"Are you sure?"

"Those of us who are protected by the president always end up in a ditch in the countryside."

He included himself. Looking for complicity.

"So you're protected by the president. What nonsense have you committed in order to be the object of such grace?"

Elmer blew out a puff of smoke and smiled.

"A lot of it. I can assure you I'm ahead of you in that regard."

"Let's see," Manuela said tensely, without leaning back in the easy chair. "You and I admire the president. This must be the meeting of the president's fans. Is the man in black another hero? Does the president admire you or do others admire you? At least I've been admired by two or three presidents and I intend to gain the admiration of future leaders."

The room was silent. Lorca moved closer to Manuela. Elmer let a big smile spread across his face.

"I assume you have a fan club."

"You can assume whatever you'd like. Meanwhile, I assume that I've been kidnapped."

"We're in a free country and you can think whatever you'd like."

"And this man? You haven't answered my question. Is he another person the president admires?"

"Will you answer her?" Elmer said to Lorca.

Lorca didn't move or make a gesture.

"We're wasting time. Let's discuss what we need to, I can take care of my own admirers."

"So, you're not admired by anyone?"

"You can think whatever you'd like," Lorca spat out, always at her side. "You can begin, for example, by telling us what you think of Lourdes and Sergio."

Manuela leaned back into the easy chair. She was confused. She was starting to feel nervous. She knew she was in trouble and that she wouldn't come out of this unscathed.

"Well," Elmer said, moving the cigar around his lips, "we have objectives in common, dear Manuela, and we'd like to come out of this in the best way possible. That means, safe and sound, and with the rest of our lives ahead of us. Doesn't that idea appeal to you in controversial times?"

"As much as it does to you," Manuela responded. "My instincts tell me that you're both comrades. Do you follow me when I say the word comrade? It's not a matter of semantics, no. You are The Comrades. And comrades seek out their comrades. The affairs of comrades are worked out among comrades. Isn't that true? I'd like to interview you. Could we set up an interview?"

"First we should resolve some other things, dear Manuela," Elmer answered while he brought the cigar to his mouth and pulled a generous mouthful of smoke.

"I prefer Lorca's style." Manuela lifted her eyes and saw the unmoving figure of the man at her side. "He's a man who doesn't beat around the bush."

"Definitely. He's an executive in our business." Elmer emphasized his smile, nearly laughing. Lorca remained without a gesture, beside Manuela. "So then," he puffed his cigar once more, "let's just say that we have friends in common, which makes us comrades. Right?"

"That's your point of view."

"Lourdes and Sergio are comrades who are very scared," Elmer continued, "and they're wandering around the country committing absurdities. They're out of control."

"Roca's comrades?" Manuela asked.

"Yes. And yours and mine and his," he pointed to Lorca. "That makes us responsible. Some colleagues think they should be dead."

"And what do you think?" the journalist interrupted once again.

"I don't think they should die. You're an educated person and you remember that verse by John Donne, if they die we will also die, if I were to write a novel or an article about this case I'd be tempted to repeat the name of Hemingway's novel, the bells toll for us, dear Manuela. If they fall, oh Manuelas of the world, if they fall!" He smiled when he thought of how he was using literary references in his own haphazard way, and that all the references were somehow taken from the literature of the Spanish Civil War. "Let's just say that I've spent a long time in this business of making revolutions, that I know how the mechanisms of this not-so-complicated clockwork function. It shouldn't catch anyone by surprise."

"Are you talking to me about purges?"

"I'm telling you that one group wants to impose itself on another and because of that it's seeking alliances with other groups, then the allied group will be taken out of the political picture by another alliance and so forth until the end."

"The end?"

"Yes, that's the detail. The end doesn't exist. And we, dear friend, you and I and our friend, we aren't even halfway between the beginning and the end, we're intangible."

"Are you a group? I only see people who are killing each other."

"You can see it however you'd like. But you should be aware that you're no longer outside all this."

"So then, what are we doing here at this informal gathering?" Manuela's mouth stayed open, searching for a word. "Could you give me some water, or a soft drink? I'm thirsty."

The air had become thick, after the rain, the humidity, the saltpeter and iodine were gaining mass, becoming an unbreathable matter. Lorca was barely gone for a few minutes and came back with a plastic bottle of mineral water.

"Evian. Though you might not believe it." Manuela saw a trace of a smile on the hard man's face.

"Let's say that we're demolition engineers and we're trying to take apart the clockwork that will make a big bomb explode," Elmer continued as though he hadn't been interrupted. "There's a way of stopping this mechanism. It doesn't matter now if we're individuals or groups killing each other, what matters to us is that we're doing it and that the means of stopping the mechanism actually exist."

"How?"

"By killing the president."

"You're crazy." Manuela stopped herself from screaming. "I don't know what the true nature of your game is, maybe you just want to involve me in a conspiracy, to make public opinion see me involved in a conspiracy, maybe you've gone crazy and have reasons for killing the president. I don't know. I'm not interested, I don't want to know anything else. Do you understand? I want out of this stupidity."

"It's late, Manuela, and it's true, you're alone, just as out of control as Lourdes and Sergio. It would be easy to make it seem as if you were involved in some ridiculous event. But just the same, let me repeat, there's an implacable clockwork that will mark the hour for each of us, unless we stop the mechanism."

"I'm inferring that we'll do this by killing the president."

"No, my friend. I'm not asking you for so much." Elmer knocked the ash off his cigar. "A while ago, Sergio started a job he needs to finish, and we can clear the way for him. The problem is that neither my colleague nor I can get close to the comrades, we would end up killing each other. But you, on the other hand, can do that, offer them an interview, an exit toward freedom, their declarations would help them escape the hunter's net, the dismal plague, in your interview you could provide them with details about the presidential visit and they would spend some time with you."

The darkness was turning blue, turning pale, turning into salty light. The atmosphere was of a clear moon grey. Manuela realized this was a situation that could banish her from the world of the living and the dead. She was about to make a pact and didn't know with what, if they were forces of good or evil, if that man with the cigar was Mephistopheles and she was Faust. Who might Margarita be? She glimpsed at Lorca and smiled. Regardless, she felt like she was up to her neck in a muddle. She thought the part about power's clockwork was true, she had verified it throughout her career, though never in such a dramatic manner.

"We know where they are. We've located them." Lorca was speaking for the first time. "As you can see, we haven't wanted to liquidate them, though it would have been easy."

"And wouldn't you have finished a job, wouldn't you be relieved without the pressure from Manuel Roca?"

Elmer sighed deeply, so much that he made noise.

"My dear friend, you haven't understood anything. You're right about one thing. If we had finished our job the pressures of this world would be over for us. See, behind us stand our killers and behind them stand others, and so on. You have a golden opportunity, the golden opportunity in this life is to survive, surviving once you're in this business is a hard thing, it's a complicated matter, do you understand?"

Manuela nodded. The mist installed itself in the white darkness of the room. She was thirsty again. She would always be thirsty. She let her head move and nod. Her sense, her life, what the Greeks called *aletheia;* her truth, her hour.

VISITATION

Just the same, time hadn't passed. This is what I was thinking. And if it had passed it was manifesting its course in a
flat manner, with no other dimensions. Time manifests itself
and is not. That's what I was thinking. I thought a great deal,
I had no space to think, but I would do it, it was the only way
of maintaining some sanity. When we were in Puerto Píritu,
Sonia answered my questions about her evanescence, I had a
mistaken appreciation of phenomena. Time, existence, sanity. I
was measuring it all from my claustrophobic temporality. She
had begun to disrupt my certainties. I had many of them, I had
been formed in the light of a thought that allowed no fissures.
At what point did the fissures start in my thought? When Silvestre opened his mouth and put the barrel inside and blew his
head off? When Sonia took me to the house in the fishermen's
village? That night when Olga placed her haunches in front of
me, opened herself, devoured me, made pain and death of me
in the empty room of the old house with high ceilings? When
I saw Carla's small and well-shaped legs, her face? When I understood they were on the other side of the mirror and that I
was dealing with shadows? When I didn't question the pas-
sions of the group of somnambulists and I included myself?
When was the fissure? During the visitation of Lourdes, her
smile, her imposition, the escape? The casualties, too many of
them, one after another as though I were acting in a bad novel?

The fissure was real and I was no longer myself and my house was not my house. I was walking far away. I was in Puerto La Cruz, I wore a shirt with palm trees and very blue and yellow colors, shorts and my hair a mess, full of gel. I was a tourist on Colón Boulevard. We were doing all right. We survived on the hope of going to Trinidad. We had managed to stabilize ourselves, we rented a room on the outskirts of the city, we took up residency next to a community of artisans, we didn't look like artisans, but that never interested them, we bought their trinkets and went out to sell them. I felt safe once more, we could spend as much time as we wanted among them, doing small robberies to supplement ourselves, quick details, a store, a hairdressing salon, any small business that had its cash register full of money would do for us, we'd make do with the crumbs until we had enough to be able to go to Sucre, reach Güiria and take a launch to Trinidad. To head toward my origins, where my grandfather's father had come from, to try to make it to London and lose ourselves, she and I each on our own, that's what we would do; it would be for the best. For now we needed each other and we loved each other because we needed each other, necessity is terrifying, Ayuso says, and necessity is the real incentive, the only one, the one that imposes itself. The worst had already happened. Escaping from Elmer and Lorca, breaking through the trap around Puerto Píritu, making ourselves invisible. Lourdes was waiting for me at home. I was supposed to return with oil to clean the weapons. She kept insisting that the time had come to do something bigger than robbing grocery stores and gas stations. We needed money to leave the country. Lourdes wouldn't stop pestering me, I should have stayed with Carla, I would have died with them, Carla smelled of bullets or gunpowder and blood, she had the smell of gunshots, of weapons and the wounded. Now I wanted to spend some time among the artisans, but Lourdes kept insisting and talking, she said we couldn't waste any time, that Roca's men were probably already about to find us, and that's why we wouldn't expropriate any more in Puerto La

Cruz, or yes, we would pull off a big robbery in the port of Guanta. We would break the pattern. She had all the details covered, she had bought a legal car and through our artisan friends had contacted a guy who would give us four passports. I was furious. By having passports made for us we had left traces. She said that at a certain point we had no choice but to leave traces, in any case, we wouldn't stay long enough to be hunted down. I stopped at a kiosk and bought a newspaper, the *Clarín de Oriente,* I looked at the crime page. The president had said that the conspiracy of the assassination attempt had been dismantled. That the interests in opposition to the revolution remained active and were conspiring to kill him. He was giving a press conference, Manuel Roca was at his side, they claimed that the media had kept up a campaign against him, after being notified that some constitutional guarantees remained suspended ever since the assassination attempt on the Day of the Homeland, with the goal of discrediting the policies set forth by the Minister of Internal Affairs to stabilize the country, to rid it of the counterrevolutionary threat and restore democracy and a sense of security. Roca responded to a journalist, his comrades were doing fine, they had been integrated into the process. That he would accompany the president to Puerto La Cruz to inaugurate the work of the government in the state of Anzoátegui. He would be there with his comrades. I felt a chill down my back. My glasses lit up with the sunset, I had the intense orange glow trapped in the darkness of its crystals. He was speaking of his comrades, a journalist had asked him about his comrades and he said they were doing fine and were integrated into the revolutionary process. They would come to Puerto La Cruz to be among comrades. The sovereign people, the governor, the president and him. The people of Puerto La Cruz, all his comrades, would come to us and then I felt as though the revelation were descending, the state of grace, the truth. Roca's arm was long and we would never escape. I went back to Lourdes with the newspaper. I told her that the journalist who had asked the compromising

question had disappeared. Why would we pull off the big robbery? They would always be able to reach Trinidad or they
would kill us in the suburbs of London, Lorca was the type of
man who never tired of walking and he would go around the
world, once, twice, three times if necessary, until he found us.

We left to meet with the man who would have our passports, I had placed a .44 at my waist, under my baggy beach
shirt, Lourdes was taking her indispensable .38 in a cloth hand-
bag. We had built a better arsenal, we even had grenades and
an Armalit AR-50 rifle. I had learned how to shoot with those
detachable, 12-pound rifles. That's why I chose myself for the
attempt against the president, because I had been the best, the
only one who could change the course of history, of events, with
a single shot, I had shot at targets from long distances and I had
never missed, moving targets, cars, and I hadn't missed, I was
the best; I didn't know much about hand to hand combat nor
explosives, but I knew how to shoot, I remembered Lourdes,
her inspiring mouth that accompanied me day and night when
I would shoot, her mouth that would come to me and burn my
glans at the same instant as the hammer burned the cartridge's
gunpowder in the chamber; the mouth that saved me on the
day of the assassination attempt; Sonia's mouth? The day Paris
was burning.

The place where we decided to meet the guy with the passports was near the terminal for the ferries that cross to Margarita. The man never showed up, I began to feel paranoid, fifteen
minutes went by and I was already grabbing Lourdes's arm to
pull her by her hand, to push her if it was necessary, waiting
could mean the end; nothing good ever came of it. The night
was going by heavily, the noise on the boulevard was insidi-
ous, the music coming out of the cafes, the ice cream shops, the
sky was cloudless and a thick breeze was flowing. *It will drag
me along*, I thought, it made my beach shirt cling to my body
and reveal the outline of my .44.

"Let's go. It was never a good idea to have passports made
for us."

"These guys are always late," she calmed me down.

"You know the guy?"

"Five minutes." I opened my fist and showed her my five fingers. "Five."

The night was no different from any other night. People were swarming along the boulevard, nothing strange was happening; and yet, I was trembling, I felt feverish, the closeness of a dream, a presence from somewhere else. Olga? Who's coming? Someone's coming.

Lourdes and I were there. Why didn't we go back to the fishing village? We were waiting for someone, I thought. But for whom? A woman approached Lourdes, she was tall, dressed in a thin, white linen suit, wearing a striped shirt, she looked a lot like Olga but she had short hair. I told myself. Who was she? Olga? I felt an erection. Who's coming? I said to myself.

And she goes and talks to Lourdes and they gesticulate, Lourdes moves her hand toward her bag, and you move yours toward your waist, the woman speaks, gesticulates, her movements are almost desperate, her movements accuse us, draw attention, we have to leave, you think, and you ask yourself what the hell this woman is doing there, why don't you just shoot her and leave her without a face, why don't you flee, disappear into the night, you know there's a trap being set, you intuit the nets they've launched, at any moment they'll pull them in and a hail of bullets will fall and the bodies will drop perforated on the landing, near the terminal, amid the tourists, you'll bleed until you're dry. You'll end up dry as codfish, you know you'll dry out and lie there until the sun comes up. You'd like to run to where Lourdes is talking to the woman, she's crazy, starting to gesticulate wildly, loses control, puts her hand on her head, shakes her red curls, passes her hand across her chest, touches her lip, they both look like mimes, silent film stars, you need to go up to them and find out what's going on, you find out the woman has come to give you the passports, but she doesn't have them on her. What does she mean she's come to give them to us? Who the fuck is she? She wants to speak with you both alone, somewhere else, a cafe, a tavern, you could have a beer, after all, having a beer on the boulevard won't raise any suspicions. Why is a woman who looks like Olga the contact for the guy with the passports? At any moment they'll pull the strings and it'll rain bullets, and then you understood it was Olga, you were back in the shadow game again, she looked like her, with fine features, her thin, red mouth, face of an Anglo-Saxon teenager, a public restroom pickpocket, it was Olga and it wasn't and you were debating yourself in that dilemma and you weren't acting when you needed to act and grab her by the arm, drag her to an alley, check her for weapons, see what she has in her bag, a big bag like a journalist's, at least that's what you thought you heard during a conversation under the withered grape vines in the big house and she said she had come to give you the passports that would get you out of all this trouble, she came to take charge of your lives, she was a journalist, you said it, thought it and you and Lourdes, shouted, What! You threatened her, you started pulling her away, you put your arm around her shoulders. Then you felt the warmth of her skin, a skin you already knew, skin of fever and daydreams, the skin of the women from the fishing village, she looked at you out of the corner of her eyes, you felt a warm erection, you weren't in danger and you felt an erection; you should be in danger because a succubus always appears when you're in danger. Since when? But she's not Olga, she's Manuela, the journalist who asked that son of a bitch Roca about his comrades, she nearly screams it, she begs you not to kill her in one of the alleys; she wants to interview you and propose something, that she had no other option and the game was locked.

"What game, you fucking bitch?"

"The one you began to play when you became comrades and which will never end unless you do a few things to stop the goddamn clockwork system."

"Are you crazy?" She repeats the phrase about the clockwork system, a tick-tock, the march of time that really does exist, fuck, try to understand Sergio, you look at Lourdes, she's just as disconcerted as you are. You corner her in an alley, pull out your gun and point it at her just below her nose, it's a shame to destroy her face, to kill Olga, *break the mirror; even though you've killed a lot of people, you would become a murderer if you killed her. Manuela said she was here on behalf of the comrades, with one option, one exit.*

"What fucking comrades?"

"Elmer and Lorca," she said, you clocked the hammer, you'll become a killer if you shoot her. Where was Elmer? Why wasn't a hail of bullets falling on you from Lorca's automatic pistol? And your rainstorm, Sergio, you had water and fire to keep up the work for days, no, don't shoot her, Lourdes says to you. If Elmer or Lorca had wanted to kill you they wouldn't have sent an emissary, much less the journalist who was making Roca's life impossible. Think, goddamn it, think. All you can think about is taking a bus back to the fishing village, taking Olga and Lourdes, grabbing the porno Venus's legs, licking her like a dog and asking her to intercede, that she cover it with her body smelling of burnt gunpowder on an open wound. Sonia! You clamor and see Lourdes, come here, help me calm down. It's a fucking song!

Lourdes grabs the journalist's arm, leads her through the streets and you're lost among the people, she takes other darker streets, decides to abandon the car, tightens her grip on Manuela's arm, she's a hook that pulls her through the labyrinths of Puerto La Cruz, you arrive at a pizzeria. In front, on the sidewalk, some kids are drinking beer and listening to music sitting on the hood of a jeep. You slap one of the pizza pies, and it flies through the air towards the tables on the terrace, the kids open their mouths and yell at you asking if you're crazy, you pull out your gun from your waist and hit the first one who comes up to you in the face, you curse and invoke his mother, you cock the hammer and kick the beer cans, they start to run and you catch the driver and take his keys. You open the door to the jeep and climb in as though you were mounting a horse's saddle, Lourdes shoves the journalist inside and climbs in after her, you take off with the wheels screeching, chasing after the kids running away, you hit a trash can with the bumper. Hasn't Olga ever seen a similar sequence? She's in the back, you can feel her, her heart's beating fast and she's sweating profusely, her face is covered in sweat. The top half of Lourdes's dress is soaked, you're all covered in sweat and smell the same, the smell of Carla makes it a communion, you're brought together by the night as you lose yourselves in the outskirts of Puerto La Cruz, headed towards the University of Oriente.

I stopped in a clearing, turned around and looked at Manuela, the journalist. What was Manuela's purpose? She told Lourdes she had no intention of being an emissary for Elmer or Lorca. So what the hell was she doing there? How did she know we were trying to get passports to leave the country? Everything was becoming clear. Elmer and Lorca had never lost sight of them, they had always been in their hands. Within shooting range. So I asked myself again, *what are Lourdes's motives? What are Elmer's motives? And Roca's?* I could feel the net spread out beneath my feet, I felt like a fish about to become dinner. They had placed the information in the mouths of fishermen in the Port of Guanta, somehow they had planted the idea in Lourdes that they should give up the modest robberies and pull off a big heist in order to get passports. Lourdes showed up one day at the house in the fishing village. What a great, incredible coincidence. I felt safe in the big house, I had lost track of time and had no other intention besides staying there, trapped between the glare of the sun and the darkness, in the warmth of an immortal embrace with those shadows that gathered beneath the cherry tree and the withered grape vines. Why Olga? Up to what point had he been a victim of a macabre plan ever since he had tried to take the president's life? Life wasn't lived chained to a succession of fortuitous events. Or maybe it was.

I couldn't conceive of Sonia and the reality in the old house as a stage set, a montage, at least not Lourdes's visit. The net was spread out under everyone's feet, Manuela included. He turned around and pointed his .44 at Lourdes.

"Neither one of you is going to fuck me over!" he yelled.

"You're losing your mind," Lourdes confronted him.

"Unhinged. Is there an explanation for this shit?"

"There's no explanation," Lourdes replied, "you're with me or with them."

"And who are they with?"

Manuela had kept herself to the margins in the back of the jeep. She'd remained silent. I thought it was part of the enigma and that she should have given us some indications.

"And you, what do you have to say about all this?"

She shrugged. The air conditioning was freezing our hands. He felt feverish and was starting to ask himself if he was facing delirium. Where was the house with the wide corridors? Where were the shadows?

"I say you should give me an interview."

"What's the point?" Lourdes asked.

"If you give me an interview and I publish it in the press, you're saved. We're exposing a tactic, right?" Manuela rubbed her hands to warm herself up.

"What sense does it make for Elmer and Roca to use you in all this?"

Silence.

Lourdes pretended to go along with the game. You could say she was a character actor.

"Shut up, Lourdes. Don't fuck with me anymore. Tell me once and for all what we're playing. When will I find my bullet?" I insisted.

"You should ask her that," she pointed to Manuela. "Your bullet is in Elmer's gun, I could swear that's where it is."

Another brief silence. The journalist looked at me with her round eyes, her hair short; it shone under the clear moon.

"I told you what I wanted," she paused and looked straight into our eyes. "They want something else and I'm something like their interlocutor." She cleared her throat, she looked beautiful. "It wasn't what I wanted, but I had no choice."

"Stop talking nonsense. Let's talk about us, " I pressed her. "What's the message?"

"Will you give me the interview?"

"We'll see, " Lourdes answered, "everything depends on how much more time we have left to live. Give us the message."

"Elmer and Lorca want you to finish what Sergio started. And for you to also kill Roca."

I felt like emptying my gun. Like kicking. Abelardo used to say that senseless affairs take on meaning as time goes by, it's a matter of being patient, of allowing that Zen materialism that my mentor was so proud of to flow. At one point Abelardo didn't know how to let his Zen materialism flow and he ended up on trial and in a ditch with four bullets in his body. I resented his death but I kept quiet, there was a reason for this revolution, they told me at the time; to understand the reasons for the revolution was to postpone your own death, I now realized, I would die for one of these reasons, I imagined Manuel Roca had good arguments, all of them within a revolutionary logic, now a logic of State; I imagined that Elmer had his own. If he wanted to assassinate Manuel Roca, why was he using me? Lorca was a man of higher capacities. Manuela was talking about the deeds they would accomplish. I could also take out the president. How much time would pass before they killed me? Lourdes remained silent. The night enveloped us, I was tired, I wanted to sleep, seek out a fishermen's shelter and spread my body on the sand, I told Lourdes and Manuela, *I just want to sleep, I don't care what happens, what they do to me while I sleep. I could give a shit.* I would let myself be taken by sleep or by the tide, by Carla's odors, by Olga's ass, by Sonia's tits, by Andrés and Humberto's reasons, we would make a circle, the one drawn by witches, a five-pointed star, a candelabra with seven arms, we would gather magical elements and leave reality outside, that one, the implacable element, the one that closed compartments and filled its reservoir with tragedies. Accepting Abelardo's death meant accepting my own and I wanted to understand, at that moment in which I had no exit, that accepting anyone's death is accepting one's own, but we all have to die, that's not the issue, accepting someone else's violent death is to accept your own violent death, the idea was more coherent when seen in this light, but it was missing something, it had to sound philosophical. I needed to find a fishermen's shelter, lie down on the sand and the fishing nets.

Dawn was coming with the mist from the tides, we rolled down the windows, got out of the car and started to argue. Manuela told us that Elmer was saying that he himself was risking his life in this movement, that we'd only stop the deaths if we killed Manuel Roca and of course, the president. Why the president? We no longer wanted to go beyond, we didn't want to change the course of history. One shot to Roca and then we'd all go back to our fishermen's refuge to spend the rest of our lives sleeping. That was the logic. The minister was the link of the chain that needed to be broken. But why us? Because we were out of the game, we were renegades, comrades who had gone out of control, Lourdes said. They, Elmer and Lorca, had to keep playing the role of being our exterminators and who would guarantee they wouldn't do it once we blew the heads off our men of State? That's where Manuela came in, she would write about us in the press. She was also doomed, I told Lourdes, like they say in bad movies, there's already a bullet with her name on it, she has a ditch or the bottom of the sea for a tomb.

"That depends," the journalist said, "they can't harm me if I'm able to consign my work to a third party."

"They'll already have the third and fourth person flagged."

"But I doubt they'd be able to flag an entire newspaper," she replied.

She was talking as if she were one of us, as though she moved within our current, if such a thing existed, this group of ours. A current of shadows. She made it clear that she was following the news, so then I asked her if a journalist should follow the news or make the news, she was making it, she was an accomplice. Which means she wouldn't be able to publish anything. No, she wasn't an accomplice, she had only been a mediator, but she told us where we could find the Grizzly .50 rifle with the laser sight, the fifteen rounds, the automatic weapons, the motorcycles and cars for the escape, she gave us the target, this was what an emissary of death would do, to mutter an overused term—she brought us the plan, we needed to fire at our targets from a hotel room, we had a reservation and the passports of Spanish tourists, Elmer had taken care of the details. He had surely taken care that Lorca would make us disappear without any scandals and that he would do the same with Lorca. It's logical that in this manner he thought he had dismantled the clockwork machinery.

"That's the game," Lourdes said.

"And we have to play it?"

"If there's no exit, " Lourdes replied. "But with our own rules. Let's go have some coffee and think of a plan, I think we can go back to our house, neither Elmer nor Lorca will act for now. And you," she touched the tip of Manuela's nose with her finger, "welcome to the club, we'll form a ménage à trois."

We only had one day to remake the plan. A long day. I didn't trust Lourdes, but I had no choice. Manuela was unhappy, she wanted to send her first notes to a correspondent, we asked for the name of the correspondent and she refused to reveal it, a journalist doesn't reveal her sources and she became furious when we told her she wasn't a mere journalist, she was a comrade journalist. We didn't pay attention to what she was writing, we didn't check her notes, we guarded her so she wouldn't escape, but she understood there was no escape, the only way was forward, the flight of the butterfly made the luminosity of the port, the inferno of light in the sky. There's no return, Manuela, at least the practice of journalism remains, perhaps, if we're able to set fire to reality, the possibility of writing an investigative piece, though I would rather write a novel, I told her, they're more truthful. For now, the comrade would drive the car.

You're looking so pretty, Lourdes, the flowered dress clings to your body like a second skin, you come down the hotel hall with the characteristic swaying of a girl from Murcia. You don't need to learn anything, you look like a Jew from Tangiers, your eagle nose, wavy red hair, the pink lipstick on your thick lips, you're fragrant and sexual, you're all decked out, girl. How could she not be. The dress is lovely and your legs are perfect, worked on in gyms and waxing salons, overwhelming under the light of the tropics, absolute. You're alluring, the rest of the tourists can't help but look at you, you slut. You're walking close to the security zone, near the area where the ministers stay and give their declarations to the press, you raise your chest and it seems as if you're daring all the males and females of the species.

Sergio, you're walking towards the opposite side, you're heading to the basin, you're a barbarous man from Buenos Aires. Your hair is slicked back, more hirsute than ever, that's how it should be, che; you look younger than you are, you're a stud. On your way to play tennis. Your strong back makes a place for you among the crowds, the chicks look at you and bite their lips. You look at the ass of the twins wearing a bandana at their waist through your sunglasses. Marvelous, you're the man, kid; everything is relaxed, you loosen your body; you don't walk, you dilute yourself, you make the racket case swing like a pendulum with the grace of a gigolo who makes a living as a tennis instructor, you smile, make your entrance into history as if this were Cannes, facing photographers and journalists.

And you, Manuela? You feel uncomfortable, it's not the chauffeur uniform you're wearing, since after all you like men's clothing, you look like an Adonis wearing a cap, with a bellboy's suit, about to be photographed for a Calvin Klein publicity campaign, you're irritated by the turn life has taken, you've skipped the ethical codes and for the sake of comforting your conscience you tell yourself that it was the result of an excessive love for your profession, you feel as if it weren't true that you were facing a dilemma or the hour of truth or the truth of your life, you understand that you're just a piece of straw in the wind, you remember the president and you understand him and know that one doesn't act according to will, that one is subject to hidden and mysterious forces, he would repeat that phrase of Bolívar's because of demagogy, he was a lava rock amid the chaos of national politics, he understood himself as well-intentioned, arbitrary, capable of taking charge of history's reins, you understand it much too late, you see passing in front of your eyes, one after another, the pages of the immense volume of War and Peace *and you recreate yourself in Tolstoy's thesis; arbitrary and unknown forces define historic events; always unpredictable, despite the will of those who make history. You can't make an omelet without breaking someone's balls; you realize that in this story, your own, the shells are fractured, spread out and pulverized, while the actors are not in their original roles, impelled by brute force, a fever, the morass or a dream, you're like General Kutuzov; you're dressed like an Adonis car driver, a model for a New York fashion house, at the wheel of a security van for an oil company, a protagonist in a muddle and maybe, if everything works out, you'll perpetrate the escape.*

Impeccable, as always, with a comfortable suit, you're a reflection of your old comrade, Elmer, you're wearing a blue blazer with gold buttons and wide flannel pants, you blend in with the security personnel, the head is shiny, your baldness is the luminous baldness of emperors, your smile is perfect as always, that's what you looked like in the desert training camps, you said you preferred death to losing glamour, you spoke of revolutionary glamour, you scan the auditorium with your eyes and wink at a girl dressed as a photographer, with that war correspondent attire that makes you recall certain situations on the Gaza strip, everything will be fixed for you soon, you'll be lost in the immense anonymity, you'll give the revolution a kick in order to save your life, at certain extreme mo-

ments chaos is the indicated door, the exit that fits the ultimate ends of those who no longer wish to be a part of any other project or goal whatsoever.

You greet people without emphasis, always faithful to the coldness that has brought you to the top, you're Manuel Roca, the Minister of Internal Affairs, if everything works out, if Elmer executes what you've agreed upon, you'll be the Ambassador to the United Kingdom, you see yourself wearing a frock coat in a carriage crossing the gardens of Buckingham Palace with your credentials, you'll stand in front of the Queen of England and drink tea and you'll stare at the majestic and affected gladiolas beneath the timid spring sunshine. Your life will have made some sense, you're headed in a certain direction, revolutions are postponed but revolutionaries remain, that's the goal, you have to weed the garden, keep far away from those childhood smells, from the despicable room in that sad school. You go to the press conference where you'll speak of your short and effective mission, of the new order that has begun and of the new mission the process has imposed on you in a country that has always been very strategic for revolutions in the Americas. You look at Elmer mixed in with the security functionaries, he gives you a thumbs up, you understand that everything's going well, Elmer, you look at Roca and give him a thumbs up and place one arm behind your back so you can cross your fingers, you look at both of them, Lourdes, you approach, you make your way amid the multitude, you break the first security ring, you see it and feel as if the cold is conquering you, what's she doing there? You seek an answer in Elmer's eyes, you make your way without revealing any uncertainty; you uncross your fingers, she should be in the hotel room waiting for the presidential limousine and you're assembling the small rifle on the tennis court, you begin to shoot randomly, the detonations make the glances meet and the journalists call the cameramen so that they'll follow them; the microphone and camera cables are crossed, people fall and security rings open up, you go and drop the handkerchief you were playing with as you walked through the hotel halls, Lourdes reveals an automatic pistol, she hits you in the face, you fall back toward a sure death, minister, as a poet said. Elmer, you look at her with the same mocking grimace painted on your face as always, you approve of her, you can't waste any time, your hand moves inside your coat, but it makes no sense to take out your weapon, your second shot hits the inveterate instructor in the stomach, and he falls face-forward, toward death, as a poet would say, within the fatal acoustics you think that Lourdes was one of your best students. Why should you be petty at the moment of death? She's hit you in one of the seven mortal points, your pulse is firm, you shoot again and run, leave the tennis court and run through the halls, you load another cartridge and discharge it into a window display, launch a burst of bullets over the heads of journalists and cameramen, they drop to the ground, they don't register you in their machines, you're a shadow, you keep firing into the window displays of the stores, Lourdes, you run toward Sergio, Sergio you run to Lourdes, it's a good scene, moving slowly and beautifully, amid the chaos, despite the disorder, on top of the bodies throwing themselves onto the floor, you pass an automatic to her, you catch it and run parallel to your comrade, the columns in the hall cover you intermittently, they've begun to shoot at you, you make your way through the cars, take off your cap, let your short, red hair loose, the tires screech, you turn, change lanes and reach the agreed upon spot, you watch them arrive as you suppose all cataclysms must, giant, beautiful windows that burst into pieces, you can't hear the shots being fired at them, you're not surprised by your coldness at the wheel, your hands aren't shaking, foot on the accelerator, they open the door to the van and climb in, grab the weapons that are laid out inside and toss some smoke grenades out the window, you let the tires squeal, you set the van in motion. You escape without any blunders, change cars in the yacht club parking lot, Lorca's waiting for you there, unruffled, with the rifle set at his waist. He doesn't shoot.

"And what about you," you ask him. He points at your chest, you see his finger eaten by Leishmania, shaking.

"Did you kill the president?"

"We took out Roca and Elmer," you answer and add, dryly: "Let history take care of the president."

"Give me a reason not to shoot."

"We've burst the clock's springs into pieces," Manuela screams from behind the wheel, "step aside, Lorca, or get in; from now on time is precious."

The house beaten by the wind kept itself from the day. Outside, the fishermen's houses, the fishermen's refuges, the tumbleweeds that bounced along the village's only street, the stone kitchens, fires from which smoke rose in fine columns toward the sky. The clouds were running beneath the afternoon blue that's growing into pink, the sun fell into the sea again. We were back at the ramshackle shelters. Time was flat, I already said it, nothing had happened, time wasn't even circular, it hadn't rotated, time was the single drop that fell over and over into the cauldron. When the sun sank into the sea and the fishermen gathered around their nets, at the moment when the women gathered the shrimp and crabs; in the silence and understanding, in the light that ceded, from the fissure of an imprecise moment; Lourdes, or Sonia, smiled, she was wearing a see-through gown, she called everyone from the big house, to the patio flanked by columns covered in star jasmine, she brought everyone to the meeting spot in front of the cherry tree, under the withered grape vines, I'd have liked to move closer and touch her body, I wanted to place my hand on her waist, feel her chest, listen to the silence of her heart, stare at the dark green eyes and understand. I needed air, I walked with the parsimony appropriate to the moment.

I was an angel of death and I wandered the mountains with an assault rifle on my shoulder and I went down to the cities and wreaked the havoc that my limitations or the circumstances allowed, it was my sign, the meaning. I now understood that this place of not being born was the correct place, the instant when you merely feel the intoxication, the second when you become pleasure; I walked out, showed my teeth and then I suffered failure. We all give in, at a moment of fracture we will be humiliated, unless we stay under these nets, in the place where the winds are to be found, in the anonymous land of the shadows.

Christians do good deeds in order to be resuscitated and live forever in paradise, at the side of the Lord; Muslims become martyrs and observe every last detail of the norms dictated to them by the Koran in order to know the eternity of saints and the love of houris; Marxists hope to see the just society without any classes, the solidarity of peoples; Liberals procure a world run by the laws of the market. When we read Hesiod's *Works and Days* we let ourselves be convinced by a past life in a Golden Age; one day we will live under its empire, we merely have to do what is just.

Standing there in front of the cherry tree was Carla, dark and pale reason, smell of sulfur, of blood and bronze, an obscure smell, right there, covered by a transparent veil, she was order, the night that contained the day, the death that contained life, sensuality that flowed from her smile and remained at the moment when Manuela blended into Olga and Lorca was indistinguishable from Andrés, I was a shade and I rejoiced in her. Manuela, Lourdes and Lorca have sat around Carla's feet, I heard them say that whatever we dreamt happened to us, that we had to watch out for our dreams. There was nothing to fear in this place ruled by shadows. I looked at them and thought that we'd been like this forever, which translated into a drop that fell, over and over, into a cauldron. Olga blew me a kiss, Humberto and Andrés performed acrobatic stunts in the middle of the patio, Sonia would not be leaving anymore, the harmony was perfect, fright did not exist. I felt I was at the center of the world, in the place where the four winds were to be found and the night became definitive, I was not assaulted by anguish for the life I abandoned, I felt very close to Carla, at her feet and I began to dream.

In Buenos Aires they called it mist. In Mexico City they called it smog. When the wind from the Sahara blew and covered Santa Cruz de Tenerife, the islanders knew it as haze. In Caracas there was soot, and I was moving through smoke and ashes on the day I went out to kill the president.

10/14/2001
Caracas-Barquisimeto

Israel Centeno was born in Venezuela in 1958. He has published ten novels and several books of poetry and short stories. He is regarded as one of the most important Venezuelan writers of the past fifty years. He has won the Federico García Lorca Award in Spain and the National Council of Culture Award in Venezuela. Since 2011, he has lived in Pittsburgh with his wife and two daughters, as an exiled Writer-in-Residence at City of Asylum Pittsburgh. *The Conspiracy* is his first novel to be translated into English.

Guillermo Parra is a poet and translator. His translations include José Antonio Ramos Sucre's *Selected Works: Expanded Edition* and *Air on the Air: Selected Poems of Juan Sánchez Peláez*. His own books of poems include *Phantasmal Repeats* and *Caracas Notebook*. He lives in Clearwater, Florida.